THESIS

—— OF ——

EVIL

PATRICK KEITHAHN

ISBN: 978-1-7323882-4-6

Cover design by Brandi Doane McCann/Ebook Cover Designs.

❁ Created with Vellum

CONTENTS

1

———

THE THREE

Warren walked down the center of the Minnesota backroad without concern, as if he didn't exist. Dusk was beginning to dim the road, summer humidity releasing a potpourri of wildflowers and aging asphalt as crickets and swallows called for evening with their white noise.

Warren's white naval attire—baggy trousers and loose jumper shirt—was immaculate enough to pass the most stringent of inspections. White Dixie cup hat cocked left, his arms hung to his sides, shoes clomping and black neckerchief flapping. His boyish features were disproportioned to his large frame, his lips parting naturally. But if there had been a soul around to witness him, it would have been his face, pale as flour and freakishly bloated, that first would have caught anyone's eye.

If I were to go back, if I could only go back right now, what would I do first? he thought.

There were visions of cheeseburgers and soda pop, simple pleasures now gone. He longed for them not from hunger or thirst but from wanting what he once had. There were memories of sipping lemonade on Granny's porch in the summer, record player lobbing tunes through the open living room window, porch swing swaying to the cadence. There was the touch of Louise, draping his arm around her shoulders, the sweet smell of her perfume far too distant, his soul incapable of reproducing the scent.

And chocolate. To have a chocolate bar one more time!

Despite these deficiencies, he had a profound understanding of this world, once his own, now just a place to visit. It was appalling to consider the great changes since the war, a nation that had progressed and regressed since 1945. How was it possible that this was still his nation? The foundation remained, but the people had become different, some key ingredient lost.

There was a rustling in the woods ten feet ahead, the source of the noise hidden by the thick undergrowth. Fear was not an emotion Warren owned anymore, so he continued to walk with nothing at risk. A doe and fawn crept into the road, doe cautious in the absence of cover. Even though Warren was close to them, neither paid him mind. He stopped to admire them, the orange hue of their coats, the slope of the doe's neck, the graceful gait. He walked past, holding out his hand to pet the doe. She was oblivious of him, as though he were invisible, the doe intent on leading her fawn to the other side of the road where they slipped into the woods.

A half a mile more of walking and the final shards of daylight were swept by the hands of darkness. Warren continued over railroad tracks that crossed the road, then around a curve to the right. Here the roadside woods thinned and the terrain sloped up. On top of a hill to his left was a stone mansion in the chateau style, with its castle-like peaks, outcroppings, and a porte cochere abutting a long driveway, light from many of its rooms casting rays across the estate. A pristine lawn dominated the foreground, perimeter secured with an iron fence.

Warren stopped to study the lavishness, his neckerchief blowing in the breeze. He whistled a quick chirp, the way he might whistle to himself when seeing a beautiful woman. "Fancy, fancy, fancy," he added.

He passed through the open gate and ascended the driveway. Despite the slope, there was no quickening of breath, no sweat issuing from his temples. He approached the mansion as if floating, driveway becoming level in front of the porte cochere.

There were expensive cars parked here, all makes and models polished to perfection. Their owners were inside dining, bragging, laughing. Today was the mansion owner's birthday. Somehow the man had survived another year.

Another year can't be allowed. He is a dangerous, dangerous man. He has to be stopped.

Warren's thoughts were interrupted by a blinding flicker of lightning and a crack of thunder from a storm enveloping the west. It was a doozy of a storm, a Midwestern giant rising without warning to swallow the region whole.

A figure materialized and walked across the shadowy lawn toward the mansion. It was a woman in tattered business attire, her eyes gray and lifeless, yet the swagger in her walk expressed that she wouldn't be deterred, as though she had waited a long time for this. She stepped not to Warren, even though she acknowledged him with a nod, but toward the mansion, taking it in with a sulk, like it was an obnoxious piece of modern art.

Another figure appeared at the other side of the yard. Warren and the woman nodded to him when he came into full view, a soldier in a blue wool coat and light blue pants. His face was deflated from malnourishment and trauma, a sizable and festering wound branding his forehead beneath his short-billed cap.

The man stepped up to them and stopped, cocking his head toward the house, saying nothing.

"Time's a wastin' folks," Warren said. The others remained transfixed on the mansion.

The sky lit with another lightning strike, a bolt ripping through the atmosphere, suspending darkness with a brilliant torrent of light before restoring night. Thunder followed, nature's carpet bombs and cannon salvos, seeming to threaten the world with annihilation for a moment before falling away to benign echoes.

As if nature's strike had triggered something profound, Warren's body began to fade from the top of his Dixie cup hat to the soles of his shoes, until he looked like a reflection in a dirty window. The woman underwent the same transformation, her body disintegrating into the Earth so that only a shadow remained. The man in blue followed suit, his form melting away.

Then all three vanished completely, gone but never forever.

2

———

DIAGNOSIS

Reid Larkin watched the storm from a window inside his White Bear Lake mansion. Lightning lit his face as he swayed in a leather rocker-recliner surrounded by his expansive personal library. Decades of personal neglect and overwork had left his face blemished with spots and wrinkles, receding hairline giving way to gray and wavy locks on the sides of his head. The surplus flesh of his chin and neck drooped into his white oxford shirt, his tie draping down into his buttoned jacket.

Larkin coughed a labored hack as an echo of death reverberated off the library walls. He reached for his handkerchief in his breast pocket and wiped the spittle from his lips, a trace of blood staining the cloth.

"Damn it all," Larkin grumbled, returning his handkerchief to his pocket.

Dim spotlights from high above uncovered a shine from the walls of dark mahogany. An unlit fireplace framed in wooden pillars was topped with a painting of a French seashore. Surrounding the library were shelves of antique books and glass cases displaying rare militaria. A circular iron staircase led up to the library's catwalk running above the perimeter of the room.

Larkin reached for a cigar in his inside jacket pocket and nestled it unlit into the pucker of his mouth. Then he reached for the end table next to his chair and opened the drawer. Finding a photo album tucked inside, he took it out and opened it, trembling hands paging through shots of Greece, China, and New Zealand. When he came to the picture he wanted—a snapshot of Mona Lisa at the Louvre—he reached in the sleeve and pulled out another photograph hidden behind it.

Larkin raised the photo and held it close to his face so his failing eyes could see it. It was not Mona Lisa, but someone far more beautiful.

Amanda.

Even though the picture was taken thirty years before, he recalled every detail of that day. Amanda had looked as stunning as ever, brown hair pulled back into a ponytail, blue topaz eyes catching reflections from the sunset. Swirling in that picture were memories of how it had felt then, his finest hour, when there had been hope that he would spend the rest of his life with her. How different might things have been had that happened? He couldn't even fathom it.

No matter, he had lost her. Had he really even had her? He had thought so, but hindsight brought doubt, the unshakeable feeling that he had been fooled. All he had to show for it was a photograph that teased of what may have been, inducing misery and hatred.

These feelings grew when he saw the *Wall Street Journal* folded in half on top of the end table. He grasped the paper with his free hand, flipped it open with a snap of the wrist, and glared at the enemy. John McMichael's photo commanded the front page, the article's headline proclaiming another victory for the Center for Immigration Assistance, McMichael's thriving nonprofit immigrant advocacy group. Larkin hated the man for a million reasons. Mainly, McMichael was a liberal philanthropist causing quite a stir with his self-righteous but effective activism. Yet, seeing the photo of McMichael reminded Larkin of one reason for the venom beyond all others: Amanda. He could never forget how McMichael had weaseled his way to her.

Larkin had no stomach for this tonight. He tossed the paper onto the floor and wiped the newsprint from his hand onto his black slacks. He tried to return to the bliss of Amanda's photo, but it was no use, the bad memories had taken over as they always had. He stuffed the picture back into its hiding place in the sleeve, shut the album, tossed it back into the drawer, and closed it with a defiant slam.

He rested his head back and sighed, stifling another cough as he rolled the cigar in his lips. Unable to resist the temptation any longer, he reached again into his inside jacket pocket, pulled out his stainless lighter, and lit the cigar, smoke drifting up into the cavernous library ceiling. Larkin sniffed the air, eyes shut. Instead of taking a drag he let the cigar smolder in his trembling grasp. Smelling it would have to suffice, but even that forced another gruesome cough, which he again tamed by pulling out his handkerchief and pressing it to his lips.

Three raps at the library door interrupted the moment. It was Marcela's characteristic knock. She would enter after giving him a moment, so he ignored her rapping. When she decided it was time to come in, one side of the double doors opened, the scent of her perfume announcing her presence. She had come to retrieve him for the night's festivities.

Without turning to look at her, he spoke: "Not yet. Close the door, I have something to tell you first."

Marcela closed the door behind her and walked inside

with clicking heels from black pumps. She was an exceptionally tall Hispanic woman, flowing black hair contrasted by its streaks of gray, her dark eyebrows casting a permanent frown. She wore a black dress with a sheer shawl, her darkened form seeming to roam across the room like a storm cloud. In her fifties, she was some twenty years younger than Larkin, but her life had been lived almost as hard as his, and it showed in her sagging frame. A scar ran down the right side of her cheek, veiled insufficiently with the smother of makeup.

Larkin studied her. "My God Marcela, black is a ghastly color on you."

Marcela gave her outfit a quick inspection, then offered a sneer. Larkin noticing anything about her was as close to a compliment as she had come to expect all these years, and she brushed it off as if nothing had been said at all.

"Problems with your newspaper?" She retrieved the paper at his feet and placed it back on his end table.

"I found the lead article lacking. Cancel my subscription."

"Of course," she said, snatching it up. "Do you want the *Times* again?"

"The best use for the *Times* is for wrapping fish guts," he said. "But as you know, I'm no fisherman. No, I'm giving up journalism. Ought to be a Surgeon General's warning on the front page."

"All right."

"Marcela, sit down. I can't speak to you hovering above me."

She stepped to the chair across from him and sat, crossing her legs tattooed in varicose.

"Most of the guests are here. We should greet them soon," she said.

"Are the bars well staffed and stocked?"

"Absolutely."

"Well then, it's my birthday, let them wait. That crowd prefers liquor over my company anyway. I have news."

Marcela watched Larkin's cigar smoke drift up from his hand in a single stream. Her expression was impenetrable as usual, her stoicism worth every penny he paid her.

"This will be my last birthday celebration," Larkin said.

"Well, it's about time you came around on that. Birthday parties only irritate you."

"Let me finish my goddamned thought please. You've missed the point. It's not about parties, it's about me."

Marcela, unscathed by the man few on Earth would tolerate, raised her chin and waited.

"As you know, Karl has been taking me to the Mayo."

"They have the finest reputation," Marcela offered.

"Overrated. But that's beside the point. They have made their diagnosis, such as it is."

"Diagnosis?"

"That's right. Marcela, I'm a dead man. Stage Four lung cancer. Can you believe that?"

Inexplicably, Larkin laughed at this confession, the kind of laugh reserved for slapstick, long and uncontrollable. But the outburst was costly, degrading into a string of suffocating hacks. He lifted his handkerchief to his mouth again and coughed into a discharge of crimson spittle.

Once recovered, he said: "It's hilarious, when you think about it."

"Of course," she said. "There must be something . . ."

"Not a goddamn thing," he said. "In my chest is a tumor as big as a fist. Like a baseball, right in my lungs, autographed by the devil."

"All right."

Despite her best efforts, the gravity of the news began to

seep through her barrier of professionalism. Larkin could see her eyes beginning to gloss.

"Oh, doctors will tell you there's a chance. But I won't have them experimenting on me."

Marcela couldn't restrain a single tear falling on her cheek, like sap running from an ancient maple. She wiped it away with a delicate stroke almost quickly enough for Larkin not to notice.

"Marcela, don't bubble in my presence. We all die, and many would have loved for me to go sooner than this."

"I'm sorry."

"Yes, I'm sure you are. This is why you've stayed my employee these twenty years. It's the respect—genuine respect—that keeps you here. Do you know how many sons a bitches I've fired in my lifetime? None of them had respect, and nothing pleases me more than handing a pink slip to the likes of them. Anyway, on to the best part."

"The best part?"

"There's always an opportunity. You know that as well as me. There's so much work to be done before my last suffocating breath."

"Work?"

"Yes. I pay you handsomely for work. I'm dying, but I'm not a corpse yet."

"Of course not."

"That's the spirit. Now, tomorrow we start. But first, swear to me, as my most trusted employee, that you'll grant a dying man two promises. You would like to hear them first, no doubt?"

"Certainly."

"Good. First, let me die the way God intended it. I will not go to one of those death camps, those *hospices*. It doesn't take an act of Congress, thank the Lord, to get pain medication.

And I don't need anyone to show me how to die. But I will need you there, as my executor, to witness my death, to call the coroner, all the fascinating morbidities."

"Done," she said.

"Very well. And secondly, I have a little project for you, one that will bring you back to the old days."

Marcela bit her lip at this unanticipated turn.

"I trust by your reaction that you understand me. And make no mistake, this one's a humdinger, I guarantee it. Makes me giddy."

Larkin smiled a toothy, sadistic grin, happiness he hadn't felt in years.

"Now, will you do as I ask? It requires everything you have."

Marcela had never married, never been romantically involved with a man for longer than a one-night stand, and had almost no family. Reid Larkin, for better or worse, was all she had. He knew she would follow him anywhere.

"Consider it done," she said.

"Excellent." Larkin seemed to relax in his chair, absorbing her promise. The cigar smoke waggled upward, and he watched it as though it was a striptease. "Tomorrow we start. Tonight, I have a goddamned birthday party."

Larkin stood from his chair as another penetrating cough overcame him, Marcela standing with him. He wiped away the blood with his handkerchief, then stuffed it into his pants pocket so it was well hidden. Recovered, he leaned toward her.

"Not a word of this to anyone, you hear me? I won't have them knowing I'm a goner. They'll find out like everyone else when I'm in the morgue."

"Of course," Marcela said, walking to the door and opening it to the noises of the party. Larkin took a deep breath and stepped from the library to celebrate.

3

TATTOOS AND BOOKISH

Karl Pike was pissed. To him, a dinner party was like a military exercise to be planned and executed with precision. An Army veteran of Iraq and Afghanistan, Pike was wired to function with martial skill. Yet if tonight had been a real military exercise, everyone would have been killed in action. As if to demonstrate this point, two of his young servers with trays full of dishes nearly collided in front of him.

"Slow the hell *down!*" he shouted at them. "Almighty God, it's like dealing with chimps!"

The servers stiffened and carried the dishes through the kitchen and into the dishwashing room with greater care.

Pike rubbed his forehead as if he was coaxing out a nail embedded deep into his skull. He shook his head and stared at the kitchen floor as though an answer could be found in the tiles.

"And these are college kids," he told himself. "We're all hosed."

As Reid Larkin's personal chef, chauffeur, and bodyguard, Pike's job description took advantage of his many skills, but he took particular pride in culinary work. On dinner party nights, he supervised a brigade of college kids hired from a temp agency to assist. But being enrolled in college didn't guarantee that the kids were smart.

Pike took inventory of the night's errors. Things derailed first when one of the servers tripped taking out entrees, scattering five meals across the dining room floor. Only Pike's backup plates and a couple of cancellations had saved the night. Then some plates were served to guests without the couscous, despite plain English describing what should go on each one. Then some dumbass spilled a pitcher of water over a lady in a fancy gown, unleashing her shrieks of injustice. Mercifully, the dessert course arrived, the easiest part, and how in all that's holy had that gone wrong? *Cut the cake and get all of the pieces on plates before anyone takes them out.* And what happens? A genius in the group started to serve them right away.

If only he could take each kid outside and beat their snot lockers to hamburger.

It hadn't been his best work, but the damage was done. The guests had eaten and retired to more drinks in the bar so the cleanup could begin. Pike continued to watch as waves of servers clad in white shirts and black pants carried the dessert dishes and utensils into the dishwashing room. There they stacked them on a counter next to the enormous dishwashing sink where more dirty dishes waited.

Tables nearly cleared, Pike spotted two workers loitering and clueless, a tall dude with glasses and a goth-looking female, her face pale and round, bangs highlighted red.

"You two," he said, snapping his fingers. "In here."

Both followed his lead into the dishwashing room. There he pointed to the daunting stacks of dirty dishes.

"You wash, honey buns, he dries."

"By hand?" The girl seemed appalled.

"Darling, what's your name again?" Pike asked.

"Erin."

"Yes gorgeous, by hand. This china ain't from Walmart. It's worth more than daddy's retirement fund. So use those baby-soft hands to make these spotless. My man here dries and serves as quality control. Any of these don't get clean, send them back to cutie pie here, okay Jack?"

"Conner," the kid with glasses tried to correct him. Ignoring him, Pike turned on the water and waited for it to travel up the long neck of the tap and down the flexible dish-washing hose, water spraying into the sink.

Pike took no chances being misunderstood: "You treat these dishes like little puppies now, girl. Rinse with the hose—press this button for soap—then wash, rinse, soap, wash, and rinse again. When they're spotless, stack them in the rack for my guy here." Pike pulled a pile of specialized washing cloths and drying towels from a storage closet and handed them to Erin and Conner. "Don't get cheap on these, we have hundreds. And none of you gets butterfingers. Nothing more gets broken tonight."

With that Pike left to supervise the others, and the two set about their work.

"Well this sucks," Erin said when Pike was out of earshot. "And I guess this place has no sexual harassment policy."

"I've had worse temp jobs," Conner said. He watched her pluck three sterling rings from her fingers and put them in her pocket before grabbing a dirty plate with disgust. As she began to hose it down, her red bangs fell into her eyes, and she blew her hair away with a puff of air from her full lips.

"Yeah, like what? Working in a coal mine?" she asked.

"Close. I had to clean up an abandoned warehouse once. The supervisor gave me a broom and a dustpan and said have at it. There was this black soot everywhere, and I swear breathing in all that'll give me cancer some day. Afterwards it took me three hours to scrub off the filth in the shower."

"At least you weren't treated like a hooker while you did it."

"True. This house is amazing though, right?"

Erin pursed her lips. "Amazingly greedy."

"What, you've never seen how the one percent lives? They'd say they've earned it."

"I seriously doubt the owner of this place has *earned* anything."

Erin cleaned the plate with a cloth as carefully as washing an infant. Conner was hypnotized by her careful movements, her petite, wet hands restoring the plate's elegance as she rinsed it. When she placed the clean plate in the dish rack he noticed a blue tattoo on her wrist, a five-pointed star with a circle around it.

"I like your pentacle."

Erin paused to look at her wrist, then turned to him: "I'm impressed. Most people think it's a pentagram and ask if I'm into animal sacrifice."

"Are you?"

"Animals, no. But I might start sacrificing people the way things are going tonight."

"Why a pentacle?"

Her suspicious eyes seemed to consider many different responses. Then: "The pentacle is a symbol of protection, and I need all I can get."

"That's a lot to ask from a tattoo."

"It's just a symbol. I think of it as a reminder that I'm not alone."

"I've thought about getting a tattoo but I can never decide between *Mother* or barbed wire."

Erin smirked. "I take it you're not a fan of tattoos?"

Conner pondered that, dish now dry, and he set it on the open stainless counter in front of him. "Why's that?"

"I don't know," she glanced at him as if to evaluate. "Tattoos and bookish don't really mix."

"I look bookish?"

"Bookish has a place."

"Well, I'm a student, I guess it's good that I look the part."

"Where do you go?"

"I'm in grad school at the U."

Erin began rinsing the next plate. "Me too. Sociology. I'm in the doctorate program, getting my master's along the way."

"History for me."

"So that explains how you know what a pentacle is," she said.

"I think it came up in a religion course in undergrad. Otherwise, my knowledge of paganism is minimal."

They heard Pike yelling about something in the distance. Erin looked out the doorway, then turned back to Conner: "He has so many issues."

"You're the sociology person. Does he have unresolved problems with his father or something?"

"That's psych, not sociology. And I don't need an advanced degree to deduce that he's an asshole."

"Suppose not," he said.

She changed the subject. "Do you have a thesis yet?"

"You really want to talk about my thesis?" he asked.

"No, but it'll pass the time better than listening to his yelling."

"I don't have anything concrete yet, but it'll probably be something related to military history, or maybe 9/11."

"Cheery. Are you a war monger or something?"

Conner laughed. "No, I'm not a war monger. I'm the opposite. It just happens that wars tend to bring out the best and worst in people, and that's intriguing to me."

"I remember being so bored by war history in high school. What do I care about sexually frustrated men murdering each other?"

"I can't explain the attraction. It just exists," Conner said. "I suppose you'll have a dissertation for your doctorate then?"

"Eventually. That's way off though," she said. "I'm interested in doing something about the societal perception of modern paganism."

"Sounds interesting. Will it cover animal sacrifice?"

"Nice," she smiled. "You're probably as bored by paganism as I am by military history."

"No, I mean it. A dissertation on paganism is pretty original. I'd read it. Or maybe you could tell me the short version sometime."

Erin looked at him like she was trying to read his motives. As he returned her stare, he thought there was something else in her searching eyes—intrigue at least, or maybe even attraction? Or was it just his own wishful thinking? He had never been able to interpret women very well.

"Holy God, monkeys can be taught!" Pike shouted. He had come to the doorway of the dishwashing room without them hearing, and both of them flinched out of their stare.

"Nicely done with the washing, cutie. Keep this up and I might ask you to come back," Pike added. "But flirt with each other on your own time, okay folks?"

Conner saw that Erin was flushing. He could feel his own face grow hot.

"All right Lady and the Tramp, keep it going, lots of dirties here."

With that Pike left them again.

"Complete weirdo," Conner whispered to her when Pike was gone. She laughed and nodded, getting back to washing.

As they worked in silence, Conner kept thinking about her. There was so much he wanted to know.

"So where do you live?" he asked at last. As soon as he did, he realized it came off the wrong way.

"That's a bit personal, isn't it?" she laughed.

"Sorry, I didn't mean for it to sound that way. I'm not a stalker."

"Never mind," she said. "Conner was it?"

"Yes, Conner. My name is . . . Conner Shaw," he said, fumbling for the words in his embarrassment.

"Erin St. Claire, nice to meet you," she said. "No worries, I know what you meant. I live in the University and Lexington area. You?"

"Not far from there."

It was the perfect opportunity to ask her out, but it seemed like she anticipated it and changed the subject: "What will you do with your degree? Teach?"

"Either that or be a dishwasher. What's your plan?"

"I don't know," she said.

"You're getting a Ph.D. and you don't know what you're going to do with it?"

"No, it's not that. Sociology is the right place for me, but I don't know specifically where it'll take me. I believe things fall into place if you work hard and keep an open mind. The universe works things out for us."

"The universe?"

Erin blew the hair out of her eyes again with a puff. "There's a plan for each of us out there, don't you think?"

"Doubtful. And if there is, why doesn't someone share it with us?"

"Because it's supposed to be a journey. Are you the kind of guy who reads the last page of a book first?"

Conner couldn't decide if he was irritated or infatuated. The two of them had entirely different ways of thinking, yet he really liked her. He decided now was the time to ask her out: "Hey, sometime would you like to . . ."

"You know what?" Pike said, peering into the dishwashing room. They both jumped, again not hearing him approach. "You girlfriends talk way too damn much. Wash my dishes, okay Bonnie and Clyde?"

As Pike left, Erin mouthed to Conner: *I hate him.*

Conner smiled back. They finished the dishes in silence.

∼

PIKE SENT the other temps home long before Erin and Conner had finished the dishes. When they were done, Pike inspected their work and actually seemed pleased. He dismissed them, and they left the mansion to the pouring rain on the side driveway where Erin's Camry and Conner's pickup waited.

"Nice meeting you," Erin said.

Before he could respond she sprinted through the rain toward her car. He walked to his pickup, kicking himself for his inaction. He dug into his pocket and pulled out the keyring with a jingle. But instead of unlocking the door, he followed Erin over to her car. She was inside starting the engine when he rapped on the window. She opened the window a crack.

"Just a little while ago you assured me you aren't a stalker," she called through the rain.

"Yeah, I'm not. I was just wondering . . ."

He suddenly felt stupid, but the point of no return had passed. "I was wondering if you'd like to get a drink sometime?"

"Seriously?"

That wasn't what he had hoped to hear.

"Since we practically live in the same neighborhood," he said.

"Usually I scare guys like you."

He thought she was going to put the car in gear as she reached for the shifter, then she went past it and found a pen and a gum wrapper. She wrote her phone number on the inside of the wrapper and handed it to him.

"Text me."

"Great, that sounds great. I'll text," he said.

She smiled and shut the window. He stuffed the number into his pocket as she peeled away, leaving some rubber on the slippery mansion driveway. Alone, he looked up as the rain pelted his face.

"She scares guys like me," he repeated her words in a whisper. Then he retreated to the shelter of his pickup.

4

___

SCAR

Marcela Rios attempted to relax her morning jitters and internalize the task at hand. She looked out of her office window over Reid Larkin's grounds, the slope of grass groomed like a professional golf course fairway, roses and hedges freshly primped. The commute from her bedroom in the basement to her office on the second floor of Larkin's mansion took her less than two minutes, while the average American spent over twenty-five. Her situation as Larkin's live-in employee had its benefits, but the cost was often steep.

Marcela reached for the scar on her cheek, yielding to the habit of touching its rough imperfection. The plastic surgeon had been unable to hide it completely. Even though the damage had been done over ten years ago, each time she caressed the scar, the texture felt foreign, still not a part of her. Like the memory of what had caused it, she would carry this blemish until she died.

The serenity of the grounds and sunshine outside offered little comfort today. A half hour earlier she had sat in Larkin's library, wading through his coughing to hear his plans. His ire had gushed between gasps like he'd rehearsed it over a lifetime. The effect on her was a paralysis of soul and mind, demanding everything she had to remain her amenable self. When finished, the magnitude of his dying wish had smashed into what remained of her conscience, and now she searched for answers in a silence that felt toxic.

Larkin's plan would force her far beyond her darkest work yet. If all went well, there would be no worries about her future, Larkin would see to that. The work ahead was close to unthinkable, but her promise to Larkin was like an unbreakable contract, and her loyalty to him too powerful to ignore. No, like any loathsome chore, all that was necessary was to begin, the task already turning gears in her mind.

Yet, like trying to find normalcy after a bad dream, her unease remained. Did she really want to relive her former days? She had done her best to forget it all, but there it was, resurfacing in her mind, inducing itchy tickles on her scar. The past revisited like a nagging illness.

The wound on her cheek had been the work of Graham Reynolds, once a successful CEO until Reid Larkin had barged into his life. Larkin had made a fortune buying companies, identifying their fatal flaws, fixing them by any means necessary, and selling them off. This had been the situation with Reynolds' company, but his case had proven exceptional. Over his 49 years, Reynolds had rarely been told what to do, and he quickly showed he wouldn't accept anything Larkin demanded. That's when Larkin assigned Marcela to find a weakness.

Mid-memory, Marcela opened her desk drawer and retrieved a compact mirror. She looked at her reflection and saw the scar was angry and red, standing out from her tired face as if the underworld has just marked it as an omen. She had to stop thinking about the past, but it was never that simple, it always came and went as it pleased. She put the mirror away and sighed, resigned to remember Reynolds, as if she could only move forward after reconciling that part of her past.

They could have just fired Reynolds, but they had needed him. He had amassed a devoted band of followers at his company, and hundreds of employees would have defected with him gone. Finding a way to silence him had seemed simpler.

Marcela recalled presenting a well researched profile of Reynolds to Larkin: married with three children; squarely in midlife, he enjoyed spending his money to make up for his inadequacies; balding and slightly overweight, he chose adrenaline-filled vacations and antique muscle cars, and he had a mistress; supported by overconfidence one minute and insecure as a middle schooler the next, his temper was volatile, with many outbursts reported by former employees.

After describing Reynolds to Larkin, Marcela had recommended caution. Larkin had preferred a stern lesson instead, one that would cut Reynolds to pieces and leave him squirming and helpless. The gamble was that Reynolds would fall in line rather than resign. Marcela had obeyed the order with the precision that Larkin had come to expect.

In the privacy of Reynolds' office, Marcela had laid down a calculated threat to Reynolds, a devastating concoction of infidelity, embezzlement, sexual harassment, and drug abuse, most of it even legitimate. If Reynolds failed to play nice with Larkin, leaking the information would dissolve his marriage, thrust him into legal purgatory, and oust him as CEO.

"It's all up to you Graham," Marcela had said in summary. "I know what I'd do, if I were you." Her words were supposed to have been the coup de grace, but instead they had felt like the lighting of a very short fuse.

Reynolds understood the ramifications all too well. The realization had changed his expression from confident and animated to dark and brooding. Eyes squinting, jaw clenched, body completely still, a psychopath had unwrapped before Marcela's eyes.

That's when Reynolds pulled something from his desk drawer, keeping whatever he had taken hidden from her view. He stood without alarm, rounded his desk, and hovered next to her. She dared not look him in the eyes, despite her intuition shouting warnings at her.

"Nicely done Marcela," he had said, looking down at her in the guest chair. "You're a smart little wetback whore, aren't you? Larkin's best, probably. I bet that son of a bitch thinks he's won by sending you here to threaten me. But I never lose, and I never will. Too bad you'll pay the price. I have to say, though, I'm going to enjoy this."

Reynolds cocked his arm back, a stainless scissors in his grip reflecting off the fluorescents. Marcela only had time to gasp before he plunged the makeshift blade into her chest once, twice, three times. The blows punched the air from her, cold stings spraying her blood over Reynolds' suit and face, the mess of no consequence to him. She looked into his bloody face and saw something similar to ecstasy, a well-hidden fantasy superbly fulfilled.

Marcela had found it within herself to scream, a dire shriek of pain and despair that had only fed the man's fury. To silence her, he whipped the bloody scissors across her face, slashing her to the cheekbone, the blow so violent it tossed her back over the chair and onto the floor. There she squirmed in her own bath of blood, reflexes conflicted between writhing in pain or gearing up to flee from danger.

The office door slammed open, someone having heard Marcela's scream. Reynolds' secretary entered, normally a pleasant blonde who now looked like the world was imploding. She took five full seconds to process the unexpected office carnage before covering her mouth to stifle a cry, the gruesome spectacle causing her to fall to her knees. Reynolds had stared at his secretary with simple irritation, like she had interrupted a phone call to take his lunch order.

"Bonnie, what is it? You should really knock," he had told her.

Bonnie couldn't help it anymore. She screamed, whipped her legs out from underneath her, and crawled out the door, slamming it shut to blot out the repugnance. Reynolds and Marcela had been left to hear Bonnie yelling from outside of the office door. At first her cries were unintelligible wails, but then Bonnie had rediscovered her words: "Nine one one! Nine one one! Somebody call it! Call it! Nine one one! Now!"

It had occurred to Marcela that calling for help was a hopeless gesture—all that was left now was for Reynolds to finish the job before anyone else interrupted. At that moment, dying on Reynolds' floor, Marcela had fully understood how humans walked the fine line of success and catastrophe. One event in a person's life could change everything. Reynolds had initiated the endgame for both of them, he had only needed to complete it.

But instead of continuing his assault, Reynolds had calmly returned to his desk. Marcela panted for life as she struggled to lift her head to see what he was doing. She saw him reach into his desk drawer for a bottle of scotch, which he swigged empty as if dying of thirst. Satiated, he withdrew a pistol next, pausing to speak:

"Marcela, tell Larkin I resign. When he reaches hell with me, I'm coming for him."

Then he had pointed the gun to his head and pulled the trigger. The gun erupted, turning his head into a cloud of red.

She saw him fall to the floor behind his desk, heard him flopping like a fish on the bottom of a boat for several seconds, then all became still.

Marcela recalled going in and out of consciousness while being taken to the hospital, those waking moments haunted by visions of Graham Reynolds lying lifeless behind his desk, leaving his wife and children behind over her attempted blackmail.

Mercifully, the rest had been a blur, blotted out by narcotics and anesthesia, weeks of surgery and intensive care that seemed vague, as if it had happened to someone else. She had made a full recovery, a near miracle, everything damaged made whole again through modern medicine and time, perhaps even more so by the healing hand of God. Only the scar on her face remained as an obvious clue of what had happened.

Even Larkin had been shaken by the event. It was subtle, but Marcela had noticed that he chose slightly more civil business strategies from then on. No more blackmail, no more specialists who could be counted on for spying, intimidation, even violence to meet Larkin's goals. It had been a fresh start into more honest business dealings, but the damage had been done, the closets of the past filled with vile deeds.

Marcela needed to return to those days now, one more time.

"Dios mío," she whispered to herself. *My God.* Spanish always comforted her at such times. Yet what did God have to do with this situation? She had long since given up her Catholic upbringing, especially during her years working for Reid Larkin. Such work was in no way God's work.

Could she do it one more time? Of course she could, there wasn't a choice. Shoving her recollections into the murky caverns of her brain, she turned to her computer to begin.

5

SOMETHING FOR US

"I've never been here before," Erin confessed as she walked with Conner toward one of the many entrances to the Mall of America.

"Never?" he asked.

"I'm not that into malls."

Conner stopped. His apprehension had been building ever since he had picked her up for their first date, and now the anxiety had frozen him to the cement. Bumbling through small talk during the drive there, he seesawed between infatuation with her and utter terror.

"We could go somewhere else," he offered.

Erin turned to face him. Her torn jeans, faded t-shirt with a goddess on the front, arm tattoos, and leopard purse perfectly contrasted his khakis and pinstripe button down. Was she analyzing the mismatch with her stare?

"It's okay, I'll survive. Plus, I'm starving," she said.

"There are other restaurants . . ."

"It's cute that you thought I'd like a mall," she interrupted. "It's just not my thing. But we're here, so let's go."

As if to reassure him, she grabbed his hand and guided

him through the entrance. All he could think about was her soft hand in his, as though it was meant to be there, and nothing else really existed. They continued to walk hand in hand through the first smattering of stores and fast-food outlets, yet he barely noticed the surroundings.

But as they reached the Rotunda, a circular conglomeration of shops at a key mall intersection, they stopped to observe the four levels of stores teeming with shoppers. She released his hand to grab the railing, taking in the view as if it was a forest fire.

"Holy cow, look at this place," she said. He couldn't tell if she was impressed or offended, but decided it was both.

"I can't believe you've never been here before," Conner said. "Why don't you like malls? I thought all . . ." He stopped when she turned to face him and folded her arms in front of her.

"You thought what?" she asked.

"Never mind."

"You think all women like malls?"

"I . . ."

"Stereotypes are fun, aren't they?" she said, showing a shrewd smile.

His mouth hung open mid-thought, a perfect still-life of mortification.

"Whatever, I'm not gonna give you a feminist lecture," she said. "I actually love shopping, I just don't think malls have anything for me. Does that answer your question?"

"Yes," he said. "I shop online, and I don't even like that. I'm not sure why I chose this place, except I came here a lot when I was a kid. I thought it might be fun."

"Then let's make it fun," she said. "Which way is dinner?"

Conner pointed past the Rotunda to the right. They made their way through the crowd to the sounds of roars and screams from the adjacent theme park. Erin stared in awe as they reached the cavernous hallway of shops away from the Rotunda. The long summer days meant that the sun was still shining through the skylights way above as evening approached, giving the impression that they were walking outside.

"This is actually pretty amazing," she confessed. "It's like its own little world. How long would it take to walk through all of this?"

"Hours," Conner said. "I still get lost. That's sort of the appeal, there's something different each time you come."

They window-shopped their way past the familiar names —Barnes & Noble, Fossil, Build-A-Bear, and Sears—before the restaurant came into view ahead on the right. The silver *Twin City Grill* letters above the entrance reflected off the sunlight. Conner led Erin to a stop in front of the restaurant, its mahogany entrance suggesting a grand world of yesterday, a young bespectacled hostess waiting behind a podium inside.

"Here?" she questioned. He braced for his choice of restaurant to backfire. Would it be an insult to some special diet? Or somehow politically incorrect? Too mainstream?

"Is this okay?"

"Beats the food court, right?" she joked. She must have noticed that he looked worried: "Sure, it looks great, let's eat."

They walked inside, Conner holding up two fingers to the hostess. "Two please."

The hostess nodded, guided them in, and seated them in the center of the restaurant. Inside, the walls and fixtures were dominated by more mahogany and images of Minnesota landmarks and icons, a large bar lining one side. The hostess plopped down menus and left them to wait for the server. Having finally arrived at their table, Conner felt a sense of ease.

"Nice place. Is the food good?" Erin asked him, opening the menu.

"The fish and seafood are great," he said. "If you like that."

"Not so much," she said, continuing to search the entrees. "Oh, flatbread. Now we're talkin'."

"Haven't had it, but everything here is good. Wine?"

"Yes, I whine a lot, haven't you noticed?" she said.

"Good one."

"Sure, wine would be great. You order it though, I don't know jack about wine."

When the server arrived, Conner ordered two glasses of merlot. In minutes the server returned with the wine and a basket of warm bread, then left them to ponder the menus.

"I'm ravenous," Erin said. "I'm gonna eat this whole basket of bread, do you mind?"

"Can I have one at least?"

"Oh all right."

Conner watched her select a piece and put it on her bread plate. She buttered it, then took a bite, melted butter dripping down her chin. She wiped it away with her napkin.

"Mmm, it's delicious, this is a good sign," she said. She passed the basket of bread across the table to him. "Seriously, don't let me eat all of these, because I will."

"I'd be sort of curious to see that," Conner said, taking a sip of his wine. "But I'm here to help." He grabbed a piece of bread and took a bite as she silently judged him for not buttering it first.

"You've never even considered coming to the Mall of America?" he said, sipping more wine to wash down the bread, alcohol beginning to numb him.

"I've thought about, it, but I've never had a compelling reason, until now."

"So that would make me . . . compelling?" he asked.

Erin looked irritated, and it panicked him before he figured out that her reaction wasn't from what he had said.

"Man these are bugging me!" she said, squinting as she pulled on one of her triangular sterling earrings. She removed the pair and placed them next to her plate, itching her ears, then frowned at him as her mind swam in contemplation.

"So that means something," she said at last.

"It does?"

A nod. "Today is Lughnasadh, right? And my earrings are Lughnasadh earrings, and they itch. Something special is about to happen, don't you think?"

"Lew-nuh what?"

"Lughnasadh. It's August first. Today is the Gaelic holiday Lughnasadh."

"I guess we needed an August holiday. What are we celebrating?"

Erin picked up an earring and pointed to it. "It's a harvest celebration in the honor of the warrior god Lugh."

"I did not know that. How is it celebrated?"

"Mostly it's not, at least not anymore. But it used to be celebrated with feasting and dancing. Here, I'll show you another way." With that she pulled a tissue from her purse, placed a piece of bread on it, wrapped it up, and tucked it away.

Conner could feel the wine embolden him. "Kleptomania?"

She glared at him and shook her head. "I'll take the bread home, put it on the table as an offering to Lugh, and that's one way to symbolically celebrate the day. It's very satisfying."

"Sounds a little less eventful than most holidays."

"It's *eventful* to me. It's all how you look at it. Anyway, a lot of current holidays come from pagan roots. We've just twisted them into something different."

The server came back to take their order. Erin ordered

vegetable flatbread, Conner the chicken parmesan, and the server left.

"So what benefit is there in placing bread on a table for a warrior god? I don't get it," he said.

There she was, folding her arms in front of herself again. "What benefit is there in hunting for Easter eggs? In carving a pumpkin? In Santa Claus?"

"Those are for the kids, for fun. Tradition."

"Exactly. For fun, for tradition, and beyond that, for spiritual harmony."

"Spiritual harmony in a piece of bread. Really?"

"Yes, really."

"If you say so," Conner laughed.

"Never mind." She scowled as she looked down at her bread.

When he saw that he'd pushed it too far, he berated himself on the inside. "Sorry, I'm just trying to understand."

"I'm not sure that you are. You can't understand, and you never will. Let's just talk about something else."

But instead of talking they ate bread and sipped wine in silence, Conner ordering two more glasses. The dining room filled with more patrons weary from shopping, toting bags filled with purchases. Looking out the front window, the setting sunlight had the effect of a city preparing for darkness. Conner's unease made him wrestle with how to rescue the date, but he came up empty.

"I have to know. What's your idea of religion?" Erin asked.

Conner thought about it, struggling for the right way to respond. The only thing that came was honesty. "I suppose I don't really have an idea. I believe in God, just not the church. People run churches, and I have a hard time trusting that."

"Fair enough. *That's* the beauty of paganism. The world is your church, and it's not even a religion. More of a way of life."

"How much are you into this stuff?" he asked, wine negating his self censors.

"*Stuff?*" she said, shrugging, "I'm pretty into it. There are things going on that the average person knows nothing about. You wouldn't know I guess."

"Like . . . putting bread on your table for a warrior guy?"

"Lugh," she snapped.

"Right, Lugh. Doesn't the bread get stale?"

"You know what?" Erin said. "I'm sorry, but I think this has gone about as far as it can."

Erin stood from the table and put down her napkin. "I really appreciate you taking me here, but I don't think we're compatible. Night and day, don't you think? I'm just gonna go."

"Not compatible? No, I'm just not very good at this," he said, standing with her. "I'm saying all the wrong things. You don't have to go."

"Actually, I do. Maybe I'll see you on campus sometime."

He considered more placating words that didn't come.

"Okay," he said. It was all he could muster.

He watched her leave the restaurant into the flow of mall traffic, her gait telling him that she had made up her mind. He sat down again and looked at her bread plate, chastising himself for being so dense.

Five minutes later, when it was clear that she wouldn't be returning, Conner considered canceling their order. But when he saw Erin's Lughnasadh earrings still on the table, he grabbed them and left for the exit. The hostess looked confused when she saw him rushing out.

"We'll be back," he said over his shoulder. "Can you hold our table?" She looked unsure what to do with that, then gave a half-hearted nod. As he left the direction Erin had gone, he pulled out his cell phone.

~

ERIN KNEW there was a light rail line from the Mall of America, she just needed to find it and get home. She shook in anger when Conner's careless words replayed in her mind. There was regret in leaving him there—the guy had seemed promising—but that was out the window now, wasn't it? What a waste. Why were guys always the same when they learned about her beliefs?

Still, part of her wanted to go back, to talk it out with him, to give it another try. She could handle it, right? What harm would there be? Maybe there was something there worth the effort?

She continued to walk past the shops and kiosks, indecision pulling her apart. But the materialism and her anger were beginning to nauseate her, so she vowed to just find an information desk and ask about a train home. She didn't need any more of this.

Then her cell phone began ringing a Bach fugue ringtone inside her purse. She plucked out the phone, looked at the screen, and saw that it was Conner. She tapped the button to answer.

"What?"

"Leaving so soon?"

"Yeah, well, I don't need to be insulted on a date, I get enough of that as it is."

She ended the call but continued to hold the phone. As she suspected, it rang again. He was persistent. She answered the call and spoke: "What are you not understanding?"

"I understand," he said. "But I need to give you something." Conner appeared in front of her from behind a kiosk, holding his phone to his ear.

Erin looked back toward the way she had come in confusion, then turned to him. He shut off his phone and put it in his pocket. "Shortcut. I told you I've been here a lot."

"Lovely. Now what do you want?"

"You forgot these." He held out her earrings in his palm. She touched her earlobes, only then realizing the absence of her earrings. Her ears started to burn and itch so severely that she pulled and rubbed her lobes.

"Thanks." She took the earrings from his hand and put them in her jeans pocket.

"Good night." She walked around him and continued on her way.

"Hey," Conner said, catching up to her.

"Is this going to end with me getting a restraining order?"

"Hopefully not. Can I say one more thing?"

"I don't know, you've said a lot already," she said.

"I think you're right about your ears."

"I'm right about my ears?"

"Yeah, the itching *does* mean something."

Erin stopped walking and faced him.

"Okay Nostradamus, what does it mean?"

"I think it means something for us. I think we're supposed to be together," he said.

"Seems like a huge leap, don't you think? And anyway, nice try, saying what you think I want to hear."

"Okay, what do you think it means?"

"It means I'm allergic to these damn earrings. I don't know."

But even as she said that, she knew he was onto something. She could feel it. For whatever reason, their meeting had a purpose.

"I won't bother you anymore then," Conner said. "I'm sorry for insulting you. I didn't mean to. I have a really bad habit of offending people by mistake."

He left her there. She watched him walk back toward the restaurant. Seeing him leave didn't feel right. There was dread, an opportunity lost, a single inaction that could cause a lifetime of misdirection.

"Hey!" she called.

"What?" He turned to face her.

"Wait up." She walked up to him.

"Is this going to end with me obtaining a restraining order?" he asked.

"Copycat," she said. "All right, I'm still mad at the ignorant things you said. But I think you were also being honest, which beats being a brownnoser any day. So I'm gonna take a risk that you're not as insensitive and dense as you've already demonstrated. Apology accepted, sort of, for now. But try to use that brain of yours a little before you speak, okay?"

Conner smiled. "Absolutely."

"I'm still starving."

"I had the hostess save our table," he said.

"Pretty overconfident of you, wasn't it? All right then, but let's take your shortcut back. I want to see this theme park."

"There's a Ferris wheel."

"A Ferris wheel in a mall? That's excessive. Let's ride it after we eat and throw up all over the place."

"That's fun to you?"

"Of course not, Mr. Gullible. Gross."

She laughed as he led her through the theme park and back to the restaurant.

6

PIKE

Appreciation of simple pleasures is an underrated life skill. Having grown up poor in Detroit, Karl Pike had learned this well. When you have nothing, you find value in what's available for free. You watch ants scuttle about the dirt in the courtyard and you sharpen Popsicle sticks on the sidewalk. Even now, as an adult living in Larkin's mansion where Pike had everything he needed and wanted, simplicity served him well, especially when exercising in the basement gym at 1 a.m. Household duties of the day complete, this was his time to enjoy the solitude of a strenuous workout.

Pike hadn't always been in peak physical condition. As a kid he had hated exercise, living a forgotten life among five siblings without hope. At eighteen, the Army had been his only option, but sometimes the only option is also the best one. The service had given him, for the first time ever, purpose and discipline. Once the idea of physical fitness had become engrained in him, it had never left. Twenty years of service under his belt, he had returned to civilian life, taking a job minding Larkin's mansion, and over time becoming one of

Larkin's most trusted employees, handling everything for Larkin from cooking, to chauffeuring, to security.

Pike jogged with long strides on the treadmill, running shoes kissing the belt, sweat pouring from his temples, earbuds piping in motivational metal. Larkin's workout room was superb: sixty-inch TV displaying ESPN, elliptical, stationary bike, free weights, speed bag, sit-up bench. Even more, this place was *his*, no one else used it.

Thirty minutes into his run, treadmill belt ascending and descending to mimic a cross-country jaunt, he summoned the resolve to endure the last fifteen minutes. His bare back and chest shimmered with a wash of sweat pouring over angry tattoos. Inspiring him was the reward of relaxing in the hot tub with a glass of Larkin's whiskey after the workout.

His run reaching a critical point, Pike decided that he needed more rousing TV than sports analysts. He reached for the remote and surfed the graveyard of programming, but he landed on a commercial for the Army, the optimistic kind meant to target young recruits. He kept it there for a moment, then shook his head and returned to ESPN.

Too late. The commercial had awakened memories that Pike had preferred to forget, and his mind regurgitated images of the Santos kid. It had happened in Afghanistan, the kid blown apart from an improvised explosive device. Pike had been the first to reach him. Still alive, yes, but Pike had known the kid was a goner, body functioning on nerves. Santos had been reduced to a mangled torso. The kid had looked incredibly young and feeble splattered in the sand, staring at the sky, bloody mouth uttering something unintelligible. Somewhere across the world a mother and father had known that childish look, their son had expressed it as far back as an infant, it hadn't been so long ago. Santos had died before anyone had been able to process it.

That hadn't been the only person Pike had seen die before, but the memory was wedged in the underworld of his brain tighter than any other. He could picture that kid down to the eyebrows, the chin, the nose, the virile body that the Army had chiseled into a masterpiece, all of it reduced to carrion.

Heart and lungs straining, Pike saw the timer on the treadmill display thirteen more minutes. He ignored his body's pleas to stop, looked away from the timer, and tried to enter a zone where time passed quickly among tangles of thoughts. But he needed even more focus than that, so he selected a point in front of him: the closed door of the gym. He studied the patterns of the heavy oak door, tried to lose his thoughts in the intricacies of its dark swirls. Feeling his body slipping in the fight to keep pace, he straightened his spine and shoulders, sucked in deeper breaths through his nose, and embraced the idea that he would rather die than quit.

After a minute, he regained his state of detachment to his body. He envisioned himself as a mule in the hot sun, laden with a heavy pack and nothing else to do but proceed, the thumping of his steps like steady pistons. So effective was the cloak of self-anesthetic that Pike blocked out the world. That's why, when the inexplicable happened, he was unable to comprehend it. He saw the gym door thrust open, knob bouncing against the wall, yet no one appeared at the doorway.

What the *hell*?

Pike shook himself from his trance, allowing his soldier's instincts to return. He tumbled off the treadmill and rolled onto the floor into a heap. He pulled himself into a crouch and looked at the doorway, finally catching a glimpse of a white mass in the darkness beyond.

Was it Larkin? Marcela? Neither. The white mass flashed to the left and out of sight, but Pike had seen enough to recognize damn well who had opened that door: a man in sailor whites.

This was as confusing as it was unsettling. Besides himself, there was no way that anyone but Larkin or Marcela could be in the mansion. Larkin's home had the best security system available, and Pike had checked the entire estate before coming down to work out. There could be no one else inside, much less a mischievous swabbie, without the alarms sounding.

Pike's martial instincts continued to guide him—Larkin had too many enemies to handle this casually. Crawling to the weight bench, he reached for his gym bag resting there, unzipped it, and found his Glock. Pulling it from the holster and cradling it with both hands, he pointed the squared barrel toward the doorway, stood, and crept forward, knees bent. Realizing his headphones were still in his ears, he tore the plugs out with his left hand and threw them to the floor, hand rejoining the other's hold on the Glock.

"Who's there?" Pike's question went unanswered. "You're gonna get plugged unless you say something! Come on out squid! I saw you."

Still no answer. Pike plunged through the doorway and waved the Glock back and forth, searching for movement. In here was Larkin's indoor swimming pool, the glassy green water illuminated by submerged pool lights. Dim as they were, the lighting was enough to see that no one was in the pool room. Nonetheless, he flicked on the ceiling lights, the wash of light revealing the glass doorway outside to his right, door to his left leading to the two bedrooms and the rest of the basement. Still no one. Pike wiped the sweat from his eyes with a shaking hand.

Whoever this guy was, he must have fled toward the theater beyond the bedrooms, so that's where Pike went. He paused to point the Glock down the hallway toward the bedrooms, but he saw that both doors were closed with no signs of entry. Satisfied, he crept toward the dark theater, stepped inside the doorway, and flipped on the lights revealing ten leather seats in front of the big screen. He waved the Glock to and fro as he walked through the room. Nothing.

The search continued past the theater to the sitting room, then the bar, and finally the game room that rounded out the basement level. If someone had been there, Pike's sweeps would have located him, he was certain of it. He knew all of the places a person could hide, but no one was there. Thoroughly confused, he doubled back through all of the rooms, including his own bedroom this time, looking for any signs of movement, any smells, any sounds. But the mansion was as vacant as ever, and eventually Pike found himself letting down his guard. The only room he hadn't checked was Marcela's, but when he checked the doorknob, he found it locked as usual. Next he returned to the pool room to check the door out to the garden, but there were no signs of tampering, no broken glass, and the door remained locked. No one had come in that way.

Baffled, Pike went upstairs with renewed precaution, assuming that the intruder had somehow doubled-back and retreated up to the main floor. But after a sweep of the main floor and the second floor, still there was nothing. He contemplated waking up Larkin to check his room on the second floor, but flustered and now questioning whether he had even seen anyone, he decided to check the security cameras instead.

He returned to the main floor and entered the small security room, closing the door behind him and locking it. The master alarm control panel on the wall indicated that the system was functioning as normal with no alarms tripped.

Next he sat at the workstation and began checking the video feeds on the computer from the dozens of hidden cameras throughout the mansion. It took him a minute to locate the pool room camera, enlarge the video window, and play back the last twenty minutes. At first he watched it in actual speed, but becoming impatient by the inactivity, he scanned ahead.

"Where did you go, you bastard?" he whispered to himself, tapping the Glock barrel on the workstation surface. Sensing that the time of the opened door was approaching, he slowed the playback to actual speed.

And then, as if witnessing his own impending death, Pike's eyes widened when he saw movement on the screen. The camera showed the gym door slamming open from poolside. The view became clearer as the gym lights shined out. To Pike's horror, it was painfully obvious that the door had opened by itself. It was as if a huge gust of wind had flung it open.

Pike stood up and clutched the top of his head in confusion. "What the *fuck*?"

He stood there watching the replay in shock. Eventually he saw himself on camera leaving the workout room pointing his Glock, and then there was no more. He hit fast-forward to make sure no one had come back, but no one had, right up until Pike himself had returned during his doubling back.

"No goddamn way! No goddamn *way*!"

Pike rewound and replayed the whole bizarre event, shaking his head and groaning to himself as he came to the same conclusion: no one had been there. He watched it six more times before he left the room in disgust, itching with heebie jeebies.

He went down to the bar, selected a fine whiskey from Larkin's supply, and slammed three double-shots. That felt better.

Then he returned to his bedroom, locked the door behind him, and kept the Glock nearby as he showered in his personal bathroom. Finished, he walked out of the bathroom, toweling himself dry. He felt slightly better, but one thing was for sure: there was no way anyone would hear about this. If this was some sort of pussified PTSD from seeing that Santos kid pop, that would be his burden alone, none of that counseling malarkey.

An hour into a late-night talk show on his TV, sprawled nude on his bed with the Glock in his hand, Pike let exhaustion and whiskey carry him to a fitful sleep.

7
____

THE THESIS

Erin wiped the china plate one last time, rinsed it, and handed it to Conner for drying. Hair pulled back from the humidity of the dishwashing room, her brow glistened with condensation.

"I shouldn't be here," she said. "I'm educated, shouldn't I be of greater value to society than a dishwasher? On a Saturday night, no less."

"I think we're pretty good at it," Conner said. "We could fall back on dishwashing if grad school doesn't pan out."

"No thanks."

Conner noticed Pike prowling the kitchen outside of the dishwashing room. Tonight being a smaller event, Conner and Erin were the only two workers he had brought in.

"So what was the big event today?" Conner called out to Pike.

Pike wiped his hands on a kitchen towel and stepped closer. "What's it to you, Mr. Professor? Dry the damn dishes."

"Just curious."

"Yeah, History Boy's always curious. I don't pay you by the question."

Conner nodded and continued drying plates. Pike came into the doorway and answered the question anyway.

"Larkin has his crew over once a month to do what head honchos do. These people got big brains and do nothing but work, but working on a Saturday is like a party for them, and they spend the whole day arguing, eating my food, and boozing. Beyond that, I couldn't say what they do. It's my job to make them comfortable, and your job is to clean up. You girls both happen to be adequate at this."

"Is his company a financial firm?" Conner asked.

"There you go again Curious George. Do I look like Warren fricken Buffet? I don't know what these guys do. Except they buy shit and they sell shit."

"A financial firm."

"Just dry my dishes," Pike said. "No wait, let Baby Doll keep washing, you come with me."

Conner put down his towel and followed Pike through the kitchen and into the adjoining hallway. They walked to the end of the cavernous hall and stopped at the two tall double doors of the library. Pike opened them and walked inside, Conner following.

Even though he had been in and out of the library earlier that night, Conner had been too preoccupied serving Larkin's staff to pay close attention to it. Library now deserted, its opulence sank in. "My God," he said, mouth hanging open.

"Stop drooling, I didn't bring you here to gawk." Pike led him deeper inside as Conner continued to survey the room.

"This collection is unbelievable," Conner said, staring at the relics in the display cases.

"And expensive, so ignore it," Pike said. He studied the room's clutter of plates, liquor glasses, and computer printouts with disgust, as if he took the mess as a personal affront. "Damn, this place is all *kinds* of messed up!"

"Looks like the day after a frat party," Conner added.

"And this little hell on Earth is all yours now," Pike said. "Take the dishes and stack them on the cart over there, throw away any garbage, and bring the cart to the kitchen. Don't break nothin, don't touch nothin but the dishes and the trash. Okay slick?"

"Right, no problem."

Pike walked back out of the library and left Conner to work. Disinterested in cleaning, Conner looked back at the door to make sure Pike was truly gone. Hearing Pike's footsteps echo down the hallway, Conner walked to the glass display cases, unable to resist the lure of what appeared to be an American Revolution section. Catching his eye first was a powder horn from the Revolutionary War etched with scrimshaw from the person who had owned it. Mounted above it was an officer's saber from the same time period. Surrounding these were an infantry drum, a colonial musket, and a British officer's tea set. He continued to follow the display cases down the row with his eyes, all of the cases loaded with historical artifacts spanning the centuries from around the world.

"Like what you see?"

Conner jumped from the words, fearing it was Pike. But when he looked toward the sound of the voice, instead he saw a sickly old man at the doorway.

"Just cleaning up," Conner said, returning to the mess.

"Looks more like another one of my employees being paid for his own amusement."

Conner began stacking dishes onto the cart as the man who Conner guessed was Reid Larkin hobbled into the library to retrieve something from his roll-top desk in the corner. Larkin coughed a horrifying bark that reminded Conner of a dog hacking on a bone.

"Are you okay?"

Larkin raised a hand and waved away Conner's concern. "Just clean up."

"Sure, I'll be out of here soon." Conner scooped up a coffee cup with a soggy napkin stuffed into it and placed it onto the cart, wondering why everyone in this place was so crabby.

"I see Karl's been trolling the colleges for hired help again," Larkin said as he shuffled through some papers on his desk. "But you look a little older than that."

"I'm a grad student at the U."

"Of course you are," Larkin said, turning to examine Conner as though he was some sort of evidence. "Let me guess more. You're studying philosophy or literature—something that will prepare you for the working world about as well as polishing my flatware?"

"History."

"Ah," Larkin said, pondering this information. "More respectable than I realized, but it'll still make you unemployable. Not much of a market for historians these days."

"Maybe not."

"And you're working on a thesis, no doubt? Something groundbreaking, like the influence of Grover Cleveland's dachshund?"

Conner was becoming annoyed. "No, nothing that amusing."

"No one cares about history anymore," Larkin said as he walked over to his display cases. "People have no use for it. Only the likes of you or me care about what happened in the past. What do you intend to do with your vast stockpile of historical knowledge?"

"Teach I suppose," Conner said. Then he remembered what Erin had said about the universe. "Or maybe something else will come along."

"Give me a synopsis of your thesis then. Wow me."

Conner wasn't expecting to present his thesis while clearing dishes. Why did everyone care about his thesis? He kept quiet and continued to work, hoping Larkin would lose interest.

"And for Christ's sake, stop stacking my dishes," Larkin boomed. "Lord knows you're probably unable to walk and chew gum at the same time. Come over here."

Conner obeyed but kept his distance from Larkin.

"That's it. Now let me have it, what's your wonderful thesis idea?"

"I haven't picked one yet," Conner said. Larkin grimaced with impatience, which compelled Conner to continue. "I don't know, maybe something about Pearl Harbor from the Japanese perspective?"

Larkin rolled his eyes.

"Or immigrant soldiers during Gettysburg," Conner said. "I've also thought about the influence of 9/11 on Islamophobia."

Larkin looked at the high ceiling of his library to consider these ideas, or maybe to calm his disgust.

"No doubt all topics your liberal instructors would want you to have," Larkin said, returning his gaze to Conner. "The colleges are all that way now, run by deranged socialists."

"Deranged socialists? I don't think . . ."

"Enemies, immigrants, and Islam," Larkin interjected. "This is what we want our students studying these days? God help us. No matter, it'll get you your degree. And your background in history explains your interest in my collection, unless you just hope to rob me?"

"Yes. I mean, no," Conner said. "You have some amazing things here, but I should get back to work."

Larkin shook his head and walked down his row of cabinets. "Not yet, let me show you something first. Consider it your OSHA break, not that I believe in them."

Conner watched as Larkin opened one of the cabinets and removed an iron contraption that clanged together like a defective clock chime. Larkin brought it over to Conner and held it out: rusty slave shackles, as rare as they were macabre, and absolutely original looking.

"If you promise not to drop this, you may look at it." He handed it to Conner with his bony hands shaking from the weight. Conner received it with both hands, shackles heavy and cold, the magnitude of what he held seeping into his sense of empathy.

"Incredible," Conner said, running his thumb over one of the wrist loops. "How old is it?"

"Likely late 1700s," Larkin said.

"Hard to imagine what the wearer of this must have suffered."

"Life is suffering," Larkin said. "These shackles represent a unique time in our history, when men could own other men. You should consider yourself lucky that you're paid for your work."

"Unique, yes, but also disgusting," Conner said. "Slavery was a brutal practice."

"Any more brutal than living in 1700s Africa? Slavers did them a favor," Larkin said.

"A favor? How can you say that?"

"Living naked in the jungle eating bugs is enjoyable then?" Larkin snapped. "They were brought into the civilized world."

"As enslaved people to be abused and denied their basic rights," Conner said.

"Slavery advanced our country," Larkin said. "Without it we may not have become what we are today."

Conner kept quiet, realizing that this discussion would go

nowhere. Sensing the standstill, Larkin took the shackles back and massaged them with chapped fingers. "In any case, it's history," he said. "Can't change it now. Can't go back, either. People have rights now, every last one of them. Too many, I say."

"People shouldn't have rights?"

"Those that the Constitution and Bill of Rights protect are sufficient," Larkin said. "But I'm talking about people going too far. Absolute equality for a society of unequals. The welfare state. People who want to be treated special for nothing they've earned. Everyone stretches their so-called rights today, and we're left with an entitled, spoiled people. America, land of the freeloaders. And if honest people speak their mind, they're crucified for it."

"That's how it works in a democracy," Conner said. "You can speak your mind, but others may disagree."

"It goes way beyond that," Larkin said. "Political correctness, government meddling, corporate policy. If you call a Black man lazy you're racist. If you call a woman emotional you're sexist. If you say you don't like homosexuals, you're a bigot."

"I should get back to the dishes," Conner said.

"Copping out of a political debate so quickly?" Larkin said. "Your liberal education teaches you to run when someone disagrees with you?"

"We just have very different ideas," Conner said. "I don't think I'll change your mind."

"No, you won't. But now we know where we stand, don't we? I call that a victory."

"If you say so," Conner said.

"My opinions are harsh to you. Good. I'm not some monster though," Larkin said. "Not yet, anyway. Maybe if Karl calls you back sometime we can discuss it more in depth. But sadly, I have other things to do now, and so do you." Larkin turned around and, with another cough, returned the shackles to the display case.

"I should also like to read your thesis when it's finished. Lord knows you'll need an objective opinion. But I hope to God you find better topics than those."

"I can send you a copy."

"Good, finish with this mess before Karl sees you dallying," Larkin said. "He's a nasty sons a bitch, just the way I like it. Don't upset the man, he'll come out shooting."

With that, Larkin walked past Conner and left the library.

Alone again, Conner took one last glance toward the display cases, shook his head, then continued cleaning the mess.

8

TAROT

Conner ascended through the darkness of the exterior staircase. Reaching the landing, he stood in front of Erin's duplex door, dim light trickling through curtains covering the door's window inside. In his left hand was a bottle of wine, and with his right he knocked, hoping he had the right place. Shadows and shuffling came from within before Erin opened the door, spicy-sweet aroma wafting out.

"Hiya," she said, stepping outside to embrace him. The hug took him by surprise, but he wrapped his arms around her in return.

"Hi," he said.

She raised her head and looked into his eyes, mouth opening in what he thought might be a kiss. She spoke instead: "I should have mentioned my porch light is burned out, and I'm all out of bulbs. Found it okay though?"

"Yep, no problem," he said.

"Come on in then," she said, pulling away and leading him inside. She shut the door behind them.

"It smells amazing in here," he said.

"That's Dragon's Blood."

"Dragon's Blood?"

"Incense," she said. "My landlady thinks I'm a pot smoker from all of the incense I burn. Anyway, here's my kitchen, stop one on the apartment tour."

He examined its simplicity: white cabinetry, worn wood floor, track lights illuminating herbs growing on a shelf above the sink, and a candle burning next to the incense on a round kitchen table.

"This sure beats my lowly bachelor kitchen," he said. Then he held up the bottle. "I brought wine."

"Yes you did," she said, moving to a drawer for the corkscrew. She fished it out and handed it to him. "You open, I'll get glasses."

She reached to open her cupboard and pulled down two tumblers, setting them on the counter. He opened the bottle and poured a healthy amount into each.

Erin grabbed her glass, took a sip, and licked her lips. "Mmm. You know your wine. Come on, the rest of the tour awaits."

She left him behind and walked down the hallway. He picked up his glass and followed.

The hallway led to a living room infinitely more complex than the kitchen: crimson walls, a black futon, worn cherry coffee table, black wooden rocking chair, and a small TV. An audio station on a shelf played new age music barely audible, more incense smoldering next to it. Commanding the room above the futon was an explosion of color from a painting unlike any Conner had seen before. It was a portrait of a cloaked woman in the foreground of a dark forest. A fog of red, blue, and yellow drifted from her head in swirls.

Conner pointed to the painting. "That's interesting."

Erin nodded and walked closer to the portrait to tell its

story. "A few years ago I was dating an artist—by the way, never date an artist—and he painted it for me. See the resemblance?" She turned back to him and changed her expression to mimic the earnest stare of the woman in the painting.

"That's you?"

She broke the stare and laughed, Conner joining in without knowing why.

"In the flesh," Erin continued. "I know it's snobby to hang a portrait of yourself in your own place, but it's not really me, it's the artist's interpretation of me."

"Looks like she's plotting something," Conner said.

"She's conjuring. She's doing what most people fail to do—letting her mind and soul reveal things that often go overlooked. If we could see those things, it might look like that."

"I'll take your word for it. Your artist guy has talent."

"Too bad that's all he had was talent," she said. "Anyway, this is pretty much the tour. There's my bedroom in there, not much to see. I call it home."

She reached for a deck of tarot cards on the coffee table and held it up. "Are you up for some of this?"

"You know how to do tarot?" he asked.

"Of course I do, doesn't everyone?"

"No. Will it hurt?"

"That depends on how you look at it. Sometimes the truth does hurt. But you're a fairly grounded guy, I don't think you have anything to fear."

"Let's do it then," he said. He took a seat on the futon, placing his cup on the table. Erin set down her wine, sat cross-legged on the floor on the other side of the coffee table, and cupped the cards in both hands as if the deck was a butterfly trying to escape.

"You need to cut the deck," she said, placing it on the table in front of him.

"I'm not sure I know the rules. Do I hit on 15?"

"This isn't like Vegas. You just need to cut the deck and I'll take it from there. If the person who is the subject of the reading touches the deck, the results will be more accurate. If nothing else, it's a symbolic gesture."

"If you say so," he said, reaching with one hand to lift half of the deck, setting it beside the other half.

"Good boy. Oh no!"

Erin stood up in alarm, causing Conner to flinch. "What?" he said.

"Hold on, I'll be right back!" She walked to the kitchen, leaving Conner to wonder what he had done.

There were sounds of cupboards and the refrigerator being opened in the kitchen. A minute later, Erin returned with a large bowl of tortilla chips and a smaller bowl of green dip. She placed them on the table and returned to her cross-legged position.

"The greatest secret of tarot is guacamole," she said.

"I think I can endorse that," he said, reaching for a chip. He dipped it deeply into the guacamole and popped it into his mouth, nodding his approval. "Delicious. Did you make it?"

"Of course," she said. "Don't buy processed guacamole. Just, don't." She dipped her own chip and wolfed it down, nodding her head.

"Okay, here we go," she said after swallowing, washing it down with a swig of wine. She placed what had been the lower part of the deck on top of the cut half. "You need to think of a question."

"Like, what's the meaning of life?"

"No, it needs to be more focused. It doesn't have to be yes or no either. If you're asking about the future, which is usually the case, it's best if it's not more than a year out, otherwise the reading gets fuzzy."

"How about, will I pass my Imperial Russia course?"

"Seriously? That's the most burning question you can think of?"

Conner considered that. "At the moment."

"So far you've given me a deep, unanswerable question *and* a really lame one. Pick something in between, an important issue that requires clarity."

Conner thought harder. "All right, how about, will my master's thesis be a success?"

Erin raised her index finger into the air. "That'll do." Then she began to place some cards face down, one in the center and others surrounding it in the beginnings of a diamond shape. But as she went to remove a card from the deck, another card fell out.

"Whoops," she said, looking down at the fallen card still face down.

"Too much wine?" he asked.

"That's never happened to me," she said.

"No harm done," he shrugged.

"Don't you believe everything happens for a reason?"

"That depends. Possibly?"

"That's pretty wishy-washy. In tarot, as in life, *nothing* is an accident. As I was laying out the cards, this one fell out. It's called jumping the deck. I'm gonna set it aside for now and we'll come back to it."

"Sounds mysterious."

"We'll see." She continued to set out the last two cards until the diamond shape was complete.

"As I overturn each card, one at a time, the question will be addressed by my interpretation of the cards. We'll turn over the card that jumped the deck after I've turned over the third card, since that's when it fell out. Are you ready?"

She looked at him as if they were preparing to jump off the Golden Gate.

"You're creeping me out slightly, but yes, I'm ready."

"Nice. Just, clear your mind, be open to what you see and hear."

Erin turned over the center card as Conner took a sip of wine.

"Huh," she said. "This is Five of Rods."

"A bunch of little people with clubs beating the hell out of each other," Conner observed. "I'm guessing that's bad."

"Not necessarily," Erin said. "The card in the center always represents hidden aspects being brought to light in relation to the question you've asked. Five of Rods indicates a battle or competition, a power struggle. It also represents obstacles that block your path or goal, and the need to acquire new skills."

"Great."

"Wouldn't you expect that a master's thesis would require some struggle?"

"I had hoped not."

"It's not all bad, in my opinion, and it's only part of the reading. We need to see what the rest of the story is."

She overturned the card to the left of the center, to his right.

"Rods again," Conner said. "A little phallic, isn't it?"

"It's not *that* kind of rod, sicko. This is Two of Rods, and it's in the position of what's developing or manifesting. The card suggests the offering of your unique talents to the world, or an idea that's ready to be launched. It can also mean education and the skills of a brilliant mind."

"Well, what can I say?" Conner said.

"This card is just showing that your thesis is in progress, which we pretty much knew. But it validates that the question is being addressed."

"So what's next, more rods?"

Erin flipped over the card above her center card. On the face was a brick tower with an explosion of light flashing at the top, with a king's crown flying from the light like shrapnel.

"This is The Tower."

"More like the Towering Inferno," Conner said. "I'm going to die in a fire?"

Erin ignored him. "This position represents the problems that have been escalating. See how the Tower is exploding? The card represents upheaval breaking apart the foundations of a situation. It can mean a human or natural disaster, where weak foundations crumble. There's an inevitable, drastic, traumatic change coming."

"I don't like the sound of that."

"This could all be figurative. Maybe the process of writing your thesis will change you somehow, maybe traumatically, but that doesn't mean it'll actually be harmful to you. A lot of personal progress can be gained through trauma, don't you think?"

Conner needed the motivation of guacamole to answer her question, and as he dipped, bit, and chewed, he nodded unconvincingly. "But again, I had hoped writing a thesis would be easier than all this. Trauma?"

"These are just words provided as part of the explanation of the cards. Wouldn't you suspect writing a thesis would involve some level of trauma?"

"No."

"It's what you make it to be. If you go into the task expecting it to be easy, maybe it will be. The cards can be wrong."

"I'm curious about the crazy card that jumped the deck," Conner said.

"We can look at it now."

Erin turned it over and gasped. Conner held up his hands, placing one index finger across the other to mimic a crucifix. Even before he read the title of the card, he knew what the picture represented: *the devil.*

"What the hell does my thesis have to do with the devil?" he asked.

Erin, too, seemed confused. "The Devil card has many meanings. It can refer to succumbing to temptation, which we all know leads to unhappiness. Those things you associate with the devil apply here: being trapped by evil, emotional imprisonment, darkness, obsession, confusion, chaos, lost souls."

"It's just a thesis!" Conner said.

Erin shook her head and squinted in concentration. "This is different, it goes way beyond your thesis. When a card jumps the deck, it represents an issue that can't be ignored. Something is going to emerge that you have to deal with, and it's of profound significance."

"If I win the lottery in the next few months, the profound significance is I'm dropping out of school."

"That's actually not a bad example, except the darkness of this card suggests an event that's not quite so cheery."

"Like, I get hit by lightning?"

"You're so negative," she smiled at him. "No, but something dark, an issue to be reckoned with."

"I have to say, I'm not getting much comfort from all this."

"The comfort should be that you're being alerted to the possibilities so you can be ready to act. But relax, there are still two more cards."

"By all means continue then."

Erin flipped over the fifth card in silence.

She studied Conner while she sipped her wine. Then: "This is the Queen of Swords. In this position it represents help you'll receive. The traits of this person helping you can be analytical, sociable, an advocate of fair treatment, courageous, assertive, determined. This could signify anyone as minor as someone who temporarily gets you through a struggle, or as major as a life partner. That's yet to be known."

"My hero. Will I know this person when the time comes?"

"I think you will. It might be someone you already know. I think it's a female."

Conner nodded. "Based on what it sounds like is coming, I'll probably go running to my mommy."

"It's not your mom, or at least I don't think so."

Conner shrugged.

Erin laughed. "You're not buying any of this, are you?"

"No offense, but it's all a little far-fetched. You turn over some cards randomly and they tell you the future? I mean, it's fun, I admit it, but I'm skeptical."

"Well humor me then," she said. "It's okay not to believe everything the cards say."

"Let's look at the last one. It can't get much worse, right?"

The final card Erin overturned showed a picture of a woman in a robe holding two swords and wearing a blindfold.

"This is Two of Swords," she said. "The last card overturned represents the resolution of the situation. Two of Swords means an important decision has to be made, but there's some anxiety involved. The pros and cons of the situation have to be pondered, and the answer is not easily found. There might be some sort of stalemate, and progress toward your goal will be halted until the stalemate is resolved."

"Maybe I should have asked about my Imperial Russia course after all," Conner said, leaning back on the futon. Erin came around to sit by him.

"Don't worry about it, you'll have help, remember?"

"Maybe elves will come to my laptop at night and cobble

together an incredibly insightful thesis paper while I sleep? Now *that's* help."

"Not very realistic though. Just open your eyes to what's around you, and the help will be there."

Conner listened to the music and inhaled the incense in the room, accented with Erin's perfume. He looked at his mostly empty cup. "Maybe it's time for more wine?"

"I think I'm influencing you already, you read my mind," she said. She grabbed both tumblers, stood up, and walked to the kitchen. Conner also stood. He turned to study the painting again, this time really seeing the resemblance to Erin, her dark eyes, round cheeks, full lips. He couldn't help but think that he'd entered a strange new world with her. He took another chip, dipped it into the guacamole, and popped it into his mouth. For all of her enigmas, though, the girl sure made a mean guacamole.

A minute later and Erin was back with more wine.

"Do you like road trips?" Conner asked as she handed him his cup.

"That came out of nowhere," she said. "Yeah. Why?"

"I've been thinking about driving to Gettysburg this summer to research my thesis. It's a long drive, but it can be done faster if it's driven straight through. It could be a weekend excursion."

"The battlefield?"

"Yeah, from the Civil War. Do you want to come? It could be fun."

"Your idea of fun is a little different from mine," she said. "How many people died there?"

"Thousands. It was horrible."

"Must be lots of emotional residue hanging around that place." Erin seemed to ponder the macabre satisfaction and horror of that. "Okay, sure, I'll go. It's not going to hurt though, right?"

"That depends on how you look at it."

"You're copying me again."

Erin reached for his shoulder and pulled herself to him. She kissed him before he was ready for it, but he met it, tasting the wine on her lips and inhaling her perfume in his nostrils. He held her as the kiss took a life of its own.

She pulled away and took another sip of her wine. "Wanna watch a movie?" she said. "I wash enough dishes to afford Netflix."

She turned on the TV and sat on the futon. He sat by her, but instead of watching TV he kissed her again.

9

———

SEMINARY RIDGE

The dog days of summer were giving way to the approaching fall on Seminary Ridge at Gettysburg National Military Park in Pennsylvania. The day had started with a hint of autumn chill, the first relief from the humidity in weeks, but now the noonday battlefield was burning with summer heat. To Conner it was perfect.

"This would have been an awful place around this time on July 3, 1863," he said.

Erin yawned. He couldn't really blame her; the abstraction of a battlefield couldn't penetrate her interest, and the grueling drive had left them both zombies. Conner's pickup almost appeared lethargic parked behind them along Hancock Avenue.

Erin took a swig of coffee from her paper cup. "And why was that?"

Conner had tried to recap the basics of the Civil War to Erin during the drive out, but she had quickly become weary of the war's barbarism and complexity. Yet he had managed to explain to her that the war, sparked by the national divide over slavery, involved many desperately fought battles, Gettysburg being the most deadly and one of the most important among them.

He pointed across the battlefield to the tree line a mile out. "Confederate batteries . . . well, cannons, opened fire out there to soften this spot for the final assault on July 3 while Union soldiers crouched behind makeshift barriers. They used rocks, knapsacks, fence posts, anything they could find to huddle behind. It would have been really loud and terrifying. There was nothing to do but wait it out and hope you weren't hit."

"What's the wisdom of men doing this to each other?" Erin asked.

"It was how things were, they all wanted to be here."

"Lucky them."

Erin stepped out beyond the Union line markers, swirling her coffee cup and staring across the open landscape.

"How many people died here?" she asked.

"Out in front of us would have been thousands of dead and wounded. When the Confederates advanced, they found that their artillery hadn't done the job on the Union lines, and it was a mile of marching right into Union fire. They were decimated, some of them vaporized by cannon fire. Some Confederates made it here, but the Union lines held. There were over fifty-thousand casualties from the three days of fighting all around us."

"What a complete waste," Erin said.

"It wasn't a waste if you consider what was at stake. Had the Confederates defeated the Union at Gettysburg, they may have gone on to capture Washington and win the war."

Erin inhaled the air, seeming to imagine the decay of battle in place of the late summer vitality. She brushed her hair from her eyes. "This place is so heavy. Can't you feel it? It's just thick with human agony, yet it's also very peaceful. I've never felt anything like it."

"See, aren't you glad you came? It's an amazing place."

"Amazing isn't the right word. It's horrifying, astonishing. I can *feel* the suffering. Can't you?"

Conner shrugged. "I feel warm, tired. Maybe a little hungry."

She walked to him. "Congratulations, you've mastered your primary senses," she said. "But that's not the kind of feelings I'm talking about. I mean the sensations inside of you. The emotions the men who died here probably felt, the misery that's still swirling around this place. Don't you feel that?"

"Not so much," he said.

She reached for his hand and held it. "It's like, when someone you admire holds your hand," she continued. "You can't explain what it does, but it's more than physical touch, it's lasting."

"Sure."

She kissed him, her lips scented with coffee and lipstick.

"Or a kiss," she said. "Tell me that my kiss is no more than a physical sensation?"

"It's definitely more," he agreed.

"That's progress," she smiled. "Not everything we experience can be described with our basic senses. So what's next?"

He pointed south. "Down there."

He led her by the hand down Hancock Avenue, leaving the pickup far behind. As they walked, they studied the open land that looked like any other stretch of farmland, but with hundreds of monuments and plaques marking battle actions. The land had transformed into something sacred ever since it was ravaged by the upheaval of war. Since those July days in 1863, the land had become an enormous living shrine and park, never again to be used for anything else.

"There it is," Conner pointed to the distance. Up ahead

towered a monument of a solitary Union soldier atop a tall concrete base, the soldier charging with a musket, bayonet pointing toward some invisible foe.

"The statue?" Erin said. "There are hundreds of them here, why is that one important?"

"That's the First Minnesota Infantry monument," Conner said.

"Minnesota fought here?"

"Yes."

"Yay for Minnesota."

"Most of them were killed or wounded."

"Well that sucks."

They reached the base of the monument. Conner looked to the right toward the direction that the soldier statue charged.

"On the second day of the battle, July 2, things didn't go well for the First Minnesota," he said. "General Hancock, the Union officer who this road is named after, was observing a huge battle between Confederate and Union forces way out in the field in front of us. But he saw that the Union lines were collapsing, and the Confederates were about to break through. That would have been disastrous because it likely would have meant that the Confederates would have swept the Union lines and won the battle."

"So what did he do?" Erin asked.

"He found a regiment on this spot that wasn't yet involved in the fighting. That was the First Minnesota. He ordered them to charge the advancing Confederates. Being the obedient Midwesterners that they were, they followed the order. Most of them were killed or wounded during that charge, but it worked. By the time it was over, it was almost dark, and the Confederates were forced to retire."

"They charged there?" Erin pointed to the gradually

sloping ground in front of the statue, a recently mowed path cutting straight to the tree line.

Conner nodded. "Down there, by the trees. It must have been horrific, bullets flying at them from the front and both sides, men falling every second, all of them knowing they were doomed. About 260 men made the charge and over 200 were killed or wounded. Some died where they fell, a lot died days and weeks later from agonizing wounds."

"Why would someone obey an order like that?"

"It was their job," Conner said. "Many had a high sense of honor. Others just didn't want to look weak in front of their fellow soldiers. And they all wanted to win."

"And life wasn't sacred, apparently."

"No, it was, but ideals were more important than living. In a way, it's kind of refreshing, isn't it, when people today mostly care about themselves?"

"Not particularly," she said. "I mean, true, people are stuck up, but dying for ideals is crazy, if you ask me." She left him to walk down the slope to see the ground for herself. He watched her sandals sweeping through the short grass, her hair blowing from a gentle breeze. He considered joining her, but he was content to observe her instead.

Erin felt the heat pound her forehead. She closed her eyes as she walked, hoping to visualize events from long ago. Her imagination recreated the excitement and momentum of the charging soldiers, young minds thinking a million thoughts in the moment of truth: fitful rage, honor, even self-preservation. She could practically hear their howls as they charged forward into the storm of combat, all of them accepting their fate.

As Erin considered these feelings, however, her thoughts drifted into something else. She felt her psyche falter as it was overrun by unbearable negativity: dread, anger, sorrow, the stain of suffering as real as if it had just happened. On cue, the vibrant daylight became overcast. Erin opened her eyes and looked up to see a solitary cloud deaden the sun. It was so out of place, a single cloud as round as a cannonball hovering in the otherwise blue sky.

Back at the monument, Conner began taking photographs with his phone. He pivoted to aim down the slope where Erin had gone, snapping pictures of her casual stroll. Then he lowered his phone to watch Erin again, and he saw her stop.

Down the slope, Erin's stomach tightened. Coffee still in one hand, she reached her free hand to her belly and wondered what havoc the cheap coffee was causing. Something smoldered in her insides, a rumble at first, then a burning followed by a wave of nausea. She lost her breath, her brain swirling in vertigo. Then the feelings receded like water sucked out to sea to fuel a tsunami. Her stability returned for a beat. She looked down at her stomach, filling her chest with a deep breath.

"Weird," she whispered. But the sensations weren't finished with her, instead returning with far greater force. She felt a jolt to her abdomen, the blow triggering an involuntary groan. It felt like she had been punched in the stomach, causing her to release the cup where it spilled on the ground. She winced and fell to her knees, fighting to regain her breath.

Conner saw her fall.

"Erin!" he called. He took a few steps toward her, trying to understand what had happened. She didn't answer. She *couldn't* answer.

All around Erin were emotions so profound and smothering that she broke into tears, as much from the pain in her stomach as the genuine anguish in her bones.

It must have been horrific, bullets flying at them from the front and both sides, men falling every second, all of them knowing they were doomed.

An altogether different sensation hit her full force. Touch receptors in her arms and legs synchronized to deliver a crippling sting. She screeched, leaped to her feet, and bounded as if evading hot coals. Now she saw them. How hadn't she noticed them before? An unyielding cluster of yellow jackets ravaged her exposed skin, stinging her incessantly. Flight response seizing control, she sprinted toward Conner, who came rushing toward her.

"What's wrong?" he shouted. She shook her arms and legs as she ran, her only response desperate squawks.

At last he saw the stream of yellow jackets following her, her limbs covered with them like splatters of yellow and black paint. He tore off his t-shirt as she galloped past, and he swatted at the passing swarm that spread to him like a virus, stinging his shirtless body.

"Get to the pickup!" he shouted, realizing a defense was hopeless. But this was already Erin's plan. She sprinted toward the truck seemingly so far away, and he followed her, whipping his shirt in the air as he ran.

The yellow jackets hung with this hasty retreat as if held to Erin and Conner by an invisible adhesive. The attackers continued to clutch and sting without mercy, driven by an unyielding instinct for violence.

Erin reached the pickup first. She opened the door and dove inside, slamming it behind her. Conner reached the driver's side seconds later, chest heaving from running. He opened the door and closed it behind him, but yellow jackets were still attached to his skin. He began to swat them with his shirt and smash them on the pickup floor until none remained alive.

Threat gone, he exhaled in relief. "Are you okay?" he asked.

"Do I look okay?" she said, rubbing the burning welts on her arms and legs, mascara running from tears. "I'm so far from okay it's not even funny!"

"Are you allergic to yellow jackets?"

"No, but I might be allergic to battlefields," she said. "Let's go, we need Benadryl."

Conner found his keys in his pocket and started the pickup as yellow jackets buzzed around the windshield.

"That was insane, you must have stepped on a nest."

"No, they just appeared. Can we go? We need to go."

Conner winced at his own stings. The thought of Benadryl and a cool bath in their motel room sounded like a very good idea. "Okay, I'll find a pharmacy," he said.

The pickup pulled away as the remaining yellow jackets returned to the sloping hill and out of sight.

10

―――

SUFFOCATE

The dream, if it was a dream, was endless torture. Legs and arms bound in chains, Reid Larkin hung upside down in the semidarkness of a filthy pit reeking of spoiled meat. Scurrying around him were ghouls in tatters shrieking in mockery as they attacked his defenseless body. They moved in a primal blur, fingernails and teeth shredding his skin, icy hands choking him to the brink of suffocation, wild blows thumping his body. He could do nothing against them except wrench and wail with each excruciating strike.

This endless suffering had already spanned days and weeks, the ground beneath him slick with his own blood. How had he even gotten there? He didn't recall. At times he thought he'd give up, just allow death to take over, but the wailing creatures were acutely aware of how far to push, enjoying his torment with tireless patience. Was this life after death? Some underbelly of the afterlife meant to torment him until the end of time? Would no one show mercy? Couldn't he just open his eyes and find himself away from this madness?

That's it, just open your eyes, he thought. *Wake up, and all of this will be gone.*

Larkin opened his eyes and lurched upright in his bed, coughing up a fright of bloody phlegm. He struggled to corral his panic, reaching for the oxygen tubes on his nightstand. He turned on the oxygen concentrator, wrapped the tubes over his ears, and attached the plastic prongs to his nose. He sucked in the air with tugging breaths, oxygen methodically reviving his starving lungs.

Coughs subsiding, he stared into the shadows of his bedroom. He could feel his pulse still working overtime, the nightmare doing a number on his circulatory system. While he waited for normalcy to return, he tried to figure out what else nagged at him. It was a feeling that he wasn't alone, that someone was in his room with him. Each square foot of his master suite looked exactly as it always had: the outlines of furniture, the open doorway to the bathroom lit by a night-light, the tall windows facing his front yard letting in moon-light. But someone was there. A man stood in the darkness by the bathroom door, Larkin was sure of it. That wasn't all. As his eyes became accustomed to the dark, he saw another man sitting in the wingback chair across from his bed just staring at him, waiting for something. Then Larkin made out a third person at the foot of his bed, a woman, so close that he could smell her noxious scent, an odd and appalling odor of burning flesh. Who were they, and where the hell had they come from?

Larkin fumbled for the reading light on his headboard and switched it on. But instead of showing three intruders in his bedroom, the light revealed no one at all. The space where the man had stood by the bathroom was empty, no one sat in the wingback, and the woman standing at the foot of his bed was gone, along with it the strange aroma. But there *had* been people there, he was sure of it! Or was he? Maybe the horrible nightmare had put him on edge, he realized, making him see phantoms that weren't there—and his eyesight wasn't what it once was. But why had it seemed so real?

Larkin spent a minute more inhaling oxygen. Its steady flow restored life to his lungs, and with the return to normal breath, he tried to shrug off the nightmare and its intruders, but they weren't easily shaken. He removed the oxygen prongs, shut off the oxygen machine, and pulled himself out of bed.

As if it wasn't enough to be dying, there were the usual creaks and snaps of age in his body as he stood. He grunted and walked to the leather wingback, bathrobe folded over the back of the chair. He picked up the robe and put it on while he looked at the wingback as if not trusting that no one was sitting there. Robe on and tied, he closed his eyes and took three deep breaths, hoping to erase the dream from his consciousness, but the stubborn visions remained. There would be no return to sleep now.

Larkin opened his eyes and shuffled to the bedroom door. He opened the door, a cool draft blowing in from the hallway and pushing back the stale bedroom air. He welcomed its freshness with a deep inhalation, the breath stirring up enough energy for a stroll. As he plodded across the wood floor, the hush of his mansion gave way to creaks from his steps.

He descended the staircase as quickly as his body allowed, which was anything but fast, but he was in no rush. Eventually he made it two flights down to the silence of the basement. Exiting the stairs, he walked past the swimming pool, the gym, and the hallway where Karl and Marcela slept in their bedrooms. He went through the theater and into the game room where he flicked on the ceiling lights, illuminating the dartboard, poker table, and pool table. Flanking the gaming area was the long oak bar, bottles and glasses winking in the light.

Whenever Larkin had trouble sleeping, a game of pool always did the trick. He walked to the rack of billiard cues in the corner, snatched one up from its slot, and inspected the tip for chalk. Seeing only slapdash scuffs of blue, he grabbed a chalk cube and smothered the tip, the applicator squeaking with each rub. Tip sufficiently chalked, he retrieved the balls from the pockets and packed them into the wooden triangle rack.

"Freeze!" Larkin heard, flinching from the distant voice. Were the intruders back? Turning toward the sound, he saw Karl Pike standing down the hallway in camo boxers aiming his Glock.

"Jesus H. Christ Karl, if you want to kill me just get it over with."

Pike rubbed his sleepy eyes, squinted toward Larkin, straightened, and lowered the Glock. "Sorry boss, I thought . . . I thought someone had broken in."

"You need your eyes examined. This is a first for me, I've never been accosted by a man in boxer shorts."

Larkin laughed at himself, bringing on fitful coughing that forced him to lean over the pool table to endure it.

Pike walked to Larkin. "You okay, chief?"

Larkin nodded, waving him away. Pike walked to the bar and put his Glock down. He found two glasses and filled them with scotch.

"This'll clear the pipes," Pike said, returning to hand him a drink. Larkin nodded and took the glass, sipping it with his dry lips pursing into a satisfied gasp.

"I've thought about firing you a hundred times over the years," Larkin said. "But it appears my better judgment has prevailed."

Pike nodded away the comment like he'd heard it often. "No one knows you like I do, boss," he said. "It'd take you years to train someone else, so you're stuck with me."

"At least I can still enjoy good scotch in my condition," Larkin continued. "Now what the hell brings you up from bed? You're a damn owl if I'm the one who woke you."

"You know me, always on my guard. Uncle Sam taught me that."

"Then my tax dollars were good for something," Larkin said. "Better to use that money to train the military than paying for welfare or throwing it at education. Well, grab a cue as long as you're awake."

"You're on," Pike said. "One of these times I'll beat you too, could be tonight." He grabbed a cue and chalked it.

"Not likely. You break. You're terrible at it and need the practice," Larkin said.

Larkin finished racking the balls and removed the racking triangle. Pike positioned the cue ball, measured it, and shoved the cue forward. Yet his approach was too powerful and clumsy, cue skipping off the side of the cue ball and sending it wildly down the table before it glanced off the balls, barely dispersing them around the table.

"Ah shit!" Pike scoffed.

"Congratulations," Larkin said. "You've set a new low at breaking."

Larkin took another sip of scotch and proceeded to knock in three balls before missing a shot. As Larkin waited for Pike to plan his shot, he seized the moment to take care of business.

"Karl," Larkin said.

"Yeah?"

"I'm really counting on you during my final days on this planet. Are you ready for that?"

Pike looked at Larkin before taking aim and sinking a ball into the leather pocket. Pike followed that with: "You know I'm ready chief, whatever you want, it's gonna happen."

"This time I'm asking for more than I've asked before. A *lot* more. I need to know that you and Marcela can do what I ask."

"I can't speak for her, but I'm up for it," Pike said. "She's a tough bird though, that lady. Probably running it all through her bean in her beauty sleep right now. She's a maniac like that."

Larkin watched Pike miss his next shot, nine ball bouncing away from the pocket.

"I thought the army taught men how to play pool," Larkin said, shaking his head.

"No, they teach you how to kill brown people. And how to drink." Pike demonstrated by draining his scotch.

"Yes, and the military can hardly do the former. How long did it take to get that Bin Laden character? Should have been days, not years. At least that moron knocked some sense into us. Taught us not to let our guard down. So he killed some people, what do I care? Worst part is I've had to be frisked like an animal to get on an airplane ever since."

"It's a new world boss, we just have to live in it."

"No, that's where you're wrong Karl." Larkin stood tall, using his cue to brace himself like a walking stick. "All my life I've seen this country go from good to lousy. Used to be you could say what you felt without someone suing you. That Civil Rights nonsense, that was the start of it. Now everyone thinks they're entitled, while folks elsewhere put in the effort. Then there's the guns, what used to be our last line of defense, but people want them taken from us because some kids are shooting up schools. Your Glock over there. Do you want that taken Karl?"

"That piece is my lady," Pike said, shaking his head. "Hell no."

"This country will do it eventually, and a whole lot more. The politicians will do more damage to the United States than Lincoln did. Look, I'm not talking about slavery—but if the masses agree to something, shouldn't it be allowed?"

"Sure chief, I know what you mean."

"So I have one chance, one dying wish to stop some of the madness. It's not about the political parties, it's about *my* party. It's my parting gift to like-minded individuals still alive in this country. We don't have to just tolerate it. So you'll make sure that it works, won't you? You'll give me everything you have to make sure this succeeds?"

"Sure boss. You just need to take care of yourself while we do it. Do you think you can get back to sleep now?"

Larkin sighed and looked at the pool table. "After this game. Leave nothing unfinished, I always say."

"That's the style, chief," Pike said.

They continued their game while Pike refilled their glasses. As Larkin took another drink, it almost washed away the feeling that someone was still watching.

11

NIGHT VISIT

"Am I going to survive, doctor?" Erin joked, stretched out on the motel bed.

"I haven't lost a patient yet," Conner said. "But you're my first patient. And I'm no doctor, not even of history."

"I officially hate yellow jackets," she said. "Little bastards."

The Quality Inn of Gettysburg where they recovered from their stings offered a price tag suitable for college students. It was also the closest motel to the part of the battlefield that they had come to see, just minutes from where thousands had been maimed and killed.

After a trip to the local drugstore, Conner had spent the past twenty minutes applying Benadryl to Erin's stings while she had winced and cursed. She had taken the brunt of the stings, her face and body dappled with angry red blotches. Welts amply covered, he applied bags of motel ice wrapped in towels to her arms and legs and gave her Tylenol. While he attended to his own stings, he could see that his efforts were beginning to work. Erin's mood settled into a complacent lethargy helped by lack of sleep from the drive to Pennsylvania.

"I love you," she said so softly that he hardly heard it. Her words took him by surprise. He hadn't been sure that the relationship had reached that level yet. Maybe she was just delirious?

"I . . ."

He was about to say it back to her when her deep breathing signaled that she'd nodded off. Instead he leaned over and kissed her cheek, but she didn't seem to notice. He watched her float farther into sleep, her mouth and lips repeating the words as if in the middle of a dream:

I love you.

As Conner rested on the bed with Erin, her sleep became contagious. Finding no choice but to surrender to it, he dozed like a child after a long day at the beach, time passing throughout Gettysburg without their permission.

～

Erin woke first.

"Hey sleepy head," she said, nudging him awake. "Let's go swimming."

"Swimming?" Conner looked at the clock to see that it was already 4 p.m.

"You're paying for this luxury resort, let's use the amenities."

"Sure, swimming," Conner said, pulling himself to an unsteady stand.

Erin got out of bed and produced a bikini from her duffle bag. She went to the bathroom to change while Conner found his pair of trunks in his own bag and put them on.

"Welted bikini bod isn't the best look," she said, coming out of the bathroom in her suit, studying herself in the mirror on the closet door.

"I think you look great," he said. "The lumps have gone down a little."

"Lies," she said. "I look like I have chicken pox. I hope I don't scare any small children."

They left the motel room and crossed the parking lot to the outdoor pool. When they reached the black iron fence surrounding the pool, they entered the gate to the tranquil blue water and saw that the entire pool area was vacant. Putting their motel towels on lounge chairs, they entered the water, Erin going first with a plunge while Conner eased his way in.

"Ahhhh, this was one of my better decisions of late," Erin said, closing her eyes to absorb the water's relief.

Conner hooked his arms to the concrete edge behind him, euphoria of the soak setting in.

"Better than my decision to bring us on a road trip here. I'm sorry for that," he said to her.

"Why?"

"We got massacred by yellow jackets, for one."

She turned over and floated on her back. "It's not all bad— we had a nice nap. Plus, it's not like you put a gun to my head to come here. Besides, what happened this morning was just . . . complicated."

"Yellow jackets are nasty, they've been known to chase people like that."

"It wasn't yellow jackets."

"I'm pretty sure it was yellow jackets," he said. He looked as though he was trying to sort through other species in his mind.

"Yeah, it was yellow jackets, but they were a representation of something else."

"You've lost me."

Erin floated up next to him and rolled over so she could

rub her hand over the water on his chest. "Put aside your skeptical nature for a second. Remember some of the things I said when we first reached the battlefield?"

"Let's see. You said something about it all being a waste, and that you couldn't understand why men would brutalize each other."

"Something like that. Spirits don't take kindly to their sacrifices being criticized."

"Spirits," Conner said, as if he had never heard the word before.

"Ghosts, the dead who can't find their way to the other side."

"Ghost yellow jackets?"

Erin huffed. "Don't be a moron. Not ghost yellow jackets. Spirits have the ability to manipulate the natural world. They could sense that I could connect with them, but they were pissed with what I'd said and they chose to show me the sacrifices they made."

"They ordered the yellow jackets to attack you?"

"Close enough," she said. "They *manipulated* the yellow jackets to attack. It was the closest thing that they could do to represent the sensations of their past pain—gunshot wounds during the battle."

"Are you sure you didn't just step on a nest?"

"Do you want me to punch you?" she asked.

"Not really."

"Then work with me here. There was no nest, I was watching where I was stepping. The yellow jackets came from nowhere, they were summoned."

"You're cute when you're all supernatural," Conner said, and he kissed her. "Okay, so the yellow jackets were summoned then. I get it."

"But you don't *believe* it. Doesn't matter, it's what I believe."

They continued to float and soak as the sun began to recede from Gettysburg. Conner couldn't help thinking how odd it was to be enjoying a pool just footsteps from where so many people had died. And now there was this ghost talk.

"You said you love me," Conner said at last.

She looked over at him, winking in the fading light. "I was in distress."

He saw that she looked serious. Had he read too much into what she had said?

"Oh," he said.

Her smile took over, hinting at how much she reveled in teasing him. "I'm kidding," she said. "Do you really think I'd just blurt that out?"

"I'd hope not."

"I meant it," she said. "Thanks for taking care of me. I don't handle pain well."

"You cussed like a felon. It was impressive."

"We all need to vent sometimes, to express our pain and needs," she said.

"I'd say you expressed it."

"Speaking of that, I'm starving. What's for dinner?" she asked.

"It's sort of a surprise," Conner said, remembering another drugstore purchase.

"I like surprises," she said.

"I mean, it's nothing fabulous," he cautioned.

"I don't care, I still like surprises," she said.

He watched as she pulled herself up and waded toward the pool stairs, stepping out and looking back at him. "Well come on, let's eat," she said. "Don't keep chicken pox lady waiting."

Conner looked befuddled that the swim was ending before it had started, but he followed her out. Draped in their motel towels, they made it back across the parking lot, asphalt still warm from the heat of the day.

They returned to the room and the odor of salve and cleaning solution. Conner walked toward the plastic drugstore bag on the motel desk and pulled out a loaf of white bread, a jar of peanut butter, and a squeeze bottle of jelly.

"Dinner is served," he said with a smile, plus a hint of doubt that she'd be pleased.

"You sure know how to impress a girl," Erin said.

"I warned that it's nothing special."

"Don't knock peanut butter and jelly," she shrugged. "It actually sounds great, all things considered. No bananas though?"

"Bananas?" he questioned.

"Never mind, it's an acquired taste."

"Then I just need to find something to use as a knife and the PB and J bar is open."

"Later, okay?" Erin said, gripping his waist, kissing him, guiding him to the bed, the feel of her cold, wet body pressing against his.

"I thought you were hungry," he said, pulling back from her as they sat on the bedside.

"I am," she said. "But I said I love you earlier, and I didn't hear you say it back."

"I did, but you fell asleep," he said.

"I'm not sleeping now. Say it again, if you mean it."

"I love you," he said.

"Sounds kinda serious," she said, kissing him again, easing back with him onto the bed, their thoughts veering far from yellow jackets and battlefields.

~

CONNER FOUND it nearly impossible to sleep. He tried to focus on the hypnotic hum of the air conditioner spilling cool air into their room as he watched late-night talk shows. This failing to put him out, he tried watching Erin sleep in the bed next to him, hoping to be inspired by her dozing. Instead he was dazzled by her beautiful complexity, her active mind most certainly in a curious place even at rest, the realization hitting him that she loved him, or at least she'd said she did. But above all else was something truly unsettling about this room, this place at night, thoughts of the dead searching for something that always seemed to elude them. It was ironic that Erin had found the ability to sleep in such a supremely unnatural space.

When Conner finally found sleep, he barely even noticed it, television still interacting with his half-asleep mind, air conditioner continuing to push a frigid gust across the room. His sixth sense was aware of a mass of soldiers ambling in tattered clothing, seeping into the room as if the walls were not there at all, the room itself not a room anymore but the battlefield. Some of the soldiers stopped to look down at the couple sleeping in the bed, but then they continued on their way, drifting like bubbles in the breeze.

One soldier took special note of Conner and Erin. He came to them and stood at the foot of the bed, his shadowy form blocking the scattered light from the television. Conner's dreaming mind found it confusing but not alarming that someone was staring down at them, the anesthesia of slumber fooling his senses.

The soldier, musket at his side, stepped to a sideways firing position, his motions precise, musket stock rising to his shoulder, rifle extending in front of him. His right thumb pulled back the hammer of the Springfield with a click, and he took aim at a spot just above their bed. He stood motionless, the passage of time meaning nothing to him. He seemed to wait for an unseen target to advance closer, listening for the order to fire. His steady arms and broad shoulders were those of a strong pioneer man, recruited for the war from farm country in the west, the chevrons of first sergeant proving that he had risen from among the enlisted men to become a leader in his company.

He fired.

Conner flinched awake to notice that the television, once barely audible, was now blaring a shootout scene, a cop show where the tough detective was trying to blast the bad guy in the stereotypical closing scene. Conner twisted toward the nightstand and found the remote, muting the sound so it wouldn't wake Erin. He turned toward her and listened. She turned away from him and mumbled something about *loud*, but he heard her sleep breathing return, and he relaxed.

As Conner rolled away from Erin to get back to sleep, something caught his attention. Was it a sudden movement near the bathroom, or just the shifting light from the television casting shadows? He stared where he thought he'd seen it and saw the television shadows dance, but none of them looked exactly like what he had seen.

Conner pulled himself out of bed, shivering at the room's temperature. He looked at the thermostat on the wall. "Gah," he whispered, seeing 54 degrees. He turned up the thermostat, and the air conditioner powered down with a hum and rattle, quieting the room.

Conner rounded the corner to the bathroom sink and counter outside of the doorway for the toilet and shower room. He flicked on the light and saw himself in the mirror, the frightful welts on his skin, hair badly messed from his disturbed rest.

Feeling half asleep, he was unprepared for the noise

creeping toward him from the shower room. It sounded like the shower curtain was slowly closing, the scraping of metal hooks over the bar like someone was trying to hide. He looked into the darkness of the shower room and saw that the curtain was closed, but its edge still moved almost imperceptibly.

Had someone broken into the room? He could feel himself tighten up from the prospect.

Then came a whisper from the shower, very faint, male, and terrifying: "Stop him."

Conner flinched from the sound, uncertain what to do about it. He waited and listened, trying to piece together what he had heard. Was it someone from the adjacent motel room, the sounds coming through the wall or a vent? It had to be.

Conner mustered the courage to step forward and turn on the light to the shower room. He stepped inside, the smell of sweat and mildew giving him pause. He hadn't recalled the bathroom having that smell earlier in the day, and it was fresh, like a perspiring man had just walked through.

Stop him? Conner didn't know what it meant. He wasn't sure if that's what he had even heard.

He reached for the shower curtain, took a solid grip, and yanked it open. Inside was the empty tub, pool towels hanging to dry from the towel bar inside.

Yet in Conner's mind was an explosion of visions as if planted there: the charging of soldiers across a field, bullets from muskets launching toward him, men being hit and falling, sobbing and yelling. Then he heard more words as if someone had whispered them right into his ear:

"Stop Larkin."

Conner jerked back and stumbled, his knee hitting the porcelain of the toilet rim with a thud.

"Ow!" he yelled, clutching his knee.

Conner heard Erin walking up to the bathroom from the bed.

"Are you okay?" she said, the light making her squint.

"I hit my leg," he grumbled.

"Conner?" Erin looked deathly serious, eyes going wide at the realization of something.

"What?"

"Someone's here."

Conner barely understood his own words when they came from his mouth, his response was that surprising to him: "I know. I think he just spoke to me."

12

CHARGE AT GETTYSBURG

I watched as if trapped in a daydream veering toward nightmare, the rustic expanse of Pennsylvania swallowed by the storm of combat, tide of vicious humanity sweeping ever closer. Confederates swarmed the Union lines with a roaring cloud of musket and artillery fire and that infernal Rebel yell, blotting out all natural sounds and obscuring details like one of those fancy paintings.

For our First Minnesota Regiment, the task was only to crouch, wait, and watch the battle from the distance.

"Ain't we gonna get into this fight? Stead of all this squattin' and watchin', Sergeant?"

I wanted to ignore Private Galvin, but the question was certainly on the minds of every man in Company H. "Too late, it'll be dark soon," I said.

Thomas Galvin, an affinity toward drunkenness, seemed to itch for a nip as he licked his lips from the heat and tried to view the carnage in front of him. I studied him, wagering with myself how long it would be before the man deserted, if he lived that long.

Company H hunkered on the right wing of the regiment,

enduring the Confederate artillery lobbed our direction at intervals. The regiment was filed in double ranks spanning a hundred yards, myself and Galvin representing the far right of our company. Next to us lay the boys of Company G, right flank fully exposed. On both sides of the regiment the Union battle lines were empty, except for a single battery far to our right. The calm organization of my regiment demonstrated every bit of what it meant to be crack troops, but we were still very much alone.

This was the duty of a soldier, to wait and wonder, never knowing what was to come. I know I wasn't alone in speculating whether the end result of this day would be the same as it always had been: defeat and bitterness. The creeping inkling festered among us like a sickness, the knowledge that we had seen hints of loss such as this before. The Army of the Potomac had secured that reputation from the past years of thrashing at the hands of the Confederates, our army too cumbersome and poorly led to bring victory. Was there a man in the Union who could bring us success? The best chance had been General George McClellan, but President Lincoln had ousted him for good. Now word had come that George Meade had taken the reigns on this fight. Meade was an able general, but how would he be any better than the handful of ousted commanding generals before him? God help us all.

In front of my regiment the smoke of battle spat shell-shocked Union soldiers of the Third Corps scurrying back. The retreating men darted behind the refuge of the First Minnesota, and the pangs of defeat crept in deeper. The bloodied, terrified men in blue didn't stop there, as if they intended to run all the way back to Washington. Only the stubborn men of Third Corps remained in front, but soon even they saw no hope in hanging around, retreat coming all at once like the bursting of a dike.

With this final collapse I saw an officer on horseback emerge as if from nowhere behind our regiment, bellowing in desperate anger. "Back in line, all of you! Reform! The line is here!"

But none of them were prepared to listen, the fear too intolerable, safety so perceptibly near.

I recognized the officer as General Winfield Scott Hancock. He dismounted and approached Colonel William Colvill, our regiment's commanding officer.

"Colonel, rally these men!" he shouted, pointing to the stragglers. Colvill leapt to action with sword and pistol drawn, officers of his staff coming to his aide, training weapons on their own retreating soldiers of Third Corps. Some of the retreating men continued running without a thought of being shot by their own officers, while others cowered at the prospect but maintained their course to safety. Some few stopped and dropped to their knees, spirit and mind spent by the debacle of shame. But in seconds all who witnessed the retreat could see that there was nothing left to rally.

Hancock faced the Rebel lines three hundred yards distant, the horde virtually silent now with nothing in their way. All of us could see the Confederate war machine inching forward—thousands of butternut and gray, Confederate flags waving, generals belching orders. The Confederate storm would sweep through in minutes, and nothing would prevent it.

If there was a perfect specimen of a general, it was Hancock. Beard and black hat, he was a master of his trade, among the finest the Union could muster. But even Hancock couldn't hide the desperation, and he succumbed to the gloom. He turned to look at the First Minnesota. "My God, are these all the men we have here?"

It was a question that didn't require an answer. Perhaps

Hancock had meant it for God himself, rebuking the absurdity of the predicament thrown his way. He glanced to the northeast where his reinforcements would be coming. Nothing. Perhaps they were on the way, but when would they arrive, if at all? Once again the men of this army were not where they were needed most.

Colvill and the other officers, seeing the futility of rallying men who no longer had guts, lowered their swords and pistols and watched Hancock, who seemed at pain over a decision.

"What regiment is this?" Hancock asked.

Colvill stiffened and stepped toward Hancock. "This is the First Minnesota, sir. What would the general have us do?" Colvill's mutton chops hung thick on his firm cheekbones, the Scotch-Irish blood evident in his straight mouth and thick brow.

Hancock pointed toward the advancing Confederates. "Colonel!" he shouted for the entire regiment to hear. "Charge those lines!"

Colvill looked toward the oncoming Confederates as if unaffected by the order, the enemy skirmishers now close enough to discern their features.

"Yes sir!" Colvill said, saluting Hancock. The general returned the salute, found his horse, mounted, and galloped to the northeast in pursuit of the reinforcements he needed so badly.

Colvill, sword still drawn, walked to the front and center of the regiment.

"Oh Lordy, here we go," whispered Galvin. Everyone else was silent, weighing the meaning of the order everyone had heard: death or wounds awaited us all, and the reckoning would be upon us in minutes.

"Quiet Galvin," I whispered.

Colvill spoke: "Atten*TION!*"

All of us took to our feet in rapid succession, snapping to attention with muskets at shoulder arms, dust falling from our uniforms in the summer wind.

"The order has been made!" Colvill said once we were all still, eyeing each of his men lined before him. "I will obey it," he continued, raising his sword. "Will you go along?"

"Yes *sir!*" came the reply from the regiment in unison. I heard myself shout it, thinking: *Is this how easily men seal their fate?*

Colvill nodded, about-faced to the direction of the enemy, and shouted: "Fix, *bayonets!*"

The officers repeated this order down the ranks. In response came a great rattling of bayonets onto musket barrels until the last clank signaled to Colvill that all were ready. Junior officers stepped forward with Colvill in front of their companies, swords raised and gleaming.

The last order came from Colvill, louder than any we had yet heard: "Forward, *double-quick! March!*"

Every step in unison, practiced to perfection on grounds from Fort Snelling back in Minnesota to Washington to the many battles the regiment had endured, the First Minnesota advanced like a marvelous machine before its time, a wave of humanity emerging with a purpose, no one faltering, not one misstep.

I felt the weight of the advance as I descended the almost imperceptible slope with Company H. I thought now that the Rebels would feel the impact of a real Union charge by men trained and hardened to do it. The Rebel skirmishers in front of us were the first to feel our strength. Shocked, the dirty Confederates froze, turned, and sprinted back toward cover. I felt myself smile at this, then returned stoic, no place for levity.

A former riverboat pilot near my hometown of Hastings, I

thought our advance was similar to a steamer laden with cargo surging down the Mississippi, an unstoppable force intent on crushing anything in its way. But now I could also see the colossal force of Rebels in front of us, many times more than we were. My thoughts changed to the riverboat steaming toward a rocky shore, a great collision awaiting. Something would have to give.

We all heard and saw the ranks of Confederates open up with musket fire. Peripherally, I saw dozens of our own fall, the hisses of lead punching the delicate flesh. The randomness of war chose its targets, minié balls inducing grunts and shrieks from the unfortunate. A shot found Galvin's arm, just inches from my own. He dropped his musket and fell to his knees. For the fallen, the charge was over, pain and death would be their task now. For the living, it was only the beginning. None of us stopped, none looked at those who fell. The companies closed ranks to fill the holes, and on we advanced, the buzzing of musket balls reminding us all that we were targets many times over, our only escape to keep going and drive the enemy away.

Somewhere hidden deep in my subconscious were thoughts of home in Hastings. What were my parents and brothers doing and thinking, completely unaware of events here? I knew the answer to that. Something terrible had consumed my family that past month, the grief inescapable. Little George, the youngest of my family, had drowned, the proof of it in a letter I still carried in my pocket. How could that be? I still remembered George alive and well as he had said goodbye to me in 1861. There had been the feeling at the time that it had been a final farewell to all of my family, but I had never considered that it would be because George would die.

"Are you gonna get killed James?" George had asked me.

"Nah Georgie," I had told him. "I'll be all right. You just don't worry about that, listen to ma and pa, do your chores each day, and I'll be back before you know it."

"Pa says I can write letters."

"Yes you can, and I'll write too."

With that, I had given George a hug, and I can still remember what that had felt like, embracing the bony frame of my little brother.

Poor child. I wished a thousand times to be killed in war if it meant little Georgie hadn't left us. If there was a way to do it, I would.

Our regiment reached the edge of a wheat field, the stalks crunching under our brogans. I didn't miss the metaphor of this, the men of my regiment soon to be reaped like crops on this Pennsylvania slope.

In front of the main enemy line the Confederate skirmishers were scattered among the mossy rocks of a dry creek bed. Sent down our lines was a command that all of us expected eventually. "*Charge!*"

Muskets tipped with bayonets were lowered, the speed of the regiment quickening to a sprint. The enemy in the creek bed, feeling the roar of charging men, froze and braced for doom.

"Fire!" came the command. As we were nearly on top of the skirmishers, there was no need to aim. Muskets shot from hips, scarcely a ball was wasted as the enemy wilted into the rocks. The charge folded into the remaining skirmishers like a great Lake Superior wave, bayonets piercing flesh, musket butts cracking onto skulls and jaws. I saw the first of this carnage to my right, Company G smashing into the line and devouring the men in gray. I saw the horrified, grubby men huddling in the ravine, some firing, some tossing muskets in favor of bowie knives, some uncertain what to do.

So this is what it all came to, divisive rhetoric across my nation giving way to savage bloodshed. I could feel the anger for the enemy untether a monster inside me, an overwhelming desire to wipe out the entire treasonous mob, accented by the exasperation that my country had failed to find some other way.

I came upon a Confederate. Musket spent, the rebel removed a bowie from his belt and lunged at me, but the bayonet struck first, ripping into his stomach. The bowie fell from the rebel's grip, clanking to the rocks. I kicked the dying man from the skewer and pushed him down. There was too much commotion to see if the man was dead, as all of Company H fell upon the Confederates with crunches and wails of animal combat. My musket butt found another Confederate, the rebel's cheekbone shattering from the blow.

Before anyone in the regiment could take stock, the rebel skirmish line dissolved. Those not falling to the onslaught scampered up and out of the ravine and back to the main line of Confederates. Seeing their retreating skirmishers, the main Confederate line opened fire again, pelting the targets in blue with punishing smacks.

We sought protection from the rocks and brush, reloading our muskets to return fire from the enormous main line pouring shot. The minié balls whistled forth, a great many slamming into men, some shots flying harmlessly overhead.

Are you gonna get killed James?

Somewhere in my mind, while I tore open a paper cartridge with my teeth and poured the powder down the musket barrel, I remembered little Georgie.

Nah, Georgie.

My words had come so quickly. I remembered the tone of my response sounding more confident than I had actually felt. There had been doubt that I would ever return home.

I'll be all right.

When the thump came to my forehead, a minié finding its way to me at last, it strangely made sense. I fell backwards, hardly feeling the jagged, mossy stones punch into my back when I toppled to the ground.

James!

The voice of little Georgie rang clear in my mind. It was all I heard despite the battle that continued to rage around me. My entire head felt hot and wet, and my mind grew confused, broken.

"Georgie?" I felt myself whisper.

For a moment, through vision that was blurry and dark, I thought I saw someone kneeling over me, saying something with a tone of comfort, but the words didn't make sense.

"It's okay James, come with me. I know the way."

I could feel my body slipping away. Nothing I could do about it, nothing to stop my muscles from going limp, my life shutting down, giving in to the irreparable damage, death smothering me with numbness.

"Georgie?" I whispered, and something of a smile came to my quivering lips. "Hello, little one."

Then I died.

As daylight waned to darkness on July 2, 1863, the scant survivors of the First Minnesota fell back, retreated up the slope they had charged down before, precious time bought for the Union defense at an incomprehensible price.

13

———

RETREAT

A gloom hovered inside the cab of the pickup. Conner wore the dread of the night before like a musty shirt.

"Are you okay?" Erin asked.

Conner watched Gettysburg disappear in the rearview mirror, the Lincoln Highway desolate in the early morning light. Only after hearing Erin's question did he realize that he had been rubbing his temple with his free hand.

"Headache," he said.

Erin reached for his leg and caressed his knee as she watched him cope with whatever demons he wrestled with. Then she reached for his head and ran her fingers through his hair.

"Maybe I should drive?" she said.

He shook his head, no. She seemed to understand that he needed silence for the moment. She withdrew her hand, rested her head on her headrest, and closed her eyes.

The pickup cut through the humid Pennsylvania countryside, a patchwork of lush fields and tangled woods looking the part of the battlefield outskirts. But Conner's interest in this place was lost for the moment as the headache and weariness from an awful night's sleep consumed him. There was another sensation that he couldn't put his finger on: an aching heaviness, like the beginnings of a head cold.

Conner thought it was fitting that the direction that they traveled was the same route that thousands of wounded Confederates had taken on July 4, 1863. The bloodied and broken men had been hauled away in wagons while the rest of General Robert E. Lee's defeated army had retreated farther south and west. Lee's grand plans for a decisive victory on Union soil had been smashed along with one third of his army. The residue of that mournful retreat still loitered about in the loneliness the modern road.

Conner nestled into the driver's seat to brace for the long ride back to Minnesota. He rubbed his tired eyes with his free hand and exhaled, guiding the truck into the turns with minimal effort from four fingers on the steering wheel. He hardly noticed that he rested his head comfortably against the headrest, eyes fighting to stay open.

An involuntary movie began to replay in Conner's mind. He saw himself sleeping in the motel bed with Erin, the room dark except for the TV light. He saw a human form seep into their room in a way that the living couldn't understand, a night fog that passed through the cracks. The figure materialized into a man, a soldier draped in Union blue, as if a black-and-white photograph of two hundred years had come to life.

Oh no, Conner thought. Panic swept into his bloodstream as he realized, barely, that things were not quite right about the vision he was seeing. He felt as if he was supposed to be doing something important, but the vision had taken its place. His anxiety mounted as he tried to understand the problem. Was there even a problem? His thoughts were compromised, confused. But yes, something was very, very wrong.

But what?

Then, like an explosion inside his chest, he felt the punch of reality.

I've fallen asleep!

Invading his nostrils was the smell of sweat and mildew, the same odors that had permeated the motel bathroom—scents of a man who had spent far too long in a hot, wool uniform on summer marches. Conner saw him in a surreal vision, a soldier guiding him into a luxurious library that Conner had seen somewhere before. The soldier beckoned Conner in, wanting to show him something important inside. Then Conner remembered it: Larkin's immaculate library with its stockpile of antiquities. The soldier walked right up to him, as if Conner wasn't there. Their bodies joined together, Conner feeling the man's fears and sorrows as if they were his own. From inside him, the soldier spoke:

"Stop him."

The words were so clear that they could have been coming from the radio, but the radio was off. Conner flinched awake, all reality returning.

I've fallen asleep, but I'm driving, and someone just whispered in my ear!

The truck shook as it veered off the road and into the grass. Conner jerked the steering wheel left, but he overcompensated, and the Ford's front wheels gouged into the turf. The pickup slid into a bouncing fishtail as weeds pelted the front grill.

Erin opened her eyes, jolted upright, and screamed as she clutched the dash for support.

Conner mashed the brake as the pickup chose its own course through the ditch. The Ford slid over ruts, Conner and Erin bouncing in their seats like popcorn. Conner gritted his teeth as he fought with the wheel that seemed perfectly useless. Erin's screams became louder while Conner growled and tugged at the wheel like holding the reins of a wild horse. For a terrible moment it felt as if the truck would roll, and with it came the sickening foreshadow of tumbling over the ground like a Matchbox car. But the pickup seemed to defy gravity in its twists and bucks before the resistance of the terrain dragged the vehicle down. A few seconds more and the truck rolled to a stop.

"Holy shit!" Conner said.

"Are you trying to kill us?" Erin yelled.

"Sorry, are you okay?"

"Not really!"

"Are you hurt?"

Erin looked down to inspect herself. "I don't think so. What the hell happened?"

Conner saw in the rearview mirror the ruinous swath that the pickup had carved behind them. The engine still hummed, so he urged the Ford back to the asphalt. The broken truck barely managed it, and the sinking feeling that the pickup might be badly damaged set in. On stable ground again, he put the Ford in park.

"Are you sure you're okay?" he asked.

"Yes, damn it, I'm fine! Did you fall asleep?"

"I don't know."

"You must have fallen asleep. Is the pickup okay?"

"I'll check," he said, cutting the ignition and getting out. Erin opened her door and joined him at the front of the pickup. Conner began picking debris out of the bumper with hands that shook.

Erin pointed to the front tire on the passenger side: "Um, that doesn't look good." Conner peered around to look where she pointed. There he saw the tire was flat and the rim badly warped, as if chomped by a dinosaur.

"Son of a bitch!" he said.

"This trip keeps getting better," she said.

"I'm sorry, okay? I didn't mean to fall asleep. I hardly slept last night."

"Then you should have let me drive! Great, now what?"

"I don't know."

"I sure as hell hope you have a spare."

"I have one. As long as the wheel isn't too warped to remove, I can change it," Conner said.

"Mister history knows how to change a flat?"

"I know lots of things."

"Apparently not driving."

Conner shook his head and opened the passenger door. He pulled the seat forward and flipped open a compartment behind it to reveal a jack. Erin folded her arms and looked around the desolate landscape of crops and woods.

"Did you hear a voice before we crashed?" Conner asked her as he freed the jack, which was in several pieces. He began to spread the parts in the grass to study how they went together.

"No, why?"

"Nothing."

"Not nothing, what did you hear?" she asked.

"Just the crazy voices in my own mind."

"The same one you heard last night?"

"What I heard last night was someone's voice from the room next to ours. It traveled through the ventilation."

"Are you always this dense? I told you that's not what happened. You heard a voice that said 'stop Larkin,' and you were meant to hear it."

"I'm not even sure that's what the voice said."

"Was the voice you heard before the crash the same voice you heard in the bathroom?"

Conner didn't answer, busy in thought assembling the jack.

Erin exhaled through his silence. "It was, wasn't it? He's following you."

Conner started to itch his head, uncertain how to assemble the jack. He went to the glove compartment and found instructions. In scholarly fashion, he studied the manual, scrutinizing the parts in the grass at intervals. Then he began assembling the jack as if it was some sort of science experiment.

"How could he be following me? That's just not possible," he said.

"He's attached to you."

"Not buying it."

"I know you don't believe this stuff. How do you explain it then?"

"All up here," he said, pointing to his head. "The mind is a powerful thing."

Erin reached for his arm and rubbed it. "I know this is hard for your logical brain to process, but it all makes perfect sense to me. And furthermore, this is happening for a reason."

Jack assembled, Conner took the lug wrench and fit it over one of the lug nuts. He pushed with all of his force, squinting, face turning red, until the lug loosened with a pop. He left the nut attached and began to loosen another one.

"What reason?" he asked while he labored with the second one.

"I'm not sure yet. What did the voice say this time?"

"Well, I think I heard 'stop him.' And I think that was my mind telling me to wake up, to 'stop him,' or stop me, from sleeping."

Erin wasn't so sure. "In the bathroom it was 'stop Larkin.'

'Stop him' means he wants us to stop Larkin, the rich guy we work for, from doing something."

"Just in case that's true, what am I supposed to do about it? I barely know Larkin, much less what the old coot is plotting."

Erin bit her lip as she pondered it. "Don't know. There's no way to know that yet."

Conner finished loosening the lug nuts, then he placed the jack under the pickup frame behind the mangled tire. He cranked the jack handle until the jack kissed the metal under-side, lifting the chassis ever so slightly. With more turns the wheel raised inches above the ground until it spun freely. He removed all of the pre-loosened lug nuts and, with a tug, he pulled off the wheel and let it fall into the grass.

"There's a wheel that will no longer work as designed," he said.

"This could have been a lot worse than a tire," Erin said, rubbing her arms still welted from yellow jacket stings.

Conner walked behind the pickup and removed the spare from the pickup's undercarriage. The tire was undersized, intended for use over short distances. He brought it to the front and fit it onto the lug studs.

"We're in business," he said. He began to attach the lug nuts.

The heat was already starting to set in as the sun began to rise higher. Beads of sweat appeared on Conner's brow as he worked.

"Is that flimsy tire going to make it all the way back?" she asked.

"Do we have a choice?"

Erin didn't answer. She watched him lower the jack and tighten the lug nuts for good.

"I have to admit, I'm impressed," she said.

"Me too," he said.

In minutes they were moving again. The Ford wobbled as the wheels turned in earnest, Conner monitoring the gauges as he brought the truck up to speed.

"Seems okay," he said with a nervous smile.

"All right, but we need to stop at the first gas station and get you some coffee before you kill us."

"Good plan."

"And in the meantime, tell me what you know about this Larkin guy. Besides the fact that he's a rich asshole," Erin said.

"You really want to talk about this?"

"We have hours of boring travel ahead of us. What else are we going to talk about?"

Conner sighed. "History?"

"In your dreams. I've had enough history, thank you."

Conner retrieved from his mind all he knew about Reid Larkin and laid it forth for Erin like a thesis as they drove the endless Pennsylvania countryside.

14

MENGELE AND MACALLAN

In the late night stillness of Reid Larkin's kitchen, Erin and Conner placed china into diamond quilted storage cases, weariness from another Larkin dinner party leaving them silent.

"Hey college boy, boss wants to see you," Karl Pike said, walking into the kitchen. "Let Baby Doll here finish this."

"I have a name you know," Erin said.

"Yeah, it's Baby Doll."

Erin looked as though she wanted to smash a plate over Pike's head. "No, it's really not."

Pike puckered his lips to make a kissing face at her. "Anyway, he's in the library," Pike continued. "Never keep the man waiting."

"Right," she said, looking at Conner. "Never know, you might learn something."

Conner stood, walked out of the kitchen, and made his way down the hallway to the double doors of the library. Doors open, he walked in. Larkin's laptop was opened to a screen saver on the roll-top desk, but Larkin was nowhere to be seen.

"Up here," came Larkin's gravelly voice. Conner looked up toward the second level of the library but couldn't see the man. "Today. I don't have all night."

Conner walked to the spiral iron staircase in the corner of the library and ascended it to the clank of his shoes on the steps. On the second level he saw Larkin sitting in a rocker with a book open in one hand, scotch in the other. Like the lower level, the upper level was lined with cases of antiquities. A small bar tucked in the corner next to Larkin was well stocked.

"Nothing like a good scotch before bed to get the dreams flowing," Larkin said, and he took a hard pull on his glass, ice cube knocking. "I don't suppose a prissy college boy would indulge?"

Conner stepped toward him and looked at the bar. "I'm still working."

"Not anymore, you're talking to me," Larkin said. "If Karl hassles you for it, he'll hear from me."

Conner went to the bar. He lifted a glass, opened the ice bucket, fished out three cubes with a tongs, and plopped them into his glass.

"What do you recommend?" Conner asked.

"It's all good or I wouldn't own it. Just pick one and sit down. Actually, have the Macallan. Two-thousand bucks a bottle, so don't spill it."

Conner lifted the bottle of Macallan as if it were filled with plutonium, filled the glass, and settled into a chair next to Larkin.

"This is an intriguing read," Larkin said, tapping the cover with his bony index finger. "Ever study the man?"

Conner saw the words *Joseph Mengele* on the cover, and shook his head.

"No, you probably wouldn't. The colleges keep the likes of him well away from their curriculum."

Conner took a sip of the scotch, strong and woody, in the back of his mind trying to calculate the cost per swig. "I'm not sure what value there is in studying Mengele in depth. But I'm aware of what he did."

"Are you?" Larkin either looked surprised or pleased. "So let's hear it then. Why should a man like Mengele, the Angel of Death, one of the most ruthless of Nazi concentration camp doctors, not be studied in depth?"

"He was a murdering lunatic, for one. He put to death innocent children for sake of experimentation."

"Lots of murdering lunatics get the spotlight. Al Capone, Charles Manson, hell even O.J. Simpson. People enjoy the macabre, they feast on that sort of diarrhea."

Conner sipped his scotch again, feeling its lavish potency hit his bloodstream. "Yes, but when the murdering lunacy is done in the name of genocide, that sort of rubber-necking becomes all the more absurd."

"Ah," Larkin said, raising a finger. "Genocide. Yes, that's the kicker, isn't it? Killing off an entire race of undesirables leaves a putrid taste in the mouth."

"I should hope it would."

"And yet, when the undesirables leave an unwanted taste in the mouths of hard-working folks, what's done about that? Is there any recourse for those of us who contribute something?"

Conner looked confused. "You've lost me."

"Yes, well, I'll stop beating around the bush then. It's my belief that not all people are cut from the same cloth. No matter what you do with the riff-raff, they won't pull their weight. But in this nation of ours, each one of us has been given a promise of equal treatment. Entitlement even. And it's people like me who pay the cost of their entitlement, and well, the taste it leaves in my mouth would remain if I rinsed it with trillions of gallons of Macallan."

Conner watched Larkin finish his drink.

"So, you're saying what, someone like Mengele is the solution to your problems?" Conner asked.

"That's an idiotic conclusion," Larkin said with a twisted smile. "No, actually. I don't believe in genocide. Well, not yet. But I do believe in people pulling their weight in society. Apparently our government does not. Meanwhile, our nation is in debt to its eyeballs while so many citizens just skate on by. Does that not irritate you in any way?"

"I guess I hadn't thought about it."

Larkin nodded. "That's because your liberal schooling has taught you not to think about it."

"I just haven't seen it as a significant problem."

Larkin swirled his empty glass and extended it toward Conner. "Be a good lad and refill this. When you reach my age you'll see how horrifying it is to get out of a chair."

Conner stood and took Larkin's glass. "Macallan," Larkin pointed to the bottle. "One cube, no water."

Conner plucked an ice cube and put it into the glass. He refilled the glass and returned it to Larkin, who licked his lips before taking another sip.

"Did you have some reason for inviting me up here?" Conner asked, returning to his chair.

"No agenda but to get to know one of my employees," Larkin said. "Besides, I can't debate Karl, he has the IQ of compost. Tell me, who did you vote for in the last election?"

Conner met the question with silence.

"No need to answer, I can tell who got your vote. Do you realize the damage your so-called president is doing?"

"He's made mistakes, just like every president before him."

"Mistakes? These are hardly mistakes, they're blunders of epic consequence, and on a daily basis! He's off the rails."

The vitriol bounced into Conner as if it were physical. With it came a familiar scent of sweat and mildew, and it made Conner scan the room of artifacts, his paranoia surprising him.

"I agree that some of his mistakes have had consequence," Conner said, trying to return to the subject. "No president is ever perfect."

Larkin frowned and sniffed the air.

"What the hell is that smell?" Larkin asked.

"I'm sorry?"

"You smell like a sewer. Whatever deodorant you use, junk it. I won't have my people stinking up my home."

Conner's jaw dropped, realizing that Larkin smelled it too: sweaty, musty, dirty, the scent of someone who hadn't bathed in weeks. It didn't seem like it was coming from either of them.

"Yes, I'll take care of it," Conner said anyway. "It's warm downstairs tonight."

"Never mind. Tell me about your thesis. Any progress?"

"We went . . . I went to Gettysburg a couple weekends ago. Research."

Larkin seemed to envision the battlefield as he stared at the ceiling. "Your first time?"

"Yes."

"So close."

"Close?"

Larkin met Conner's eyes in the way a fisherman would glance at his line tightening from a fish. "Yes. Can you imagine the consequences of the Confederacy winning that battle?"

Conner nodded. "That's been speculated a lot. The South likely would have won the war."

"And our country would be a very different place today."

"Maybe. Hard to tell though."

Larkin scowled at the response. "Two countries, the United States of America and the Confederate States of America, both destined to compete against one another for world dominance. That, son, represents a dramatic shift from what we have today."

"And that would somehow be better?"

Larkin nodded. "It could not possibly be any worse. But, since time machines don't exist, it's futile speculating about it. We have what we have today, and everyone just has to make do."

"I suppose."

Larkin yawned and put his drink on the end table next to his chair. "The scotch is working better than I had hoped. Thankfully only you need to go back to work. I'm going to bed."

Conner stood and put his glass on the bar. "Thanks for the drink."

"Consider it a bonus for services rendered."

"Well, good night then."

Larkin coughed, and for a moment it seemed like it would be another of his gagging fits, but he held it back.

"That girl of yours," Larkin said as an afterthought.

"What girl?" Conner said.

"The raven-haired beauty with the tattoos. You've taken a liking to her?"

Conner shrugged.

"Don't be evasive with me, I know young lust when I see it. You took her to Gettysburg then?

Conner wasn't sure how he knew that, until Larkin clarified: "You said *we* went to Gettysburg. I assume it was her?"

"It was."

"And did she have a good time?" he asked.

"Not so much," Conner said, feeling weird about the conversation.

"You don't have to worry, I have no policies against employees dating one another."

"Good to know," Conner said.

"But yes, I suspect history wouldn't interest her at all. Be careful with that one," Larkin said. "Seems more trouble than the physical benefits."

"Right," Conner said. "Well, good night."

Conner turned without looking back, descended the stairs, and left Larkin's library. Echoing throughout the mansion came a new fit of coughs from Larkin, and it mixed with the undeniable smell of musty sweat.

15

———

MR. RED

"He's still insisting on not showing his face," Marcela said.

"What's the point of a video conference if we can't see him?" Larkin said.

"It's the only way he agreed to do this. It's prudent, our government wants him badly."

Pike chimed in: "We're probably lucky he agreed to be contacted at all, chief. These guys like to hide. Even with an encrypted call, he won't take any chances of being identified."

When evaluating human beings, Reid Larkin chose to follow his instincts. There was no magic formula In assessing human capital, but Larkin had seen people fail at the task by relying too much on facts and statistics. For this reason, before crossing the threshold of any business deal, he insisted on meeting the critical players face to face. Now, it seemed, their man refused to show his. The facts suggested that this man was a perfect fit: explosives expert, no political agendas, living well hidden as a wanted man. But Larkin needed to see more.

Marcela connected her computer to the giant monitor on Larkin's library wall and sat with her laptop on her thighs as the monitor flickered to life. Larkin slumped in his leather chair next to her, Pike sitting to his right swigging a Red Bull, morning light just now hitting the library.

Marcela's green polished nails clacked the laptop keyboard, and the display on the big monitor now mirrored her laptop screen, revealing a scattering of windows and applications that both confused and mesmerized Larkin. She opened the encrypted conference call application, tapped a series of numbers into various fields, and clicked Video Call. Her laptop, linked to the concealed sound system of Larkin's library, echoed a cadence of rings resembling a telephone. A large blank window with a smaller one below it formed on the big screen. Before anything discernible appeared, the sound system picked up the baritone voice of a demon: "Go ahead."

An image of a man appeared in the larger window, and below it came the feed showing Larkin, Marcela, and Pike, the view that streamed to the camera at the other end. Larkin stared at the monitor, jaw cracking a half smile. In the foreground of the larger window was the upper torso of a surreal figure: face covered in desert camouflage paint, framed by a tangle of dirty blonde dreadlocks, hair as thick as the ragged wool of an old ewe. Darting from the man's chin was a matching blonde beard that extended into a cone. His eyes were covered by tiny mirrored sunglasses, perfectly round, giving him the appearance of a shark. Above his sunglasses were chevrons of thick eyebrows of perpetual anger. Behind the man were sharp peaks of gray-black mountains, as if he were taking a break from mountain climbing to join the call.

"Look what the goddamned cat dragged in," Larkin said.

"Mr. Red?" Marcela asked the man.

"In the flesh," came Mr. Red's synthesized voice, his computer rigged with voice modulation.

Larkin found this entire interaction bizarre. "Good Lord.

Are you kidding me? Mr. Red? Couldn't you have come up with a more personable alias? Tom, perhaps?"

Mr. Red was unaffected by the comment.

"Yes, well thank you for joining us, Mr. Red," Marcela said. "I'm Marcela. This is Mr. Larkin. Also joining us is Mr. Pike, who rounds out our internal team."

Mr. Red provided no reaction, the only movement the mountain wind lifting his messy locks.

"Mr. Red, has the cat also got your tongue?" Larkin asked.

"If there is a purpose to this call, time is waning," said Mr. Red.

"Let's proceed then," Marcela said, looking at Larkin to see his subtle frown. Larkin sighed and leaned back in his chair, content to let Marcela do her job. She continued: "We have a few logistical questions, now that you've agreed to perform the work."

Mr. Red cocked his head to listen.

"Can we be sure that you know how to use the materials we'll be sending you?" she asked. "My source assures me that this is not an issue, but I'd like to hear . . ."

"You don't need to worry about my skills," said Mr. Red. "I can and will use your materials well. Next question."

"The instructions for delivery of the materials, are they clear?" Marcela asked.

"As clear as your pretty face marred by the scar on your cheek."

Marcela responded with an uncomfortable smile. "Good. Now, the timing for the task is unknown as of yet, and we will inform you of this information within the coming months. That will give you time to assemble the materials and strategize your mobilization."

None of this seemed to matter to Mr. Red.

"I have a question," Larkin said. Marcela stiffened as Larkin pulled himself upright in his seat.

"Mr. Larkin, allow me to ask your question for you," Mr. Red interrupted.

"Oh, you read minds too, Mr. Red?" Larkin said. "Well, by all means then, ask *my* question."

"You would like to know if I have any objections, even hesitations, about performing the task you've assigned to me."

"It appears you *can* read minds then," Larkin said. "I won't pay extra for that. But yes, that's about the size of it. I can't have your girly-haired brain submit to second thoughts at the moment of truth."

Mr. Red seemed to consider this. "I'd vaporize my own mother if the price were right. No, I'm not the type to have second thoughts, my business doesn't allow for that kind of distraction."

"And is the price right, Mr. Red?" Larkin asked.

"Right as spring rain."

"Good," Larkin said. "You strike me as much too cautious. When your caution gets in the way of my plans, I sincerely hope it won't louse up the operation."

"How many people have you killed with your bare hands?" Mr. Red asked.

Larkin looked down at his hands. "None. It's not my thing."

"Well then, when you've lost track of how many you've done by hand, as I have, maybe you too would become cautious. Not at the thought of being caught, but at the prospect of never again being able to feel another life slipping away in your grasp. Once you've accomplished it enough, you'll crave it as much as your precious tobacco that's formed a cancer into your lungs."

Larkin looked at Marcela, outraged at the thought of Mr.

Red somehow knowing about his cancer. Marcela's expression of surprise told Larkin that she had said nothing about it to Mr. Red.

"Any further questions?" Mr. Red said.

Larkin shook his head and leaned back into his chair.

"Do you have any questions for us?" Marcela said.

Mr. Red seemed to consider this. "I'd like to know why."

"Why what?" Marcela said.

"I'd like to know the reason for unleashing this horror show."

"I have my reasons," Larkin said.

"Secrets are fun, aren't they Mr. Larkin?" Mr. Red said. "Never mind. I happen to know the answer. It always seems to come down to a woman, doesn't it Marcela dear?"

"I'm not sure what you mean," Marcela said.

"Yes you do," Mr. Red said. "The trouble with men is the fairer sex always brings out the worst in them. That scar of yours is no doubt a perfect example. So your employer has chosen me to be his ally in this game of revenge, and I will carry out his wishes with prejudice."

Mr. Red cut off his feed and the larger window went dark, leaving the library silent, the three of them looking at each other in confusion.

Pike crushed his empty Red Bull with a metallic clank. "That's one spooky bugger, boss," he said, pulling himself out of his seat.

Marcela looked at Larkin, preempting his inevitable rage: "I didn't tell him anything Reid, I swear."

"Well how the hell does he know about it then? I seem to recall telling both of you morons that no one is to know about my health. Was I unclear about this?"

"The guy's good, that's all boss," Pike said. "He's gotta be ex-military, has connections and knows his shit. Cool as a cucumber too, gives me the willies."

Larkin sighed and squinted. "Doesn't matter," Larkin said. "It's getting harder to hide it anyway."

He began a coughing fit, Marcela and Pike waiting for him to cough himself into near suffocation.

"Goddamn this cough," he said when finished, breathing heavily.

"I know our man is irritating, but are you satisfied with him?" Marcela asked.

Larkin nodded. "Personal grooming and nosiness aside, we have our man."

MR. RED REMAINED STILL after disconnecting from the conference call, then he closed his laptop.

"I don't know Mike, this might be a new look for me," he said to his bulldog sitting on the concrete floor of the Idaho bunker.

Mr. Red turned off the oscillating fans and elaborate lighting that rounded out the effects of the mountainous backdrop on his wall, a huge photograph projected there to look like a real mountain landscape. Mr. Red pulled off the blonde dreadlocks wig, revealing closely cut black hair. He ran his hand through the spikes and pulled the fake beard off his chin.

"Oh well, another day another boatload of dollars."

The bulldog sat up and hobbled toward Mr. Red, who knelt down to stroke his dog's smooth head and back.

"Time for lunch." With that, Mr. Red escorted his dog out of the room and toward the bunker's kitchen, thoughts of steak and eggs on his mind.

16

MIGHTY MISSISSIPPI

Conner walked past the white farmhouse, the last light of dusk reflecting off its faded side boards. Whoever lived there seemed not at home, so he paid it no mind as he strolled across the yard toward the woods. There he entered a narrow path, not knowing why, yet understanding that he had to go that way.

Upon entering the woods, he found that the chill had chased away the mosquitoes, while the leaves in the trees had begun to turn and thin out from the suggestion of fall. The path descended before he was aware of it, causing him to stumble harmlessly before recovering. He adjusted to a more cautious pace, and he allowed himself a look farther ahead at what appeared to be his destination: a river flowing in silence like some giant gray predator.

A mournful wail as if from a prehistoric water beast erupted from the river. Conner stopped in alarm, but when the sound came again, he realized it was a steamboat whistle. Through the trees he saw the vessel surge downriver, rushing to reach its destination before nightfall. He resumed his pace and made it to the riverbank as waves from the steamboat's wake washed onto the shore. There he looked downriver to see the steamboat round a bend out of sight.

Even in the river's silence, he could feel the power of its current flowing in front of him. It invoked an incredible thirst, his lips and mouth so painfully dry that he wanted to inhale the entire river. He stepped in the water, reached his hands down and scooped up mouthfuls, water splashing down his face and chest, the iron-rich fluid washing away the cotton phlegm in his mouth and throat. Then he waded in deeper, the river bottom dropping quickly so that he was up to his waist, and then his chest. The current began to tug at him.

Again came the shriek of the steamboat whistle, much farther away this time but nearly as piercing as the first.

"Seems you can hear 'em for miles, evenings like this," came a voice from behind him on shore. Conner turned to see a man watching him, just enough light to reveal the stranger's blue coat and the stubble of his beard.

"Are they always so loud?" he asked the stranger.

"Most of them," said the man.

"What river is this? I was so . . . thirsty."

"This here's the Mighty Mississip. And not to worry, there's more than enough water for a man to drink, and it's cleanest here, unlike down south."

He watched the man in blue standing on shore, and suddenly it occurred to him that there was so much he didn't know.

"Hey, can you help me with something?"

The man on shore didn't respond, which seemed as good as a yes.

"I don't really know where I am. Doesn't that seem strange?"

The man on shore still said nothing.

"I feel like I don't belong here."

Then the man in blue spoke: "No sir, you don't belong here. Sometimes we go where we don't belong, or we're taken there for a time because it needs to be. You can stay a bit longer. Long enough for what I need to tell you."

"Tell me?"

"Yes, and it goes like this. Some people just ain't right with the world, and those who are of right mind have to step in and turn things around."

"They do?"

"Yessir. Otherwise those people will cause harm, and that can't be had."

"Why are you telling me this?"

"Because there's someone you have to stop. You might be the only one who can."

"I don't understand."

"You have to find out what he's doing and put a stop to it."

This all seemed like nonsense, incoherent babble from an eccentric stranger. He didn't know what to think anymore, this river, this place, and this stranger in blue making no sense.

There came a disturbance in the water upriver followed by another thunderous steamboat whistle, this one more deafening and low. The enormous ship appeared in the shadowy distance, paddlewheel impelling the massive hull forward.

"Good Lord that's loud," he said looking back at the stranger again.

The man on shore nodded but said nothing.

"Can you at least tell me how I got here?"

"You're here because I brought you here," said the man in blue. "I was born and raised in that farmhouse back through those woods. Used to fish on this shore, watching those old boats pass on by. Used to pilot them when I got older."

"You brought me here? How did you do that?"

"Some things are better not explained. And it's time to go now, I'm afraid."

The steamboat bellowed again. Conner turned away from the stranger and stared at the great ship.

"I don't understand. You brought me here? I don't know you. Stop who?"

But when he turned to look at the man, no one was there. In fact, his entire view seemed to cloud over into darkness. He may as well have had his eyes shut. The only sensations were the cool water lapping against his body and the chugging sound of the steamboat.

CONNER WOKE TO A TERRIFYING REALITY. He stood waist deep in the outdoor swimming pool of his apartment complex, body beginning to shiver from the night cold. Instead of the steamship whistle from his dream he heard a train horn, boxcars clanking over the tracks across the street from the complex. His mouth tasted like chlorine, the sickening realization hitting him that he had been drinking pool water.

He tried to understand how he had made it to the pool without remembering. Was he drunk? No, slowly it came back to him. It was Monday, or maybe Tuesday. His last memory was going to sleep. Erin had stayed the night.

Sleepwalking.

As a kid, Conner used to walk in his sleep, but it had been temporary and benign. Sleepwalking outside of his apartment and finding himself in the swimming pool was a whole new level of weird.

It got worse. Conner looked down and saw that he was completely nude.

"Oh come on!" he scolded himself.

Suddenly the apartment building seemed exceptionally far away.

The schoolyard panic of shame was inescapable. He tried to calm himself as he scanned every direction for movement. Except for the train, there was no activity anywhere, and it gave him hope that he might slip back to his apartment undetected. He waded out of the pool, crouching like a naked ninja as he ascended the pool steps, fully alert to any sounds or movement, trying to stifle thoughts of being arrested for indecent exposure.

As he approached the pool gate, Conner noticed a crushed cardboard box in the middle of the parking lot. Not having time to think it through, he exited the pool gate and slunk toward the box, gingerly stepping over loose stones of the asphalt. When he reached the box he saw it was a crushed Leinenkugel's case, and for once he thanked the careless beer drinkers of the world. He picked up the box, tore it at the seams to enlarge it, and wrapped it around his waist like a loincloth. Then he continued across the parking lot, maintaining a crouch as he kept to the shadows until he reached the door of his complex. He found the call button for his apartment and punched it three times with his index finger.

Nothing. He waited thirty seconds before he mashed the button again, wondering if the buzzer was working.

"Hello?" came Erin's voice sounding annoyed and sleepy.

"Hi it's me, can you buzz me in?"

"Conner?"

"Just buzz me in, press and hold the button on the intercom."

Conner looked behind him to make sure no one was coming, teeth chattering from the cold. There came a buzz and a click as Erin found the entry button. Conner pushed the door open and sprinted for the stairway, climbing to the third floor in record time. When he opened the stairwell door to the hallway leading to his apartment, he saw Erin opening the apartment door three doors down.

"What in the world is going on?" she said, stunned by the unexpected sight of his nude body clad in a beer box.

Conner slipped into the apartment, breathing heavily from equal parts terror and exertion, closing the door with relief. Erin looked him over with baffled amusement.

"If this is some sort of kinky streaker Peeping Tom fetish . . ."

"No," he said, removing the beer box from his waist. "I think I was walking in my sleep."

"Sleepwalking? Where did you go? You're soaked!"

Conner left her and retreated to the bathroom. He pulled a towel from the cupboard and began wiping himself dry.

Erin followed him there. Unable to repress it any longer, she began to giggle.

"This is funny?" Conner wasn't amused.

Erin stopped laughing and reached for his arm, caressing it gently.

"Sorry," she said, hiding her laugh with her hand. "But really? You just up and left the building naked and carefree?"

"And I ended up in the swimming pool."

This pushed Erin over the edge, and her laughs came so strong that she had to bend over.

"Wow, I'm glad this is so hilarious!" he snapped.

"I'm sorry," she said, trying to recover. "Are you okay?"

"No, I'm not okay," he said, walking away and into the bedroom. He retrieved his underwear and pajama pants from the floor. Erin followed him and watched him dress. Finished, he sat on the edge of the bed, and she joined him there.

"Tell me what happened," she said. "Are you hurt?"

"No, but I'm totally losing it."

"No you're not. You're the sanest person I know."

"Then why does this stuff keep happening?" he asked.

"What's the last thing you remember?"

"It felt like a dream, one of those crazy, realistic dreams."

"What was the dream?"

"There was a river, the Mississippi. I waded in, and there was this steamboat."

"Steamboat? Like one of the old ones?"

"Yeah, one of those. And there was a man there. I talked to him. He was wearing a uniform."

Both of them understood the significance.

"Did he say anything?"

"He said what he always says."

"So it was the same guy?" she asked.

Conner nodded. "He said I have to stop a man from doing something. I guess he meant Larkin again."

"Then maybe you need to start thinking about how you can do what he says. He's just going to keep at it until you do."

Conner seemed to feel her words as if it was a sentencing.

"It's okay," she said, kissing his cheek. "I know you don't want this, but he's selected you for a reason. I'll help you."

Conner's confusion led to frustration that he could no longer contain. He tried to hold back his anger, knowing that he'd say something he'd regret, but nothing could prevent it.

"I don't believe any of this. This is not some bullshit ghost thing!"

Erin stood up. "Well what is it then? What more do you need to hear to understand what's going on?"

"I understand perfectly, and I've heard enough of your phony ghost crap! So just stop with all of your weird beliefs already, I don't buy any of it!"

Conner stood and left the room. Erin watched him leave,

shaking her head and slapping a palm to her forehead. "Some people are just *never* gonna get it. Nice."

Conner didn't know how long he'd sat alone in the darkness of his living room. The silence was interrupted by the sounds of Erin's footsteps, then the unlocking of his front door.

"Erin, wait," he said, standing up.

"No *you* wait!" she said opening his door and turning to face him. He saw that she was dressed and carrying her stuff. "I keep asking myself if we're really meant to be together, and tonight you answered it loud and clear. So I'm leaving."

"Come on, don't leave!"

But she was out with a slam of the door behind her before he could say more. He rushed to chase her, opening the door to see the stairwell door closing.

"Damn it!"

He wanted to follow her, but he became painfully aware that he had blown it badly. He closed the door and stood in his escalating misery.

"Well that's perfect. Nicely done."

From the distance he heard the train horn outside, haunting the night.

17

THE FAIR

The octagonal gazebo overlooked northern Wisconsin's Raven Lake, its waters familiar to only the handful of residents who owned cabins onshore. A steep cedar staircase trailed up from the gazebo to Larkin's A-frame cabin commanding the hilltop. Seated on a blue deck chair in the screened-in gazebo, Larkin wheezed and felt his stomach bursting from another one of Karl's fine dinners.

Out on the lake came the familiar sight of an Alumacraft drifting by, 10-horse Mercury sputtering smoke in a troll for gamefish, one of Larkin's retired neighbors trying one last sweep before giving up to darkness. Campfire smoke from somewhere along the lake drifted into Larkin's nostrils, and it reminded him how badly he wanted a cigar. He pulled one from his shirt pocket and popped it into his mouth unlit. Usually he would have had Karl fix him a drink before coming down to the gazebo, but not tonight. For once, he hadn't wanted one.

Somewhere in the ebbing light hitting the highest tree-tops, Larkin saw the past split open in his mind, and he recalled the exact details still locked there from so many years ago.

"I'm not eating all of these myself," Amanda had said, offering him the plastic bucket filled with Sweet Martha's chocolate chip cookies.

"Why in the hell did you buy a whole bucket then?" he had asked.

"When in Rome," she had said. "Come on, they're delicious." He had taken a cookie and plopped it into his mouth.

The Minnesota State Fair was never kind to arteries. Anything that could be deep fried and skewered on a stick was served there, but that was only the beginning. Cheese curds, French fries, mini doughnuts, corn on the cob, fried pickles, foot longs—all of it forcing a greasy tonic into thousands of sweaty fairgoers. The place nauseated Larkin, but Amanda wanted to be there, the roots of the Fair deep inside her from annual visits throughout her childhood.

"Remind me what people find so breathtaking about this dump," Larkin said as they traveled down Cooper Street and turned onto Judson Avenue. The infestation of people down the Fair's main drag looked almost impassable.

"Oh stop Reid, do you even need to ask?" she said, clutching his arm and guiding him into the International Bazaar. As if to stifle him like a child, she fed him another cookie. Sunglasses and baseball cap, ponytail of straight brown hair flowing out the back of it like a cape, she looked especially gorgeous that day, and she had been all his.

The Bazaar was row upon row of shopping stalls with imported fashions and trinkets: handmade Hmong clothing and jewelry, carved African crafts, South American handbags. Larkin stopped to study the curiosity of it all, instantly knowing this was not where he wanted to be. He spied a beer counter across the Bazaar plaza. "You go ahead and look," he said, leaving her there.

"Reid, you don't want to see this?"

All he mustered was a wave over his shoulder. If he was able to see her, he would have noticed her disappointment. Then she shrugged and started shopping.

Larkin ordered a beer at the beer counter, which was served to him topped with a frothy head in a plastic cup. He took the brew to a table under an umbrella within view of the stage where Ojibwe performed a traditional dance. Glad to be free from the sun, he sat and swigged his beer half empty while watching the performance. Invigorating thumps came from a solitary drummer while a dancer clad in feathers and a flowing robe stomped and spun, another man chanting to the cadence. To Larkin, the dance was fascinating and primal, but equally irritating. He had grown tired of the white race apologizing to these people. He had long ago deduced that their time in North America had come to an end, and Americans today owed them nothing.

Larkin searched over his shoulder for Amanda, and with it came the regret that he hadn't gone with her. He pulled out a cigar and lit it, ignoring the sour looks of others when they caught the scent of the smoke. True, he hadn't wanted to shop, but he could have taken the time to just be with her. This was a strange revelation, actually missing someone, when the weight of one's actions or inactions evolved into remorse. He had spent most of his life not loving anyone, and then along comes this woman, threatening to change his ways, and he was helpless against it. He began to think about the wedding ring he had been considering buying, the huge one that would have fit so nicely on her thin finger and pale hand. Would she say yes? He didn't actually know. But there had been something beyond fear of rejection blocking him from doing it, some sort of sixth sense warning him that there was risk in marriage. Larkin was a calculated risk-taker, and he wanted more time to think about such an important transaction.

A half hour later, beer long gone, cigar snuffed, Ojibwe performance finished, Larkin continued to watch for her, the nervousness of not knowing where she was making him paranoid. Had she left him there, finally finished with his antics?

"Reid, look at this," Amanda said from behind him, pulling a beaded necklace from a plastic bag. "Isn't it beautiful?"

"Hmm? Yes," he said, pulling himself up from the table.

"Can you put it on me?"

He took the necklace from her, feeling the cool stone beads rattle in his palm as he unhooked the clasp. She turned and pulled up her ponytail, revealing her smooth neck that he had kissed before. As gently as he could muster, he secured the necklace to her neck, and she turned around with a smile. Every article of clothing or jewelry had always looked as if it was made to exist on her.

"I love it," she said. "Don't you?"

Larkin nodded, thinking once again of that wedding ring and imagining how big of a smile *that* would produce.

"All right, better get you out of here before you get too cultured," she said, leading him back onto Judson Avenue. They passed the haunted house and the dairy building, then stopped in front of the DNR building where a crowd gathered to see hundreds of freshwater fish lazing in a viewing pond. He grabbed her hand as they meandered north, realizing at last that he didn't want her to leave his sight.

"Look," she said, pointing to the Democratic-Farmer-Labor (DFL) booth. "Reid, I have to stop."

Larkin eyed the booth as if it were Satan's lair, but he released her while he waited next to a Pronto Pup stand. How was it that someone so perfect for him was so imperfect politically? Politics was the one thing that they were unable to discuss. But Larkin felt something even more repugnant as he watched Amanda talking to a handsome young DFLer, both of them laughing about something: jealousy.

He turned to the Pronto Pup vendor. "Give me one of those," he said. The vendor plucked out a corndog and handed it to him. Larkin paid, soaked the pup in mustard, and found a bench as he nibbled away at the hot dough and processed meat.

Amanda signed something the DFLer produced for her, probably a careless petition that would somehow ruin them all. Larkin found himself shaking his head, the act feeling like a grave betrayal. Finished, she returned to Larkin, who stood and threw the barely eaten pup into the garbage.

"Well, what's the DFL up to now?"

"Clean water petition," she said, looking back at the man she had talked to. "You want clean water, don't you?"

"How much will it cost?"

"Oh Reid, never mind. They're so nice over there."

"Right, that's what politicians do. Mr. Slick over there sure knows how to put on the charm."

"Jealous?"

"Of him? Hardly."

"That's John McMichael," she said. Somehow the way she said it—proudly—placed an exclamation point on Larkin's defeat.

"Am I supposed to know who he is?"

"Nope, but I have a feeling you will some day. Very smart man."

"Well what's next?" Larkin said. "Our ideological differences are showing."

"Do you like sheep?" she said, clutching his arm.

"If cooked right."

"Not to eat, you cruel man, to see. Let's go see the animals."

"If you insist," he said, and he let her lead the way toward the animal barns.

As Reid Larkin continued to look out over Raven Lake in his daydream, he was surprised how quickly darkness was coming. The fisherman in the Alumacraft revved the engine and headed back to shore without a final catch.

There are certain points in life that are imprinted so squarely that the residual emotions endure forever, and that day at the Fair was one for Reid Larkin. It had been the beginning of the end of his relationship with Amanda. Months later she had started volunteering her time to the DFL, a hobby that evolved into a career. When exactly had she betrayed him? He had never been able to pinpoint when she had fallen for McMichael, but likely not long after she had met him at the Fair. As far as Larkin was concerned, the day she had first seen the man, it had been all over. Now, so many years later, she was John McMichael's wife, a title that formed a rot in Larkin's dark soul whenever he thought of it. No, he would never be able to forgive that transgression.

Larkin ripped his unlit cigar from his lips and tossed it onto the gazebo floor, his face red with anger as if the Fair had all just happened. The crickets and mosquitoes welcomed the night as Larkin coughed his deathly cough, a sickly bellow that hated the world.

"You okay boss?"

Pike had snuck down the staircase, drink in his hand. He opened the gazebo door and entered. Larkin nodded, regaining his breath. "I do hope that drink is for me," Larkin said, the need for booze coming at last.

"Just how you like it, potent enough to burn down a castle."

He handed the drink to Larkin, who accepted it but didn't sip it, content instead to gaze out at memories that wouldn't leave.

"I think I'm going to miss this place more than any other when I'm gone," Larkin said.

Pike looked out at the lake and didn't speak.

"If there were only such things as ghosts," Larkin said, "I'd haunt the hell out of this gazebo."

"I'll set out a drink for you, chief. Ghosts sure as hell need a belt now and then, too."

"Waste of good liquor," Larkin said. "Just drink one for me."

Neither of them seemed to notice stars beginning to appear.

"Do you want me to stay down here with you?"

"No Karl, I need to be alone with my scotch."

"Are you okay sir?"

"Fine, fine. Only some regrets. Do you have any of those?"

Karl thought about it. "Not really. Can't live regretting what you hosed up. You?"

"Just one."

Pike nodded. He knew enough about Larkin's past to know exactly the regret Larkin meant.

"Okay boss, call if you need me. That scotch is good and strong, so go easy on her." Pike opened the gazebo door and ascended the staircase back to a baseball game playing in the cabin.

Thank the Lord for fine scotch, the elixir against regret, Larkin thought. He took a full swig, feeling as if every living thing in the darkness around him watched and pitied and loathed him.

18

A GIFT

A week following the night Erin had left him, Conner slept in the disarray of his apartment. Earlier in the night he had finally found sleep on his second-hand couch while listening to music in the darkness. At 2 a.m., his phone's playlist had ended, leaving him to a lonely and quiet sleep. It was deep enough that he hadn't noticed the disembodied disturbances in his apartment: the rattling of his keys on the kitchen counter, the opening and closing of a cupboard door, and footfalls from hard-soled shoes on the kitchen linoleum. If he had heard them, he may have put stock in a logical explanation anyway.

Even in sleep, his subconscious tried to solve his crisis. His mind replayed the dozens of unanswered phone calls and texts to Erin, each one telling him all he needed to know about the relationship. He had blown it. Each day he had inched closer to driving to Erin's apartment on the chance that she would answer the door, but he knew she wouldn't. Even if he were to pound on the door for hours like a lunatic, she'd only ignore him or call the police. But he wasn't ready to give up on her, as if some unknown outside force urged him forward, aided by the realization that his existence without her had become ordinary again, even intolerable. He had to believe that there was some sliver of her that felt the same way. How was it possible that one dumb statement could end it all? He knew the answer—their beliefs were too incompatible, and he had allowed himself to be a jerk about it.

At 2:30, with his mind overrun by his dilemma, something forced Conner to pull himself from the couch and stand, eyes closed, deep asleep and aware of nothing but the sense of loss inside him. His eyes opened, yet he saw nothing but the ramblings of his tormented thoughts, the room not existing in his vision. He stood a full twenty minutes, perfectly still and facing his front door, hypnotized by something he couldn't see or understand, propped up by a motivation he didn't control.

The door buzzer echoed in the entryway. Conner stiffened back to the world, heart jolting his body awake. He took inventory of his surroundings, and it felt as though it had at the pool: complete disorientation, chest heaving with impulse. Another sleepwalk.

The buzzer sounded again, this time with three impatient buzzes. Cobwebs withering from his mind, Conner understood the significance of someone ringing his buzzer at nearly 3 a.m. It could only be one person. He walked to the door, pressed the intercom, and addressed Erin as friendly as he could muster: "Hi."

"Hello," came a man's voice, the unexpected rasp startling Conner.

"Mr. Larkin?"

"Now that the pleasantries are out of the way, how do I come in?" Larkin answered.

Conner mulled why on Earth Reid Larkin would visit him, especially at this hour. He had no answer, but he decided no good could come of it.

"I'll buzz you in," Conner said anyway, pressing the button to unlock the complex door downstairs. Then he turned on the light to reveal the mess that was his apartment. He looked down at himself and saw only his underwear. That wouldn't do. He had time to grab his bathrobe from the bathroom before three firm knocks hit the front door.

"What the hell is he doing here?" Conner whispered to himself as he went for the door. He unlocked the deadbolt and door chain before opening the door to the frailty of Reid Larkin, shadowed by Karl Pike, arms folded in front of him like an expectant hitman.

"Did we wake you?" Larkin asked.

"Sort of," Conner said.

"No matter, you're young, sleep deprivation won't be the end of you," Larkin said. He turned to Pike: "Karl, wait down at the car."

Then Larkin stepped inside uninvited while Pike hovered about the hallway for a second before leaving. Conner closed the door.

"It might be time to have a chat with your cleaning staff," Larkin said, examining the mess of wrappers, cans, books, and dishes on the coffee table and floor. It occurred to Conner that Larkin had probably never been in such a shabby and unkempt space before. Larkin found a spot on the couch and sat with great difficulty, the blood rushing to his ashen face.

"Doesn't that girl of yours clean up?" Larkin added.

"We had a falling out."

"Ah yes, I should have guessed. This place has an *I don't give a damn anymore* look to it. Well knock it off, there are more fish in the sea, as they say. And that fish was trouble anyway, as I've mentioned. Better to throw her back and keep fishing."

"Right."

"But I didn't visit at three a.m. to give you advice about

women," Larkin said. "I've not been well lately, so a full night's sleep is rare. Since there are errands to be run, I took the opportunity. Luckily Karl is used to night missions."

"Errands?"

"Yes, well, I'm getting to that. You don't need to be a bright college kid to see that my days are numbered. When you get this old, you'll begin to wonder when your time will come."

"I'm sure you have a lot of time left," Conner said.

"Not as much as you might think."

From outside came a train whistle. Conner had once learned to block out that sound, but nowadays he heard it every time.

"Lord Almighty, how do you sleep with Grand Central Station across the street?"

"It's getting more difficult of late," Conner said.

Larkin swatted away the topic with his characteristic wave of the hand. "Anyhow, I've been thinking about your thesis."

"My thesis?"

"Indeed. I've never been much for charity. Why part with my money on those who will only squander it without learning a thing?"

"Charity?"

"Yes, you know, parting with cash to those who think they need it."

"Charity is all some people have," Conner said, bracing for an argument that felt off the point.

"No, charity is all some people *think* they have."

"I'm sorry, what does this have to do with my thesis?"

Larkin raised his index finger as if Conner had asked a critical question. "You should really have some funding in order for it to be a success, God knows you need it." Larkin looked around at the shabbiness of the apartment as if to emphasize his point. Then he pulled an envelope from his pocket and handed it to Conner: "You seem like the type who won't suck off the charity teat without making the most of it. So here."

"Mr. Larkin, you don't need to . . ."

"Shut up and open it."

Conner felt the pristine texture of Larkin's personal stationery as he tore open the envelope carefully.

"It's an itinerary for your trip to Oahu, expenses paid," Larkin explained before Conner could open it fully. "You are to visit Pearl Harbor while you're there. Maybe seeing first-hand the location where so many American boys were slaughtered will inspire a thesis topic other than the Japanese perspective."

"But I . . ."

"If you knew how little this actually cost me you wouldn't even want to thank me."

Conner pulled out the itinerary and began reading it. "Erin's name is on this too."

"Yes, well, the arrangements were made before I knew you'd dumped her. You did dump *her,* rather than the other way around?"

Conner's silence answered the question. Larkin only shook his head. "She did you a service then, don't dwell on it."

"This is unbelievable. Thank you."

"Consider it your holiday bonus, not that I've ever done those. You can either go alone, or, if you find some other floozy in the meantime, call the number on the itinerary and have the name changed."

There came a crash from the kitchen. Conner stood and looked that way, seeing nothing to indicate a cause.

"Sounds like you have a rat problem," Larkin asked.

"I don't have rats," Conner said, leaving Larkin there and walking toward the kitchen. As he entered he saw what had caused the noise. The cupboard door was open and on the floor was a broken water glass, shards everywhere.

"What the?" Conner whispered, trying to deny for himself that his senses smelled sweat, as if someone was standing there next to him.

"As long as you're out there, I could use a beer," said Larkin.

"At 3 a.m.?"

"Why not?"

Conner shook his head, reached into his refrigerator, and pulled out his last can of cheap beer. He brought it to Larkin and handed it to him.

"It's hardly a Guinness, but it'll do," Larkin said, taking the beer, popping it open, and taking a swig. "So what's with your kitchen?"

"A glass fell from the cupboard. I'm not sure how."

"You live in squalor and you dismiss that a rat is in your kitchen?"

"I don't know," Conner said. "I guess I'll buy some traps."

The train whistle came again, barely audible.

"Well then," Larkin said, taking another sip from his beer and setting it on the coffee table. "I have more errands to run. You're not going to go groveling back to that girl, are you?"

"I don't know."

"Move on," Larkin said, conjuring the memories of his own past. "You'll always be pissed off at her, but move along."

"I guess so."

Larkin pulled himself out of the chair with a grunt. When it looked as if he might topple over, Conner stood to help.

"I'm fine," Larkin said, shooing him away. Larkin walked toward the door and opened it. "Now make the best of that trip, don't waste my money."

"Right, and . . ."

Larkin went out the door and closed it before Conner could thank him again.

"Weird," Conner whispered to himself, looking at the envelope in his hand. He went to the kitchen with thoughts of rat traps on his mind, distant train whistle moaning into the night.

19

MOVE ON

Conner felt the chill of the fall afternoon as he rounded the building to the entrance of the Ginkgo Coffeehouse along Snelling Avenue. At any moment a blizzard would assume ownership of St. Paul, snow already slogging across the state from the west. But for now it was dry and windy, Minnesotans in denial that an early winter was near.

Conner saw the patrons through the windows of the coffee shop. Was she in there? Part of him hoped she wouldn't be, his fight-or-flight reflex battling itself. But there she was, conspicuous among the handful of others. She sat at a square table in an eclectic purple chair, coffee cup steaming on a saucer beside her open laptop and a textbook, hand running through her black hair and red bangs as she grappled with sociological theory. He was both mesmerized and terrified to see her, indecision bonding his feet to the sidewalk.

Move on Larkin had said. At the moment, it sounded like good advice. But this was *his* life, not the sad life of a bitter, old tycoon. Instead an ultimatum skittered into Conner's consciousness: get back what he had lost or fail miserably trying.

He pushed open the glass door to the smell of fresh coffee and scones. To his left was a long counter along the wall. Behind the counter was an impressive lineup of coffee dispensers, bottles of syrup, and bean containers. Hanging on the wall above was a chalkboard with handwritten menu items of gourmet coffees and exotic teas.

No one seemed to notice Conner enter, especially Erin, so entrenched in her studies that nothing else seemed to exist. He was grateful for this as he approached her table, taking a seat across from her without causing her to look up.

Then she spoke to him, words coming in bland indifference without her even looking at him. "What do you want?"

"I didn't think you saw me."

She tore her attention from her work to look at him. What was hidden in her blank stare? Anger, disappointment, impatience? Sorrow?

"You wouldn't understand anything about it, but I can sense trouble when it walks in the door," she said.

Conner wished he hadn't come.

"Do you want me to go?" he asked.

"Yes. But say what's on your mind first."

"Would it mean anything to say I'm sorry?"

"No, especially if you say it like that." Erin looked at her computer and tapped the keys.

"Well I *am* sorry."

"Sorry for saying what you think?"

"I didn't mean for it to come off like that. I didn't understand what had happened with the pool."

"Do you now?"

"Not really. But I know that I need your help to figure it out."

"Oh Conner, you don't need my help. Find some psychologist. It's all in your mind, remember?"

"I don't know anymore."

She looked at him. "What do you want from me exactly? I have things to do here."

"I know you think we're over," Conner said. "When you make up your mind, that's the end of it. But I don't want it to be over. And I don't want it to end without telling you what you mean to me."

"And what's that? What could I possibly mean to you?"

"Everything."

"Everything," she said, raising her arms and dropping them to her side. "All my life I've heard people tell me my beliefs are wrong. I thought you understood me."

Conner nodded, as if he had expected this reaction. "Just look me in the eye and tell me you don't feel the same way, that nothing is missing when we're apart."

She considered it. "Right now? No, I don't feel that way. Nothing's missing, sorry. Do you have anything else to say to me?"

Conner stood and looked up at the old tin tiles of the high ceiling, then looked down at the worn wooden floor and waited for her to say something. But she was working on her homework again, itching her scalp from intense thoughts irritating her brain.

"There has to be something I can do," he said. "This doesn't feel like how it's supposed to end. Don't you feel it?"

Erin ignored him with a finality that stung. There was nothing more to say.

Conner left the coffee shop to pinpricks of freezing rain, wind whipping a prelude to the approaching blizzard. Digging for his keys, he rounded the building, unlocked his pickup, and got in, windows covered with grime and moisture. He sat as if not knowing what was next.

Move on, came Larkin's words again. But how, exactly, is that done? This pickup, his apartment, the entire city now reminded him of her. He considered going back inside, refusing to leave until she took him back. But he was frozen inside the pickup, the sleet closing out the world like nature's anesthesia, the peltings so captivating that he could only remain there, indecision irrelevant. He wondered if he could just stay until the sleet turned to snow, burying him there in the steel tomb. He tilted back his head onto the headrest and closed his eyes, feeling like he never wanted to leave this parking lot, because doing so would mean giving up.

The passenger door opened, causing Conner to flinch. There was Erin, face and hair soaked from sleet, mascara running.

"Wait," she said.

She got into the passenger seat and closed the door, turning to face him, eyes red with regret.

"You're right," she said.

"I am?"

She reached for his shoulder and brought him closer to her, kissing as if they had been apart for years.

Conner pulled away. "But you said . . ."

"Forget what I said, I'm mad and stubborn, which is not a good combo for me."

She kissed him again, then whispered into his ear: "Now I'm the one who's sorry."

Conner held her tight as he watched the sleet pelt the pickup's windows.

"Then why did you say . . ."

"I said forget it," she said. "You said the right things."

"I did?"

She nodded. "This isn't how it's supposed to end. I feel it too, and I always have. What took you so long to figure it out?"

"Slow learner?" he said.

"Super slow," she said, tapping his cheek with her wet hand. "Just, forget it."

"My apartment is a mess, I couldn't do anything since you left."

"Really?" she said, almost enjoying that. "Mr. Clean let his apartment go? This I have to see."

"I kept calling."

"I know," she said. "And texting. I saw all of them, but I couldn't answer them. Just promise me one thing. Whenever you think of some really dumb thing to say that you know will hurt me, don't say it, okay?"

"It's as easy as that?"

"It should be," she said. "It's called empathy, and tact."

Erin looked out the window. "I'm going to get soaked if I go back in there."

"Then don't," Conner said. "It can't sleet forever. We'll wait."

"But my laptop."

"No one's going to touch your computer in that place. It's way too joyful and peace-loving."

Erin grabbed a tissue from the glove box, pulled down the sun visor to see the vanity mirror, and began to clean up her face.

"You wanna go to Hawaii?" Conner asked.

Erin looked at him in amusement. "You have me back, you don't need to brownnose."

"No, I have tickets."

"To Hawaii? You're more broke than I am, how did you get tickets?"

"From Larkin."

"Larkin?"

"Yeah, he stopped by my apartment earlier in the week. It was creepy as hell, and he gave us tickets to Hawaii."

Erin let her arm with the tissue drop to her lap. "He gave *us* tickets? Why?"

"Because he's a weirdo, I don't know. He said I needed to go for my thesis. Should we go?"

Erin laughed. "Let me think about it. We can stay in boring Minnesota for the winter apocalypse, or go to Hawaii. Tough call."

"I'm dying to see you do the hula," he said.

"In your dreams." She kissed him again as the sleet pressed harder still.

20

SWIMMING

By 1 a.m., Marcela had put the finishing touches on her workday at her desk in Reid Larkin's mansion. Yet, leaning back in the chair, she began to second-guess whether she had made enough progress on her mountain of tasks. Managing Larkin's day-to-day affairs on top of his latest special assignment meant longer hours than usual, and she could feel the strain as though it was a parasite feasting away on her vitality.

"You need to get some exercise," Pike had told her the day before when he'd noticed how tense she'd looked. "Here's what you do. Take a swim in the pool, throttle on full for thirty laps. Follow it with a soak in the hot tub for an hour, then a cold shower, and I mean Arctic. Top it with a glass of Larkin's best firewater, but make it good and stiff. Then off to night-night. You'll wake up feeling like Wonder Woman minus the trashy outfit."

She had been indifferent to Pike's unsolicited advice at the time, but a swim tonight held some appeal. She had been on the swimming team in high school long ago, when she had learned to appreciate the company of the pool over spending time with people. But in adulthood, she had let the water slip away, only using Larkin's pool a few times all of these years. Now she intended to change that.

Marcela shut down her computer, pulled her stiff bones from the desk chair, snapped off the desk lamp, and shut off the overhead light on the way out of her office. There she was met by the dark and winding hallway that would eventually take her to the staircase, but she navigated through the shadows with ease, the layout long since committed to memory, soon finding the stairway and descending. When the stairs brought her down closer to the basement, she saw light down there, Karl still awake to do his usual night owl workout. She walked through the pool room and past the workout room, then made it to her bedroom. There she changed into her swimming suit, found her swim goggles packed neatly in a drawer, grabbed a towel from her bathroom, and made her way back to the pool.

Larkin's pool room was dominated by the pool's placid blue water dimly lit by submerged lighting. Marcela flicked on the ceiling lights, then rotated the dimmer until the light was sufficient for a swim, yet still subdued. The adjacent workout room door was closed, the light and sound coming from the bottom crack in the door as Karl worked out inside.

Marcela placed her towel on a deck chair, then sat at the edge of the pool, easing her legs into the tepid water. She held out her goggles to straighten the elastic band, then stretched the band over her head, fitting the goggles snuggly to her eyes.

Inhaling in preparation for her swim, she wondered how many laps she could do, having been out of shape and chained to her desk most days. She struggled to remember how many she could do in high school, always challenging herself for increases in quantity and speed. Pike's prescription of thirty laps seemed optimistic, but the shadowy memories of her past swims sent her blood into action to meet the challenge.

Just before she entered the pool, her thoughts were hijacked by something unsettling and elusive. This caused her to look around the pool room, its quiet emptiness telling her that no one was there, but her senses screamed a different story, one in which someone unseen was watching. But she knew that the mansion's comprehensive alarm system made that impossible. And the wall of black windows surrounding much of the pool showed nothing outside, Larkin's surrounding lawn presumably as empty as it always was. But why did it feel like someone was watching from out there, too, lurking in observation of her every move? Her scar begged to be itched in the name of all of her past transgressions in this moment of insecurity, her memories of that day threatening to surface again.

"Esto es absurdo," she whispered. *This is absurd.*

She scooted forward and slid into the pool, submerging away the thoughts that wouldn't serve her, focusing only on swimming again. She surfaced for a breath, then recalled her butterfly stroke as if it had never left, surging forward through the rejuvenating water.

Three laps into her swim and Marcela began to relive the seclusion of the water, the pool becoming that familiar world she had sought in her troubled childhood. The competition against others while on the swimming team had never been the appeal. It had always been this moment—the training, just her and the pool, her senses dulled by the world half underwater. The pool had allowed her to go forward through a life that had otherwise found her lacking, a tumultuous journey that inevitably had found her as Larkin's loyal servant in adulthood, her one and only success in life.

Five laps now, or was it six? Marcela had already lost

count, but no matter. Her body was facing the challenge of the water with dignity, heart revving through the workout, unaccustomed to the effort but holding its own for now. It was then that Marcela realized how much she missed this, her and the pool, and she vowed to make it a routine again. Very soon she'd have a pool of her own, a place of her own, a life of her own, and the promise of a free life until her dying days. She'd install a top-notch pool on her own estate, lean on being in that pool as her purpose and crutch, restore her health again —live for herself for a change.

But in time, even the insulation of water couldn't keep her from her own darkest thoughts, and at lap twelve (or was it thirteen?), she switched her stroke to a more leisurely crawl. After she did, she began to consider the magnitude of her latest work for Larkin. How would it feel, when all was said and done? Larkin's plan would be sprung, just before his death, and after his last breath, she would be released into the world a multimillionaire, albeit in hiding until the residue of his plan had cleared. What would her conscience have in store for her in those days, knowing what she'd helped to accomplish? The scar on her cheek was one thing, a physical mark symbolizing the pain and destruction caused by her own actions. But what other scars would there be, the hidden ones that would crop up in the middle of the night to haunt her, no one there but herself to try to rationalize them away?

Something odd occurred at what may have been lap fifteen. A moment of darkness crept in, as if all light was erased for a millisecond. Had someone turned off the pool lights, if only for an instant? If so, she could see that they were back on now, nothing abnormal going on. In the back of her mind came a fear that the workout was too much, that she was beginning to black out from the strain. Yet her body appeared to be holding up, the workout forcing her breaths to come more quickly now, but she felt nothing drastic. Maybe she was overdoing it though, and her muscles would certainly pay the price in the morning. This caused her to ease her pace, long strokes floating her forward like a lazy rowboat on a placid pond.

When the darkness came again, there was no doubt about it this time. There was nothing but blackness surrounding her, even though her eyes were wide open searching for her bearings. Panic overwhelming her, she stopped her stroke and struggled for an answer. Was she having a heart attack? Going blind?

Before that sank in, Marcela felt a pull on her legs, as if the bottom of the pool had opened to an enormous whirlpool sucking her down. Helpless to escape it, she drew a deep breath before being yanked into the depths, her entire body dragged under and down, down, down, many times deeper than the pool should have been.

Blinded and holding her breath, Marcela fought against this terrifying new foe, like being tossed in the foam of a giant wave, left to wonder which way was up, the surface an unsolvable mystery. Struggle as she might, there was no escape, no way to even gauge her progress against it, the only realization left that her air was running out, another thirty seconds at best and she'd be forced to inhale.

A clock in her head ticked away the final seconds of life, her chest tightening as she held in air, daring to release it in short bursts to ration her time. But as she hovered on the brink, she felt a great release within the water, the pulling sensation ceasing, leaving her to float unimpeded. The realization that she was free reenergized her actions, arms and legs kicking to propel her again, but which way was the surface? She chose a direction, it was her only option, and urged herself through the water with everything she had left.

When she plunged through the surface at full force, it came as a surprise, her body launching up and then back into the water. She trod up, head and shoulders surfacing again, her mouth opening wide to suck in the desperately needed oxygen. In the darkness still, she listened to herself breathing, four-five-six breaths before she felt her body begin to recover, many more breaths needed for something close to normalcy to return while she wondered again what was happening to her.

The light returned, ever so slightly, like a candle being lit from high above her. As the shadows parted to reveal her surroundings, she was met with the astounding realization that this wasn't the pool room. It was an underground chamber of some kind, much smaller than the pool room, the size of a large walk-in closet. Instead of the smells of chlorine, the odor was an appalling rot with a hint of sulfur and machine oil, walls of dirt and rock like she had been dropped into a lonely sinkhole of decay far below ground. She looked to see the opening high above, a world left behind forever, its distant light no more than a reminder.

Marcela screamed. It was the scream of her childhood when she knew there was something watching her in her bed at night, a cry of desperation, hoping someone would hear her and rescue her before it was too late. The only response was her own echo going up and up, then out to nowhere at all.

When a hand touched her shoulder, Marcela shrieked again, kicking away from the touch, paddling through the stinking water to the wall opposite of whatever had reached for her. As the murky, dirty water rippled from her reaction, she dared to look back, hoping to God nothing would be there. Yet there it was, a figure darkened by the inadequate light, a torso protruding above the water line. It drifted toward her with unnatural ease, water not even forming a wake from its movement as the form rose even higher above her.

"Leave me alone!" she shouted, pressing herself against the wall of muck at her back, nowhere else to go. "Go away!"

The figure ignored her pleas, floating up to her until she could see its eyes. It was a man, and he seemed to defy the properties of water and gravity, his torso visible as if he was in waist-deep water, even though Marcela was unable to touch the bottom of the mysterious cesspool.

He reached both arms out and gripped her shoulders, his hands so cold and bony they actually hurt her, Marcela's screams turning to sobs. He pushed his face right up to hers, the oily stink from his mouth so overpowering she thought she'd vomit. He opened his mouth to speak, but before he said anything, a black puddle dripped over his bottom lip and splashed into the water.

"I know what you're doing," the man said, his voice sounding waterlogged by a deep rattle. She looked away from his horrible face, but had seen that his clothing was white. It was a uniform—Navy whites.

"Stop!" he shouted.

Marcela flinched. "Please don't hurt me," she said, shaking from his grasp and turning her back to him, digging her nails into the muddy wall as if she intended to claw her way through.

When there was only silence behind her, she stopped to listen, hoping he had disappeared to wherever he had come. A minute of the silence passed, lending support that he was indeed gone, but she dared not look back just the same. So when an explosion erupted behind her, it shattered whatever nerves remained within her. The blast pushed hot air and waves of putrid water her way, the sound reverberating up and up, her body slamming into the mud wall. When she stabilized, she shook from the shock, not turning to look at the cause of the explosion. Before she had recovered, another blast came, ringing her ears, the eruption shoving her into the muddy wall again. This time, among the echoes of the blast were screams of terror and pain, an entire chorus, as if people were there with her, badly maimed and hysterical from the blast.

Marcela wept, face nudging tightly into the wall like a soldier hugging a tiny ridge against an unrelenting artillery barrage. So when the third blast came, a symphony of screams following it stronger than the first, Marcela had lost all capacity to evade and comprehend what had become of her, where she was and why she was there, much less how this would end. The sobs came freely, the heartbreak of the screams behind her too much to deflect. She gripped her hands tighter into the wall, feeling her nails burrow into the grit of its mud.

Marcela cringed when she felt another hand on her shoulder. He was back, had never left. Even though she might have expected it to come, his touch was as unwelcome as the inspecting massage of an anaconda.

"I said leave me alone!" she shouted.

She turned her head part way, unwilling to look at all of him again. But as she did, she saw the cavern of muck slide away like a time lapsed set change on a stage, the hopeless chamber replaced before her eyes with the blue shimmers of Larkin's pool. The muddy walls dissolved, revealing the windows and walls of the pool room, the horrific odors giving way to damp chlorine.

"Marcela?" came a voice. It was Karl. He was kneeling poolside, arm patting her shoulder. "Can you hear me?"

She looked up at him, saw the concern and confusion in

his expression as he tried to ascertain what had gotten hold of her.

"Yeah," she nodded, sighing in relief.

"Jesus girl, what the hell happened?" he asked. "Are you okay?"

"I'm . . . okay," she said, voice low and dazed.

"You don't look okay," he said. "And you were flopping around the pool screaming like that drunken swimmer getting attacked by Jaws. I kept yelling at you to snap out of it. Did you have a seizure or something?"

She shook her head. "I don't know," she said. She watched for his reaction. Beneath his unemotional response there was a cold acceptance to her honesty.

"I think I'll have that drink now," she added.

"I'll join you," Pike said, offering her a hand out of the pool.

21

———

BOOM

"**S**omething to drink?"

The prim and painted flight attendant waited for an answer as Erin and Conner looked at each other, the opulence of first class leading to awkward silence.

"White wine," Erin said.

"Light beer," Conner said.

The flight attendant scurried away to get their drinks.

"It's not a bad way to travel," Conner said, leaning back in the spacious blue leather seat.

"It feels sort of snobby, all the rabble back there packed in coach with their pretzels and orange juice."

"That's why they pull the curtain between the classes, so we don't have to feel guilty. Could be worse, it's not like they're riding in steerage of some filthy ship. Now *that* was a horrible way to travel."

Erin looked out the window at the snow-covered Great Plains far below, the beauty of rural life reflected in secluded farms and lonely roads. The white November blanket had seized the Midwest, the snow likely to wreak havoc for the upcoming Thanksgiving travel.

"There won't be yellow jackets this time, right?" Erin pulled lip balm from her purse and applied it to her lips withered by dry airplane air.

"Just volcanoes, sharks, and tsunamis, nothing to worry about."

Erin pulled her tablet from her carry-on and placed it on her tray table. "Funny guy. And we do intend to do some fun things out there? It's Hawaii, we can't be cooped up in museums the whole time."

"We only have a few days," Conner said. Erin's frown made him reconsider his words. "But yeah, I need a day, that's it. The rest is for us." He kissed her cheek.

"I like the sound of that," she smiled. "Hawaii should be a very spiritual place, don't you think?"

"I suppose."

"I want to soak it all in. We need to do a luau."

"Do we have to?"

"Yes, we do, and you'll like it."

"Okay, a luau."

The flight attendant arrived with their drinks, setting them on napkins sporting the airline logo. She smiled and moved on to other passengers.

Erin flipped through the pages of a textbook on her tablet as if to start reading, but then held back.

"So here's a philosophical question," she said.

"The answer is six."

"No it's not. This doesn't have a right or wrong answer. Why is it, do you think, that we were put on this planet?"

Conner squinted in contemplation. "Aliens?"

"You are *so* annoying. Can you just answer the question seriously please?"

"Sorry," he said, sipping his beer. "I don't know, I think it's the result of some sort of cosmic accident."

"An accident."

"Sure, like God was experimenting in his lab, and there was this explosion, and it created the universe. That's why we're in chaos much of the time, because we represent a Bob Ross happy accident that our creator doesn't have complete control over. Once in a great while, things work."

"I'm trying to picture God looking like Bob Ross," she said. "Interesting theory, but life doesn't feel like an accident to me. I think even things we think are accidents happen very intentionally."

"So the time I accidentally stabbed myself in the eye with a stick when I was five, that was intentional?"

Erin laughed. "You stabbed yourself with a stick?"

"In the eye. I was running after the ice cream truck and mistakes were made. Now why in God's name would *that* be intentional?"

"Maybe getting stabbed with the stick prevented you from being hit by a car. You just don't know. There's something good resulting from everything if you look closely and consider the possibilities."

"All I know is I had to wear an eye patch and Pokémon sunglasses for weeks. Hardly seems worth it."

"Oh, poor Conner," she mocked, touching his arm. "Did you have to have Mommy kiss it?"

"Next subject."

Erin laughed again then sipped her wine. The flight attendants walked the aisle to supply a steady flow of liquor and food to the passengers.

"I had a point by asking you why you think we were put on this planet," Erin said, licking the wine residue from her lips.

"Here it comes."

"The voice you keep hearing."

Conner had almost forgotten about the voice. The trip had already taken his mind off of it.

"What about it?"

"You wouldn't be hearing it if there wasn't something important to be heard, some reason behind it," she said. "Don't you think it's possible that there are forces at work, trying to guide us through things we can't otherwise know or understand?"

"This discussion is getting weird," he said, and she glared at him. "But yes, I guess it's possible. Or it still could be aliens."

"Shut up," she said, slapping him gently on the arm. "I'm gonna read."

"I'm gonna finish my beer," he said.

HEY BUDDY, come here, came a whisper. It was inviting, like the voice of an old friend who wanted to share an amusing secret. *Pay attention now, this is a real humdinger. Are you listening? Hey, wake up! You gotta hear this. There I was, in my rack cutting zees against a hangover, and WHAM!*

When Conner woke it was darker in the plane's cabin, overcast skies visible from the oval plane windows. Erin slept soundly, her face turned toward him, tablet off. He kissed her forehead, and she didn't stir, deep asleep.

He looked around, wondering whose voice it was that woken him. Most of the passengers in first class were dozing, and the plane was quiet except for the drone of the engines.

Free beer filled Conner's bladder with a painful burn. He unhooked his seatbelt, the click disturbing Erin into movement, but she stayed asleep as he pulled himself to his feet. He wondered how long he had been asleep as he made his way down the aisle to the lavatory. Earlier in the day they had made a quick stop at Los Angeles, and now they were well over the Pacific.

Conner felt the plane bounce through turbulence, and for a moment he had the sensation of floating as the plane creaked and rocked. The fuselage provided an illusion of safety, the controlled chaos of the jet engines powering the plane through clouds thousands of feet above a dark and unforgiving ocean. It was best not to think too hard about it.

Up ahead was the lavatory door at the end of first class, a blue curtain dividing the classes past the door. The previous occupant hadn't closed the door fully, and it thumped with the turbulence.

Wafting through the aisle came an unusual odor: mechanical, oily, tar-like, so overpowering that it raised alarm bells in Conner's mind. Was there something wrong with the plane? The aroma grew stronger the closer he came to the lavatory door, making him wonder if the chemical toilet had overflowed. He turned to look for a flight attendant toward the front of the plane, but none were visible, probably huddled somewhere enjoying a quiet break from the passengers.

The aroma messed with Conner's mind. He imagined the plane plunging down, its nose knifing through the air from engine failure, the fall of the plane pulling at his stomach as all of the passengers at once realized their peril, oxygen masks dropping, overhead bins opening to spill out carry-ons. Like the most extreme of roller coasters, the plane would dip as if descending the main slope of track until the craft met the ocean, cutting with a metallic screech into the gray swells, sending the cabin into a roll as the passengers wailed and tumbled, the plane busting apart like a toy. Seawater would rush in, the splash of salt water and jet fuel unbearable, panic seizing the passengers that were still alive.

Knock it off, Conner thought. *We're fine.*

But even his imagination held some truth. Was it jet fuel that he was smelling? He wished he knew. He thought about walking to the front of the plane to find a flight attendant, but his bladder overruled it, the lavatory door continuing to bounce with the plane.

Hey buddy, come here. Conner remembered the words that had woken him back in his seat, the voice that he reasoned was from a dream. Now he imagined those words coming from the lavatory, someone inside, waiting.

Conner took the last step to the door, grabbed the handle, and opened it to find the bathroom empty. He stepped in, closed the door and locked it, light flickering to life, the claustrophobic lavatory incarcerating him. The tarry aroma was here, too, but now there was something else: the indisputable scent of burning flesh. The combination gagged him.

Conner saw movement peripherally in the bathroom mirror, an impossibility since he was motionless and alone. He turned to look, seeing what could only be his own reflection, but for a millisecond it wasn't.

It was a man wearing a sailor uniform.

"Boom!" the man whispered, then he disappeared, leaving only Conner's own reflection.

An earsplitting bang rocked the plane. Conner's crash premonition veering toward reality, he thought of the restroom floor giving way and dropping him thousands of feet to the Pacific. He unlocked the door and tumbled into the aisle, slamming the door behind him. The smell of fuel was gone, but everyone in first class was now awake and rattled from the bang all of them had heard.

"Ladies and gentlemen," the captain sounded over the PA. "We've hit some rough weather, and we're adjusting our course around it. I'm going to turn on the seatbelt sign, and I ask that you please remain seated with your seatbelts fastened."

"That scared the bejesus out of me," a balding passenger said as he looked at his wife laughing. "Just thunder."

Thunder. The explosion had been thunder.

Conner returned to his seat, the burn from his bladder no longer his top priority. He sat down next to Erin, who was wide awake.

"What was that?" she said, looking at him.

"Thunder," Conner said, looking shell shocked.

"Conner, are you okay? You look . . ."

"I know," he said, buckling his seatbelt. "I look like I've just seen a ghost."

22

PEARL HARBOR

Naval steel sliced through the Sunday whitecaps of the Pacific, ships closing in on their unsuspecting prey like sharks. Thirty-one vessels strong, banners of their empire flowing, the six aircraft carriers among them unleashed their fighters, a rage of sound the world had never witnessed. The planes, like dragons, groaned into the salty Pacific wind, preparing to flock south upon the island in perfect formation, Rising Sun roundels on wings and fuselages, blood red, like the Hawaiian sunrise. The generation of organized murder surged forward.

Job done for now, the crews on ships waited and wondered, prayers and the smooth burn of sake distant memories while the planes disappeared from sight and sound, the hopes of an ancient nation on the line. Suit-and-tie diplomacy had once again given way to the most simple of motives: the world has limits to what it provides, and the strongest will take what it needs.

Inside the cockpits of what Americans called Zeros, Vals, and Kates, confident minds prevailed, squashing weak thoughts of survival and replacing them with memories of training, objectives of destruction, and honor. The sleepless nights prior were over. It was a hunt like no other.

Yet among them also lingered the scrap of the unknown, the one chance of failure: sometimes the prey, suspecting danger, becomes the hunter, and the attack becomes a fight to the death. Were the Americans now lying in wait, ready to fight, the sleeping giant awakened again?

But as the planes approached Hawaii, there was nothing to indicate alarm. The island slept, the lazy tropical haze like any Hawaiian Sunday morning, the region showing total indifference to the beastly roars from above. The lush green vegetation below burst with vitality as the aqua sea tasted the shores. The simple world below seemed unprepared for what raced across the sky.

To the Japanese pilots adhering to radio silence, there was no celebration to be heard, only the realization that the trap had been set well. All that remained was to deal the fatal blow. Bombers and fighters constricted the island while the naive souls living there believed it was just another Sunday.

MEMORIES of cheap beer and the pretty nurse named Nan filled my dreams that Sunday morning. I had celebrated well with my crew mates, dancing, drinking, and enjoying the freedom Honolulu had granted away from the Navy's hold. Somehow I had found my way back to the USS *Oklahoma*, a feat I hadn't really recalled, and equally impressive was my falling into a bunk to sleep off the night.

"Will I see you again?" I had asked Nan.

Then she had stepped toward me and kissed my drunken lips, the sweetest taste I could recall, her red hair the brightest I had ever seen, damp from dance and drink.

"Some day," she had said. "Take care of yourself out there."

She had left me there to the heckling of my buddies. More drinks had erased all memories of the night except that pretty girl and the hope of finding her again on my next liberty off ship.

Mid-slumber, there came a thumping like from a drum, a crazy thing to hear on a naval base. But it was no drum, something worse, growing signs of trouble in the distance. Yet my mind would not be bothered by it. In my dreams there was a nap in the hot sun of Waikiki, the huge waves rolling onto the shore, beach filled with sailors. A gurgling in my stomach signaled that soon it would be time for breakfast. Not yet, sleep first.

But the muffled echoes of the ship's loudspeaker weren't having it:

"Man your battle stations, this is no shit!"

Panic slapped me with *who what when where why* without immediate answers to any. Above me was the familiar steel overhead of the ship, a hard bunk supporting me, tethered to the overhead with chains. That answered the where, the ship, the *Oklahoma*. But what had that guy just said? Battle stations? It was a terrible gag to pull a drill on a Sunday morning, but the Navy was more interested in molding hard men than allowing sleep.

I struggled to pull myself up, head pounding, but I only managed to roll onto my side, straddling the edge of the bunk, fighting the decision to remain there or report to my station. Looking down, I saw the other bunks were empty, men who had occupied them long since gone to breakfast.

"Hey, what did that say?" I called out, hoping someone was around to hear. The response wasn't what I had hoped. A booming crash shook the entire ship, sweeping me from the bunk and down to the deck before I could react. I landed hard, knocking the wind from my lungs. I wrestled for air in shock on the cold deck. Pulling myself to hands and knees I sucked in oxygen like I was drowning, a minute later the sensation waning as I pulled myself to my feet.

This was a cruel joke, last night's beer so good going in, now muddying my veins. I felt immobilized by the hangover's hold, body struggling to remain upright. But the urgency of the situation forced me to consider action. Where to? Topside, find a ladder and get up. Report to your station.

Boom! Another explosion rocked the ship, lifting me off the deck and slamming me down again.

"God almighty!" I yelled, pulling myself up again. Had there been a collision? If so, someone's teat would be in a king-sized wringer.

Then came an unmistakable feeling. The ship began listing to port, the entire deck swaying to one side, tilting the bunks and lockers as if being pulled by some great magnet. I reacted with knees bent and arms extended sideways as though on a balance beam.

Then came the water. It seemed to rush in from everywhere, flowing through steel and over coamings, the hiss of its wash followed by creaks and knocks of the listing ship, cries of panicked crewmen coming from the distance.

By God, I found a ladder quick—on navy ships stairs were ladders. The metal steps had already begun to twist from the list of the ship. Water up to my knees, I pulled myself up on the ladder, hanging on the railing to climb the steps angling heavily.

Another explosion slammed the ship, and I lost my footing, hanging by one arm to the railing. Recovering, I pulled myself the rest of the way up to the relative safety of second deck.

Then came another crash, sending me to the deck once again, a lousy routine now.

No way this could be a collision. This was an attack, the thumpings outside were shells, bombs, torpedoes. But from who? How would anyone have the guts? There would be a fight up there for sure, and I wanted in on it.

"Abandon ship," came someone's yell in the distance. I tried to make sense of where the yell had come from, but everything was wrong. I stood on the bulkhead of the vessel, signaling that the ship was now completely on its side. Still the water rushed in, and now it was tainted with fuel oil from below decks, the odor overpowering me, making my eyes water.

The lights flickered and died, plunging my already confused world into blackness, nothing in my view but the foaming phosphorescence of the salty, oily seawater rushing about and the light from portholes above.

"Oh God!" came a scream, a shipmate I couldn't see overcome by fear. His voice reminded me instantly of my little brother, way too young to be in a war. Both of us were.

"We have to find a porthole!" I yelled. As I looked up, the overhead now the starboard side of the ship, I could see them there, a row of circular lights that meant escape and survival. But how to get up to them?

I could feel the water coming higher with every second, now up to my chest, time running out. I coughed as the fumes choked me.

"We're trapped!" came the sailor, this time closer, perhaps now in the same room.

There were coughs from the crewman, also succumbing to fumes. Then he pleaded to anyone: "I can't swim. Jesus, I can't swim!"

"Just hold on to something!" I said, wondering why in the

hell anyone would join the Navy without being able to swim. "I'll help you out. We have to get up to the portholes."

But there came only coughing and whimpers from the other man. For some reason I remembered swimming in the lake back home, how I would spend the day with friends, challenging each other to contests to see who could stay underwater longest. A silly game, but we would do it for hours, perfecting the skill before moving on to some other game. I'd been good at it.

Now this was no game. I wished it were, and I wanted this only to be a lake on a warm summer Sunday. After swimming we might go into town for a soda and goofing off, the endless summer days spent away from home, free to wander anywhere.

"Oh Mama!" came the voice of the terrified sailor again.

How I wished this was all just a terrible dream, and that I'd wake up in my bunk sweating and gasping, hung over and heart racing from the nightmare, but safe, the galley awaiting, ready to greet me with intolerable coffee, eggs, and bacon.

I wondered where Nan was now, and if she had even remembered me. "Take care of yourself out there," she had said, so soothing last night but so ominous this morning. I couldn't remember her face, only her red hair and gentle voice, and it found me wanting to know everything about her, I knew so little.

But the *Oklahoma* wasn't finished, and her listing interrupted my thoughts. It seemed inconceivable that the veteran ship of nearly thirty years could be so abused. With more creaks and moans, she started to slide again, and I came to the terrible recognition that there was one final task ahead for her —capsize, then sink for good.

"We're turning turtle!" I shouted.

"Oh my God, we're goners! We're gonna drown. We're gonna drown!"

"No we won't, when we turn over we have to get to the portholes!" I cried. "See em there? Look at the daylight through them. We have to get to them before we flood out."

"I can't swim!" shouted the crewman.

"I know, I'll help you."

"No, we can't make it. We can't make it up!"

I zeroed in on the crewman's voice, reaching into the darkness for him. I found a mattress floating in the water, pushed it aside, and kept fishing for my crew mate. With another sweep I found him, and the man yelped from the contact.

"I'm right here!" I shouted. "Grab hold of my arm!"

The crewman obeyed with an iron clutch to my arm, and I could feel the man quivering, ironic because he seemed large and strong. "We'll get out of here, relax," I said.

Everyone has at least one weakness. All bravado leaves when faced with it, and this man's was water. Maybe for another person it's fire or snakes or darkness, and people move throughout their existence hoping never to endure any of it. But why, oh why join the Navy with such fear of water? Better off in the Army, far, far away from the sea. But I couldn't judge the man anymore. The cold darkness of the listing ship, so much now like a watery tomb, had the will to smother any man's hope, and now it threatened to have us all forever.

Riding the toppling ship, I returned my focus again to the portholes, urging the crewman toward them, supporting both of us above the water line. "I've got you, stop struggling," I said. "Just hang on to me."

In moments we were up to the starboard side, the already opened portholes underwater but right there, I could see them, the faint promise of Hawaiian daylight shining through the water.

"Listen!" I said. "You have to dive under with me, it's the only way to get out. When we go under, open your eyes and find a porthole, I'll help you through."

"No, no!" came the crewman's response. "Leave me here, I can't do it!"

The water was high now, only enough room for our heads bobbing above the water line and the flat part of the ship that was now above us, the portholes deep below.

"Will you die trying? You have to try," I said.

I heard the crewman gasping for air, coughing and fretting, reaching a painful conclusion. "I can try it. You'll help me through?"

"I'll help you through. Get a deep breath. On three. One, two, three . . ."

I pulled the crewman under, opening my eyes to the black, salty, oily water. We dove to the closest orb of light, and I labored to drag the crewman down to it. Once there, I pushed the man into it, seeing now that it would be tight. The man became stuck, writhing against it, even underwater his cries audible, a foolish waste of oxygen. I shoved once, twice, a third time and the man started to go through an inch with each shove.

There's a point when the body sends out alarms for oxygen, warning the body of dangers, forcing irrational decisions. I began to approach that point as I struggled to push the crewman through, the light of the portholes seeming to go dim. I would have to give up and save myself soon, I had done what I could. But the helpless struggles of the man motivated me to continue, the frenzy of shoving to push him forth, my chest tightening and burning for air, fighting the need to close my eyes against the burning oil.

Too late. It was all too late. I realized it now, the pivotal point of oxygen deprivation arriving before I was ready. But with one last shove I pushed the crewman out, the last sensation his wild kicks as he made it through the porthole, free at last.

I couldn't think. I entered the porthole myself, realizing that I would have the same trouble fitting as the crewman. I urged myself in, path partially blocked, if only someone else had been there to return the favor of lifesaving shoves. I couldn't make it through without them.

Maybe there was still air to be had if I went back inside, one last breath to start my approach anew. Lungs pleading in desperation, I answered by turning away from the porthole to resurface back where I had come. But even as I did, I realized that part of the ship had filled, I could feel it with the thump of my head as I hit metal. The water had taken over, there was no air to be found there, the heartbreaking realization leading to overwhelming panic.

I dove back to the porthole and shoved myself inside, shoulders knocking hard, sending twinges of pain to my frame.

No good. Just, no good.

I shoved again and again, but it was all no good.

There was a rage to it now, a burning passion for life that was being denied, and the reaction was a fierce wrenching at the hull to get out, the desire to live again and fight another day. But it was all no good.

My body had lost the initiative, the need for air too great, and I floated back into the darkness away from the porthole, praying to God to make it all end quickly. My lungs won the battle in the quest for air, taking in the salty, oily water to gasping coughs.

The wash of death swept throughout the *Oklahoma,* four hundred young and promising boys who would never again see the Hawaiian daylight, few of their deaths simple or fast.

Still the planes outside circled and attacked before leaving behind the wreckage of their victory, so many broken vessels and the survivors who would never be the same again. I met my death that day, one of many gone too soon, all of us forever loathing the ridiculous human craving for bloodshed.

23

TEARS OF THE ARIZONA

Conner found Erin sitting on a bench staring out at Pearl Harbor. An hour earlier she had left him so he could tour the visitor center at his own pace, Erin preferring to sponge up the essence of the grounds rather than its exhibits. The late morning sun and humidity were already scorching, soothed only a little by the salty sea breeze, but she basked in it as though she belonged.

Conner watched her in her zone of solitude among the palm trees and tropical hedges. Her back was to him, body motionless, all senses focused as she viewed the skeletal USS *Arizona* monument on the water in the distance. He thought they could both remain like this all day, him watching her, her soaking up all that came forward.

A profound thought came to him uninvited but indisputable. He wondered if he'd ever really understand her as well as she understood him. After what had happened on the flight to Hawaii, he had fallen out of reality again, unexplainable events seizing his nerves. Yet, ever since landing in Honolulu, she had led his mind elsewhere, drained away his fretting and replaced it with night walks along the beach, calming discussions over seafood dinners on Larkin's dollar, her embrace in the hotel bed lulling him to sleep each night. He found himself utterly grateful for her, and maybe watching her all day would keep the feeling from escaping. He never wanted to lose her again.

Erin knew he was there. "Take a picture, it'll last longer," she said before turning to look at him.

"You have eyes on the back of your head now?" he asked. "Or did you just sense trouble approaching again?"

Erin stood and walked to him. "You *are* trouble," she said pulling him into a hug. "But you're my trouble." Her lips found his, the kiss transferring a subtle message to her. She pulled back. "What is it *now?*"

"Nothing," Conner said, eyes searching the harbor behind her.

"Not nothing," she said. "What's wrong? You're tense again. This is Hawaii, you need to mellow out."

"I keep thinking I'll see something out there."

"We've talked about this," she said, taking his hand. "So what if you do? It can't hurt you. And I'm here."

"I don't see how you can be so calm about it."

"I just said it can't hurt you, that's why," she said. "Besides, isn't it all sort of exciting?"

"The world is exciting enough, isn't it?"

"Just don't worry, okay? I'm right about this, you'll be okay."

"We should get in line for the boat," he said.

"Aye aye, Captain," she said. "But after all of this history you owe me a luau."

"Deal," he said.

∼

CONNER AND ERIN rode in the Navy boat toward the *Arizona* memorial, the boat's motor bubbling beneath the waterline, vessel rocking over harbor swells. Across the harbor was moored the battleship *Missouri,* its bow standing guard over what had been Pearl Harbor's battleship row in 1941. The *Missouri* had witnessed the surrender of the Japanese on its deck, ending World War II. Now the ship's final mission was an eternal watch over the place where American involvement in the war in the Pacific had begun. Empty white moorings near it marked the locations of battleships long since gone following the attack on Pearl Harbor.

But it was the sagging white structure of the *Arizona* directly ahead that captured the attention of the tourists packed tightly onto the ferry with Erin and Conner. Many talked loud enough to each other to be heard over the boat engine, others took photos or videos, some watched in silence. Erin sat at the edge of the boat, Conner next to her watching the waterline over her shoulder.

"Perfect weather again today," Erin said, turning to him. "Just another day in paradise."

"Maybe we should have waited another day before coming out here," he said.

"It's a little late to realize that now, isn't it?" Erin said. "Besides, you'd feel the same tomorrow, it would just delay the inevitable. Think about something else. Tell me about the *Arizona.* Of all the ships, why does this one have a memorial in the water?"

"The *Arizona* got the worst of it," Conner explained. "There was an explosion, over a thousand sailors were killed. Much of the ship's structure is still out there beneath the memorial. They couldn't raise it. Many of the dead were never removed, it's their tomb now. In time a permanent memorial was built right where it sank."

"Bodies are still in there?"

Conner nodded. "And the ship is still leaking fuel oil. Some refer to it as the tears of the *Arizona.*"

"Now that's sad," she said. "But see, the spiritual world understands tragedy and reminds us of the sacrifice with a metaphor. It couldn't be clearer."

"And it's an environmental hazard," he said. "Like a toxic bloodstain that will never be erased."

"That's dark, even for you," she said. "Good simile though."

Maybe Erin could sense that he'd rather observe than talk, so they kept silent for the rest of the approach. Eventually the boat's engine throttled back to ease into the memorial's dock. A Navy seaman leaped from the boat to the dock to secure the lines while the passengers ruminated over the monument's stark white structure reflecting tropical sunlight.

Boat secured, everyone filtered onto the dock and up the gangplank to the sanctuary of the memorial, the white-washed interior conjuring the gateway to heaven. They filed past a display of honor flags and into the belly of the memorial, like the insides of a great whale, daylight producing symmetrical shadows on the floor. The memorial crossed perpendicularly over the *Arizona,* parts of the ship visible in the water below.

Conner and Erin walked up to the right railing away from the crowd and looked into the water. The rusting turret mount of the *Arizona* poked above the waterline, a battered crown of a mortally wounded king. In the green water they could see the outline of the submerged ship, its form crusted with a coat of algae. Conner couldn't help but feeling like they were standing over an enormous graveyard, both for the men still inside and for the fallen vessel itself. In his mind he could hear the cries for mercy of those not killed instantly, flaming casket of steel slowly dragging them under for good where they would remain forever.

Conner went to the other side of the memorial to look at the *Missouri* in the distance. Erin followed him there, hair blowing in the breeze. He began taking pictures with his phone down the length of the memorial, the task of documenting the site almost an afterthought before he turned back to look out at the water.

"What are we looking at?" she asked.

"Those white moorings mark where the ships on battleship row were docked. The *Oklahoma* took the worst of it among those, taking several torpedoes to the side. It turned upside down and mostly sank."

"Do you think he came from one of those ships?" Erin said.

"Who?"

"The sailor you saw in the mirror on the flight out here."

"Maybe," Conner said, not wanting to talk about it.

She left him there to walk toward the back of the memorial where the names of sailors killed on the *Arizona* were listed. Conner followed her there, took a picture of her, and joined her in front of the velvet ropes guarding the list of names.

"They shouldn't have died like this," she whispered to him. "So senseless."

Conner didn't disagree with her, but he wished she wouldn't do this again, like she had done at Gettysburg. Those who'd died wouldn't want to hear someone calling their deaths senseless. It wasn't all senseless anyway—the deaths and destruction at Pearl Harbor had stirred the United States into action, eventually helping put an end to Axis aggression. Wasn't that worth the price paid?

Conner sensed something sweeping in from behind them.

He looked back, sure he'd see someone crowding him, but none of the other tourists were close enough. Then a gust of frigid air brushed against his bare legs, washing over his feet through his flip-flops.

"Do you feel that?" Erin asked.

"I thought it was just me," Conner said. "Cool air. Where's it coming from?"

Erin put her palm toward the floor. "Right here," she said, pointing to the spot right beside them. "Something's here."

"It must be a cooling system of some sort, something we can't see."

"You're kidding, right?" Erin said. "There's nothing like that here. And it's not moving, it's stationary cold air."

She was right, of course. Still, he looked for any clues of its source, a drain or ventilation grate. There was nothing.

Erin's face turned sour, her hand moving to her stomach. She rested her palm on her belly.

"What?" Conner asked.

"Stomach," was all she could murmur.

Conner was about to tell her that she was imagining it when something rolled inside his own stomach, digestion of his breakfast temporarily put on hold. He opened his mouth to speak, but the discomfort in his gut drowned the words.

"You feel it too," she said, reading the disturbance in his face.

"What's going on?" he asked her. Other tourists milled around, completely unaffected, gazing at the memorial without a thought of what was happening to the two of them.

The knot in Conner's stomach spread, contaminating his body with a sick lethargy. He and Erin looked into each other's eyes for answers, both unable to move or speak, paralyzed by an unseen murk.

If they were on the edge of a cliff, both were teetering

there, losing balance, beginning to fall into the abyss below. Conner could feel the sensation rolling toward a startling endgame, consciousness begin to lapse, heart racing at the prospect of passing out and falling to the concrete. He saw Erin looking frail, pale, hypnotized, struggling to maintain any scrap of normalcy.

For a moment the surroundings bent, an illusion that they were no longer on the memorial. Instead they were standing in front of a two-story office building during a workday. The building was modern, tall windows revealing people working inside. There was a detached peacefulness to it, watching from a distance as humanity solved problems and conducted the drudgery of business. But that changed in one tumultuous instant when the building exploded, glass and steel succumbing to fire, the structure bursting from within, cries of hundreds nearly muted beneath the roar. Then a strange silence took over, the destruction so sudden and complete that there was little left to see or hear.

The illusion faded, Erin and Conner returning to the view of the *Arizona*. As the sounds of the explosion left his mind, Conner heard a vaguely familiar voice:

"You have to stop it."

Words echoing away into silence, the paralyzing grip on Conner's body fell away like the release of a straitjacket. He inhaled a rejuvenated breath.

"Conner!" Erin said. She, too, looked like she had broken free from the fog.

"What?"

"Look," she said, pointing to the ground.

Conner was still trying to make sense of the voice he had just heard, so when he looked to where she pointed, what was there seemed like a mirage. But as reality returned even more, he saw that they were standing in a sizable puddle of water, as if they had both been dripping wet.

"Where did that come from?" he asked her.

"I don't know," she said, stepping out of it, shaking the water from her sandals.

He joined her away from the puddle. Other tourists took notice of it, too, but only long enough to decide that Conner or Erin must have spilled something, and they went about their tour.

Erin grabbed Conner's shoulder. "What did he say?" she asked.

"Who?"

"I know you heard the voice," she said. "I heard it too. What did he say?"

"I don't know," Conner said.

"Well I do," she said. "He said *you have to stop it.*"

Conner didn't dispute it. That's what he thought he'd heard, too.

"I saw an explosion," Erin said. "A building exploded, I saw it in my mind."

"How in the hell did you see that too?" Conner said.

Erin's mouth opened wide at the significance. "You saw it?"

"We have to go," Conner said, leaving her for the other end of the memorial.

"Wait!" she called, trying to catch up to him, but his long strides that were intent on escape wove through the crowd of tourists faster than she could. She only caught up with him when he stopped to peer over a railing near the entrance. She stood next to him, Conner looking as though he'd rather jump over the side than remain on board.

"Just calm it a little, will you? It's okay," she said.

"I've gone completely nuts."

"If you're nuts, then we both are," she said. "This time I felt it too. You can't deny that it happened to both of us."

He grabbed the railing with both hands, arms extending out like he wanted to push it free. Erin reached for his right hand and massaged his grip free from the bar. Then she slid in between him and the railing, holding him and looking into his eyes. "I'm here you know," she said. "Whatever's happening, I'm right here."

He stroked the hair from her eyes, felt her body inch up to his, the lure of her face and lips coming toward his, but his body was still too numb to participate.

"Earth to Conner?" she said instead of kissing him. "Anyone home?"

"Barely," he said.

"I understand," she said. "But get a grip here. You're alive, and you're perfectly sane. Well, reasonably sane."

"Thanks," he said.

"But you're gonna drive me bats if you keep freaking out like this," she continued. "Don't you want to see more of the monument?"

Conner looked back toward where they had been. "I think I'm done," he said.

"Are you sure? We came here for this."

"I'm more than sure."

She nodded. "Then let's go to the beach. We need to get away from here, go back to enjoying this place."

"You read my mind," he said.

"I was never much of a psychic, but I'll take credit this time," she said,

They took the next boat back to shore, left Pearl Harbor, and never returned.

24

EVIDENCE

Erin stretched stomach down on a hotel towel surrounded by pristine Oahu sand. Conner sat across from her facing the ocean with his back propped on a palm tree. A cluster of palms cast uneven shade over their spot on a less crowded edge of Hanauma Bay. On Conner's towel next to him was an uneaten pastrami sandwich.

Hanauma was once a volcanic cone, long since erupting into the Pacific to form a majestic semicircle cradling the sea. A backdrop of hills behind the beach created a sense of seclusion, as if all that existed on Earth for those on the beach were the bay and the ocean beyond. Hanauma's beauty brought in tourists by the thousands, and this day was no exception, many of them snorkeling in the coral shallows near the denser crowds toward the beach's center. The serenity forced something close to comfort into Conner's mood like a slow-working hypnosis.

"If you're waiting for that sandwich to completely decompose, it could take a while," Erin said, studying him.

"Not very hungry," Conner said, looking down at his lunch as if he'd never seen it before. Despite what he said, he picked up the sandwich and took a bite. As he chewed he realized he was hungrier than he thought, so he kept eating. Erin watched him through her sunglasses without revealing what she was thinking.

"You have to admit, it was pretty amazing, right?" she said. "Something was there with us. The cold air, water materializing under our feet, both of us having the same vision—stuff like that just doesn't happen every day."

"That was a first for me, all right," he said.

"Yet I was right, nothing happened to us. We weren't harmed."

"Physically, no," he said.

They both tracked an outburst from the left, two children running in the sand. Both kids raced by Erin, a younger boy chasing an older girl, siblings maybe, girl goading the boy to chase, boy clad in arm floaties wild with pursuit. Not realizing what he was doing, the boy kicked sand onto Erin's back before continuing the chase away and down to the water. Erin grimaced and pulled herself to a sitting position, trying to brush the sand now sticking to the tanning lotion on her back.

"Little twit," she huffed to herself.

Conner laughed.

"Do you want a mouthful of sand?" she said to Conner when she realized he was laughing at her.

"I'll just stick with my sandwich," he said, holding it up. "He didn't mean it. Don't you like kids?"

"I love kids, when they aren't kicking sand on me," she said. "But since this is the first time I've seen you laugh in a while, I'll let it go."

"I like this place, it's calming," he said.

"Agreed. We should stay here, move to Oahu and become beach bums," she said.

"Beats college and doing dishes, but it's not the best career move."

"Fine, we'll go home then," she said. "Then we'll get fancy jobs with our degrees and come here every winter."

"Now you're talking," he said.

Erin came to him and knelt on his towel.

"The sun is scorching. Your spot is shadier, palm-tree man," she said.

"I like the thought of being a tree on a tropical beach," he said. "There would be this great view all day, and hardly a care except when a storm comes."

"That's no better of a career move than a beach bum," she said. "But if I can snap you out of your weird tree fantasy, I was wondering something."

"Do we have to keep talking about what happened? I'm trying to take my mind off it."

"We will, but talking a little will help," she said. "Just trust me. Do you remember the details of our tarot session, or did you have too much wine that night?"

"Sure, it showed that my thesis would be a total disaster, how could I forget?" he said.

"Not an accurate summary, but yes, that," she said.

"What about it?"

"Not to pat myself on the back or anything, but it was right on, don't you think?"

"I've hardly even begun my thesis," he said.

She removed her sunglasses to look him in the eyes. "I don't think it was necessarily about your thesis. It originated from that, sure, but something greater was interjected. I think what we've been experiencing lately is what the cards were warning about."

"The cards," he said.

"They showed us something was coming, something we'll have to deal with."

"A building explosion," Conner said.

"Exactly," Erin said. "And it has something to do with Larkin."

Conner took another bite of his sandwich and spoke through a mouthful: "Sure, but why would an old coot blow something up?"

"An old, bitter, eccentric coot? I could think of a few reasons. And maybe we're in a position to find out why and what. He's obviously taken a liking to you. You might be able to get info out of him."

"Seriously? He's creepy as hell. Plus, I'd rather not go up to him and start talking about visions we've been having about explosions. Or that we've been seeing and hearing from ghosts."

"I'm just saying we should keep our minds open to anything that may come along from Larkin," she said. "If there's something going on, we have to figure out what."

Conner looked out at the water, happy to be distracted by its serenity.

"I'm gonna wash this Godforsaken sand off, are you coming?" she asked.

"You go ahead, the palm tree needs me here," he said. "We'll watch."

"Okay, weirdo," she said.

While Erin walked to the water, the explosion started replaying in Conner's mind as vividly as when they had first seen it. How many people would die in such a blast? Maybe hundreds. And what did Larkin have to do with it? Despite everything logical telling Conner that none of what he saw was real, he had to stop writing it off, there were too many unexplained events to ignore now, especially if lives were at stake. Maybe he couldn't be as calm and enthusiastic about it as Erin was, but he could start treating it for what it was: reality, or some smidgeon of it.

Conner pulled out his phone and turned it on. He hadn't looked at the photos he had taken on the *Arizona* memorial, and something nagged at him to do it now. Maybe seeing the memorial again would help him piece together what to do next. Hesitant at first, he opened his photo app. A thumbnail of the last photo he took of the *Arizona* names wall appeared, and he tapped it open. He couldn't make out the image details in the sun's glare, so he moved his arm so that the screen was more in the shade of the palms, and the photo became discernible. It showed Erin facing away from the camera, list of names in the background.

And something else entirely.

"What's that?" he whispered to himself.

To Erin's right in the photo was a dark figure, as tall as a man and inexplicably blurred. Conner tapped the image and zoomed in. Slowly his mind filled in the gaps, cloudy shapes making more sense the closer he zoomed. There was no doubting what he saw, and it was as disturbing as it was astounding: a man dressed in a sailor suit.

Conner tossed the phone face down on his towel as though it was suddenly poisonous. He stared at it for a minute, then realized how ludicrous it was to be afraid of a phone. He picked it up and looked at the image again, hoping it could be explained as a photographic anomaly. No, the sailor was definitely still there. The camera had caught a figure that human vision had not—no sailor had been anywhere near them when he had taken the photo.

Conner inhaled and then swiped to the previous photo. The image showed the railing along the memorial, tourists peering over to see the sunken *Arizona* in the water below.

There was something there, too, and he almost didn't see it at first. But once he noticed it he got the shivers, another view of the same blurred sailor standing in the center of the tourists, seemingly staring right at the camera.

Conner swiped to the photo before that, nearly the same angle but taken a minute earlier. He flinched when he saw it, the entire screen taken up by a blurred face and body. It was the sailor again, but this time right in front of the camera, eyes darkened and hollow, mouth open as if saying something.

"Oh damn!" Conner said, holding the camera away from him, his curiosity forcing him to keep looking at the image despite his horror. He swept past the image, relieved to see it gone, the next one a mercifully benign shot of the battleship moorings in the harbor with no people in view. He swept to another image, but that was all he had taken of the memorial. Only then did he realize that he had forgotten to take pictures of the visitor center, his mind too preoccupied with the prospect of visiting the memorial. The next photos were from earlier on the trip—one of Erin walking on the beach, another of her on their hotel lanai, and a selfie of the both of them at dinner. No more ghosts, thank God.

Conner looked toward the bay to see Erin wade into the water and begin to brush the sand from her back. He needed to show the photos to her. He swiped back to the ominous closeup, the macabre and distorted face uncomfortable to view, as though the image was alive and watching him from inside his phone's camera.

Another thought occurred to Conner, one he wished he hadn't discovered. He hadn't yet looked at the photos from the Gettysburg trip. Would there be more creepy things among those? He hated to even think about it, but he began to scroll through his photos to find them. He sped through the thumbnails until he found the set he had taken at Gettysburg. This time he looked at the first one he had taken near the First Minnesota memorial. The monument image wasn't unusual, the statue of the charging Minnesota infantryman just as Conner had remembered it. But the next one was a different story. It showed Erin standing in the field in the distance when she had walked out before the yellow jackets had come. Next to her was another blurred image, someone standing there, someone who hadn't been there when he had taken the photo.

"Shit!" he said, zooming in on the blur. As with the sailor, when he zoomed he immediately determined what the figure was: a man wearing a Civil War uniform. Conner advanced to the next image, the blurred soldier remaining like a permanent fixture of the battlefield.

Conner saw Erin exiting the water and returning toward him. He didn't even try to hide his concern, she would sense it anyway.

"Now what's wrong?" she asked when close enough.

He toggled back to the *Arizona* images, and handed the phone out to her. "Look."

She took the phone and studied the picture. When she figured out what she was seeing, she covered her mouth with her hand. "It's him. He *was* there!"

"He was all around us, apparently," Conner said.

Erin began swiping back until she found the closeup of the sailor. "Oh my God!"

"There's more," he said. "Go to the Gettysburg pictures."

"Are you serious?" she asked, looking at him in shock. Then she swiped to the Gettysburg images, taking only a few seconds to see the blurred man. "It's the other one!" Erin said. "The man you heard at Gettysburg. Holy shit Conner, these are ghost photos, really good ones! The ghosts are everywhere!"

Conner had no words for that.

"Well that puts an exclamation point on things," she said.

"Never in a million years did I think any of this was possible," he said.

"Do you now?" she asked. He didn't need to answer.

"This is indisputable proof. We have to do something," she said.

"We've been through this already. What, exactly, do we need to do?"

"I'm not sure yet," she said. "But I think we'll find out soon enough."

25

OUR AMERICAN COUSIN

Larkin's mansion had the ability to make anyone feel small. Back from Hawaii, Conner realized that he'd forgotten the feeling of awe he'd always felt outside of the home. Today, there was something more: dread. He tried to ignore the sensation as he walked up the steps through the porte cochere archway, stopping at the mansion's wooden front door, its iron clavos and hinges giving it a medieval appearance. He found the doorbell and rang it, Westminster Chimes clanging from within.

"Be right there college boy," Pike's voice sounded from the intercom. Conner looked up at the security camera and waved, knowing that Pike was watching him from somewhere. A minute later and the deadbolt clicked, the handle turned, and the door opened with a creak, revealing Pike's usual expression of disgust. His arms and chest looked ready to bust through his dry-fit t-shirt, cargo pants and work boots more worthy of a special ops mission than cooking or chauffeuring.

"He's upstairs," Pike said. Conner stepped inside as Pike closed the door behind him and locked it again. He led Conner across the marble-floored foyer and up the wide curving staircase to the second floor. The hush of the mansion seemed out of place, Conner much more accustomed to the home bustling from a gathering.

When they reached the landing at the top of the staircase, Pike stopped and turned to Conner. He spoke with a quieter voice as he pointed down the hallway: "He's down there, but here's some advice Mr. Professor. He hasn't been feeling well, so go easy on the man. In and out, if you can, no dallying around talking history BS. Okay?"

"Right," Conner said. "But he invited me."

"God only knows why. He must be reliving his college days through you, but I guess that's his right. Anyway, in and out."

Conner nodded. Pike led Conner down the hall. When they reached the door, Pike rapped on it with the back of his hand as he called through the door: "Hey boss? The kid's here to see you."

"Bring him in then," Larkin answered. Pike opened the door and gestured for Conner to enter.

As Conner stepped inside, he became inundated by the splendor of a spacious sitting room. A stone fireplace commanded most of the far wall, sizable blaze warming the room and scenting it with wood smoke. Above the fireplace was a painting in a gilded frame of American Indians enduring the death walk on "The Trail of Tears." Four Grecian-style pillars occupied each corner of the room, and the base of each was a carving of an exotic maiden. Busts of Julius Caesar and Napoleon mingled with Tiffany lamps atop Victorian parlor tables. Near the fireplace sat Larkin's assistant, Marcela, in a white high-back chair. Next to her was Larkin in a red velvet parlor chair, his frail body draped in a plaid cashmere blanket. Even from this distance, Conner could see that Larkin looked ill, a paler, thinner version of the man he had seen just weeks before.

"Marcela was just leaving," Larkin called, waving Conner over. Marcela dutifully closed her laptop, stood, and headed for the exit, nodding a cold greeting to Conner as she left. Pike pulled the door closed and left Conner alone with Larkin.

"This room . . ." Conner said.

"Yes, it's astounding, I know," Larkin interrupted. "Everything is vintage and priceless, but I didn't invite you here to see a room."

Conner walked forward and sat in the white chair Marcela had left, fireplace warming the winter chill from his back.

"You wanted to see me?" Conner asked.

"It wasn't an order, you hardly even work for me," Larkin said. "But yes. I wanted to hear about Hawaii. It's still there? The Japanese haven't bombed it again?"

"It's still there," Conner said. "We just got back. Thanks again for the trip, we had a great time."

"Yes, I heard you made up with that girl. I hope frolicking around on the beaches with her wasn't all you did."

"No. We spent a day at Pearl Harbor."

"And?"

"It's a remarkable place," Conner said. Even as he spoke the visions of the apparition at Pearl Harbor took over, his words sounding detached and insincere even to himself.

"You don't sound very inspired," Larkin said. "The location where two thousand Americans were slaughtered didn't grab you?"

"I wasn't feeling well the day we went," Conner said. "Something I ate maybe. But it was helpful to see, it gave me a lot to think about."

"You still want to write your thesis about the Japanese perspective," Larkin concluded.

"Maybe," Conner said. "I don't know yet."

"Why not focus on our poor bastards who drowned and burned on those ships? Our guys deserve that, don't they?"

"Sure they do, but isn't it worth finding out what motivates enemies of the United States? We still have lots of them, both outside of the country and from within."

For a change Conner thought he'd stumped Larkin. The old man's mouth hung open as if to reply, something holding him back. What came out instead was a thick, soupy hack. Larkin winced, eyes closing to tame the cough. Finished, he swallowed hard and opened his eyes again in a daze, looking too exhausted to argue.

"Write about whatever you want, or whatever your teachers want to brainwash you with," Larkin said. "None of my damn business I suppose."

Conner looked away from the awkwardness. His view fixed upon an open laptop on the end table next to Larkin just as the screensaver activated. An image floated ominously on the screen, a wrought iron sign with infamous words: "Arbeit Macht Frei." Conner recognized it immediately, and its rough translation formed in his head: *Work Sets You Free.* He recalled that these words had greeted prisoners to the Auschwitz concentration camp during World War II, one of the cruelest lies ever to appear on signage. Why would Larkin choose that, of all things, for his screen saver? Or did Conner even want to know?

"Whatever it is, I hope writing my thesis is easier than choosing the topic," Conner said. He watched Larkin reach for a glass of water next to the laptop. Larkin's hand shook as he drank, even the act of swallowing a fatiguing ordeal.

"You've had that cough for a while," Conner said. "Maybe you need to get it checked?"

Larkin forced a smile, something amusing about the question. "Oh I've seen someone," he said, returning the glass to the end table. "I have this little affliction known as lung cancer. It's a fun ailment, if it weren't for the coughing up blood and gradual suffocation."

"Lung cancer?" Conner said.

"That's right. And it's terminal."

The words hung in the room that was silent except for the pops and crackles from the fireplace.

"That's awful," Conner said. "There's nothing that can be done?"

Larkin shook his head. "Doctors can't even cure the common cold, much less lung cancer as bad as mine. They claim to have treatments available, all with success rates far worse than slim or none, only to delay the inevitable. No, nothing can be done, this affliction will kill me, and sooner rather than later."

"How long do you have?" Conner asked.

"That's a roulette wheel," Larkin said. "Could be days, could be weeks. Only God knows. Don't dwell on it, I'm not. Can't be afraid to die at my age. Why should I? I've had a good life, and it's time to go, that's all."

Conner nodded.

"I trust you'll keep your mouth shut about it. No one else is to know, besides Marcela and Karl."

"I will," Conner said.

"I barely remember being your age," Larkin said. "But I was that young once. Right now you're thinking you'll never die, you can't even imagine it."

"It's naive to think I'll never die," Conner said. "But you're right, I can't imagine it."

"Never mind about that," Larkin said. "Just be glad it isn't you. When you go home, be grateful you have a long time left. Now, let me show you something."

Larkin opened the end table drawer and pulled out what

looked to be a long picture frame. "You might find this amusing," he said, handing it over.

Noticing right away that the object was old, Conner rested it carefully on his lap to study it: a heavy brass frame in the form of ivy vines, glass window encasing a yellowed playbill, in the center a familiar title: *Our American Cousin*. Overshadowing everything was handwriting scrawled across the playbill, its significance causing Conner's mouth to open wide in disbelief:

I do not repent the blow I struck. April 14, 1865 J. Wilkes Booth

"This can't be real," Conner said, looking up at Larkin.

"Sure about that? I happen to think it's one hundred percent authentic," Larkin said. "Almost no one knows it exists, which is the beauty of it. An original playbill from *Our American Cousin*, the comedy performed at Ford's Theater the night Abraham Lincoln was assassinated, autographed by the assassin himself, John Wilkes Booth."

"How in the world did you get this?" Conner asked. "And how do you know it isn't a fake?"

"A person can buy a great many things if he has the means," Larkin said. "This came from a reputable and reclusive dealer, signature and playbill authenticated under secrecy. Our assassin Mr. Booth signed this playbill, possibly even on the night the blow was struck."

"That's pretty hard to believe."

"I don't really care if you believe it or not, I know it's legit," Larkin said. "And in any case, now you have two secrets to keep. Don't tell anyone this exists, I don't want people pestering me to sell it. I wouldn't, not for any price."

"Supposing it's genuine, why shouldn't the world know about it?" Conner asked.

"Because the world sees that event very differently than I do," Larkin said. "An act of treason, the murdering of a great president. I see it as a man fed up with what his country had become, and he did the only thing he felt he could do."

"You're right, not many would agree with that," Conner said.

"All the more reason that piece will go to the grave with me, never to be seen again. You might be the last one to ever see it. Consider it a symbol of standing up for your beliefs, even when the rest of society disagrees."

The vision of the building exploding crept into Conner's memory as if someone had planted it there again. Thinking about any connection to the explosion and Larkin was as unsettling as the John Wilkes Booth signature he now held. What was this sickly old man plotting in his dying days? Or was he planning anything at all, everything Conner now felt just a coincidence?

Conner took one last look at the playbill, a small part of him wanting to believe it was real, most of his thoughts preoccupied by Larkin being a fan of John Wilkes Booth. He handed the playbill back to Larkin, who looked at it with an amazement similar to seeing it for the first time. Then Larkin returned it to the drawer, no one the wiser that something so potentially rare rested inside.

"What will become of the rest of your collection?" Conner asked. He realized too late that it was an insensitive thing to ask.

"Jockeying for an inheritance?" Larkin said.

"No, I didn't mean it like that. I just mean, the things you own are phenomenal. Museums would love to have them."

Larkin rested his head back on his chair. "Yes, I've considered all that. Can't very well bury them all with me like some pharaoh, much as I'd like to. They'll find their way to the right museums. My will is clear on that."

"I wish there was something that could be done for you," Conner said.

"You and me both," Larkin said. "I'm afraid I'm getting groggy. I should have liked to have learned more about what you're studying at that college of yours. It passes the time you know, using your brain to think about the past. But these drugs make me damn near comatose. I trust you can find the exit without the need for me to call Karl?"

"I can," Conner said. He stood, realizing the strange visit was to end abruptly. At least Pike would be satisfied. "Can I get you anything before I go?"

"Only to leave me festering in this chair," Larkin said. "Come again and tell me all about your liberal schooling so I can explain why it's all wrong."

"Sure," Conner said, Larkin looking like he was already falling asleep. "Take care of yourself then."

Conner turned and walked through the room, the Cherokees above the fireplace and the busts of Caesar and Napoleon watching him leave. As he opened the door, the words *I do not repent the blow I struck* occurred to him. When he turned around to wave goodbye, he heard Larkin's labored snore, so he closed the door quietly and left for home.

26

TERROR

The private study room at the University of Minnesota's Wilson library masked any knowledge of the December chill outside. Books and periodicals were spread open on every chair and table surface, images of the Oklahoma City bombing, the Boston Marathon bombing, the Las Vegas shooting, and 9/11 displaying terror on American soil in vivid detail. Conner stood up to survey it all, stretching his aching back, piecing together what he wanted to look at next, his laptop cursor blinking mid-sentence.

Much earlier that day, homework finished, Conner had begun researching anything he could find about Reid Larkin. Expecting to find loads of dirt on a man of Larkin's character, what surfaced was a boring array of business dealings, the power of the Internet failing to shake loose anything to suggest Larkin was up to something questionable. After hours of digging, Conner realized it would take a full-time private investigator to find more, if there was even anything to find.

Giving up on Larkin, Conner had then begun researching 9/11 for possible thesis topics. Before long, the task had expanded into something larger and darker, terrorism on his mind like some vague but indisputable clue, his actions driven by an undying urge to learn every detail. But the research had taken its toll on his mind, unravelling a web of toxic acts in stark retellings of destruction and heartbreak. As he stood looking at the sources spilling out terror, he could hear the pleading screams from the dying as clearly as he remembered the vision of the exploding building he saw at Pearl Harbor. Yet he also felt like he was somehow on the right track.

A knock at the study room window was so invasive to his thoughts that he flinched, knocking to the floor a book about the Unabomber. Conner turned to see Erin standing outside the study room holding up two coffees. She cringed when she realized that she had startled him from concentration. She stacked the coffees on top of one another and opened the door with her free hand.

"Someone's jumpy," she said, stepping inside and closing the door behind her.

"I didn't notice you were there," he said.

"I got you a coffee, not that you need it with your jitters," she said, handing him a cup.

"Thanks," he said, taking the cup. He looked at the time on his laptop: 8:27 p.m. "I could use some, I've been at this all day."

"And what is this exactly, a CIA investigation?" she said, picking up the Unabomber book from the floor.

"Domestic terrorism," he said.

"Don't you study anything positive?" she asked. "There must be some warm and fuzzy parts of history."

"Ever since visiting Larkin yesterday, I just can't get the thought out of my head," he said.

Erin placed the book on the table. "What thought exactly, besides the man's an intolerable prick?"

"Terrorism."

"Okay, sit down," she said, guiding him to the chair he had been sitting in. As he sat, she cleared space on another chair and joined him at the study table. "You think he's a terrorist now?"

"Not yet," he said. "He has terminal cancer, he told me yesterday."

Erin's eyes widened. "He's dying? That's terrible."

"I know. But the more I talk to the guy, the more it seems like he's not wired like us. His views are really out there. I mean, the man studies Mengele and he defends John Wilkes Booth. Who does that?"

"A crabby rich white racist narcissist," she said.

"Right, that's our guy."

"And you think he's going to blow up a building as a terrorist act," she said, stating it as though it was an answer to a question.

"Possibly," Conner said. "If we're meant to believe that the vision we saw was an accurate representation of the future, which a part of me still thinks is fantasy."

"Nothing fantasy about it," she said, sipping her coffee. "It makes perfect sense."

"What if the vision is a metaphor?" Conner asked. "What if I'm supposed to help Larkin figure something out. Maybe help him resolve his exploding emotions before he dies?"

Erin shook her head. "A metaphor in a dream is one thing. But we both saw the same vision in broad daylight among a crowd of people. Nothing about that was intended to be metaphorical. It was a clear vision of future events. I think you're right, Larkin is planning a last hurrah of evil."

"I wish we knew the details though," Conner said.

"What are you hoping to figure out by investigating terrorism?" she asked.

"Nothing," he said. "I guess it took me looking through this stuff to believe Larkin's capable of doing such a thing. We're talking about a man with unlimited funding, unbridled hatred, and nothing to lose."

"A perfect storm for committing an atrocity," Erin said.

"The problem is, what do we do? We can't go to the police, we have no evidence whatsoever. They'll think we're nut jobs."

"What about talking to Pike?" Erin offered.

"Pike is too dedicated to Larkin, he wouldn't do anything," Conner said. "Or he wouldn't believe us."

"He might even be in on it," Erin added. "There's also Larkin's weird assistant lady, but same problem there. He keeps dedicated people around him, they wouldn't help us."

"So that leaves what?" Conner said, finally taking a sip of his coffee.

"We could snoop," Erin said.

"What, like look around his mansion? No way."

"How else will we find anything?" Erin said. "Next time we work there, we could find ways to distract Pike so we can have a look around."

"What would we even be looking for?" Conner said.

"Documents, some sort of evidence of a plot, computers. Haven't you watched any James Bond movies?"

"Enough to know that you can get caught," Conner said. "What if Pike were to catch us in the act? Or there could be cameras."

"I've never seen cameras in that place, unless they're hidden," Erin said. "Besides, if we're caught all they'd do is fire us. There're thousands of other crappy dishwashing jobs out there."

"Or Pike could perform some demented form of vigilante justice on us. The man is wound up way too tightly."

"Then we just have to make sure not to get caught," she said.

"Or not snoop," Conner said. "This whole discussion is giving me a panic attack."

They sat among the humming of the library lights gazing at the books laid out. Erin reached for a book about 9/11 and began thumbing through pictures.

"I'm glad I was too young to remember much of this," she said, pointing to a photo of an airliner plunging into one of the Twin Towers in New York City. "We studied it a lot in school, and that was plenty for me. How can you stand obsessing about these things?"

"Coffee helps," he said, taking another sip. "But I think today I learned that I don't want to do my thesis about it. You're right, it's depressing. Maybe I can find something about the history of trade wars."

"Trade wars? How is that better? I want to hang myself just hearing that topic," Erin said.

Conner laughed. "It's more interesting than you'd think," he said. "What's an intriguing sociology topic, the gender stereotypes of pet clothing?"

"Nice try," she said. "Still a more interesting topic than trade wars."

Erin continued turning pages in the book until she saw a photo of a 9/11 victim leaping from one of the Twin Towers. "Oh God," she said, closing the book. "This stuff is really weirding me out, and I think it's affecting you too. Let's get out of here."

"And go where?" he asked.

"You're going to take me out for ice cream."

"It's 8:30 at night, and it's December in the Midwest, and you want ice cream?"

"Exactly," she said, leaning over to kiss him. "I've been craving mint and chip all day, and you're going to get it for me."

"Okay," Conner said. "Then what?"

"My place?"

"Help me get rid of these books," he said.

"I thought you'd see it my way," she smiled.

They cleaned up Conner's study room, departed Wilson Library, and left behind domestic terrorism for ice cream.

27

AMANDA

The morning transition from darkness to the faint glow of sunrise had begun in the woods behind John and Amanda McMichael's upscale and remote suburban home. A casual observer would never have noticed Mr. Red lying flat among the tawny brush along the tree line. He had made his way there during the night, and with the coming of daylight, his camouflage from head to toe concealed him well, tactical spotting scope on a tripod aimed at the back of the home. Face covered with a camo balaclava, Mr. Red's eyes shifted to his wristwatch between his parka sleeve and his gloved hand showing 6:56 a.m.

The mechanical sounds that Mr. Red heard in the dawn stillness were the garage door opening from the front of the house followed by John McMichael's Mercedes backing out. Next came the sound of the car accelerating down the street, McMichael leaving for work exactly on schedule, garage door rattling down and closing with a final clank.

Days of observing the house at intervals from this very spot and using his surveillance cameras hidden around the property had shown this pattern to Mr. Red. He had also made certain that the McMichaels had no security cameras of their own, and the homes in this area were too far apart to worry about watchful neighbors. His spying had also shown him that, any minute, Amanda McMichael would appear just inside the back door of the home with her two Huskies, which she walked every day. She would set the home security system, open the French doors, and lock them behind her before taking the dogs for a walk through the nature trails out back.

This morning held special significance over previous days, because as of today, Mr. Red had done enough surveillance to seal the deal, if he could obtain one final detail. An overstuffed backpack waited next to him hidden in the brush, ready for work, pistol secured to his side and combat knife sheathed on his chest for last resort use only. The angle of his location in the brush allowed him to zoom in with his spotting scope through the glass of the French doors and onto the security alarm keypad. He widened his eyes to clear his vision, then waited, challenging his mind to be ready to focus on the moment that would come and go in just over a second.

Mr. Red mentally blocked out the cold that pressed onto his back and the uncompromisingly solid ground that dug into his stomach and thighs. He dared not move to address the discomfort, instead controlling his breathing as his view through the scope remained focused. He hoped the woman wouldn't be taking her sweet time this morning, of all mornings.

Through his left eye, the one not looking through the scope, Mr. Red saw movement inside the French doors, one of the dogs hopping with excitement up to the door. More commotion followed as the second dog joined the first, both pooches vying for the coveted spot in front of the French doors. Next came Amanda McMichael in her white coat and pink knit hat, pulling on fleece gloves in preparation for her walk. She knelt next to the dogs to attach their leashes, both of them panting and competing to lick her face as she squinted and leaned away from their affection, laughing at her pets, mouthing something along the lines of how they should calm down.

Mr. Red pushed his right eye closer to the scope, all of his focus becoming that keypad, waiting for his window to observe.

Leashes attached, Amanda led the dogs to the wall and the alarm system control panel. Her gloved index finger entered the scope's view and pushed the keypad buttons. It was fast, but Mr. Red was certain he had seen it: 4-2-2-1.

Then Amanda was off, French doors opening, dogs rushing through, Amanda following and closing the doors behind her. Straining to hold both leashes in one hand, she pulled a key from her coat pocket and locked the doors. Then she said something inaudible to the dogs, a gentle scolding for pulling her so hard maybe, inducing temporary looks of shame in both of them. But maybe since no harm was done, she patted them both and led them away, dogs tugging at the leashes every which way like a discombobulated sled team.

Mr. Red followed the three of them with his eyes, admiring Amanda's carefree stride dragged by the energized mutts. It was then, for an instant, that Mr. Red regretted what he'd have to do to her, the atrocity for which he was paid so very well to carry out. This morning routine had a certain beauty to it, a happiness he could taste just by viewing it, this short moment in time a snapshot of a gratifying, stable life. But it was only an instant that he felt this. It was all he would ever allow himself to feel—it was best that way.

When Amanda and the dogs hit the trail and disappeared into nature, Mr. Red waited and listened. After he could no longer hear them, he pulled himself up to his knees. First he folded up the tripod and slid the scope into his backpack. Then he scanned his surroundings and listened to make sure he was alone. With nothing but the woods and the empty McMichael home to witness it, Mr. Red stood from hiding, picked up the pack, hefted it onto his back, then walked across the yard toward the French doors.

Too many homeowners were dumb enough to hide a spare key near their locked doors in case of an accidental lockout, and Mr. Red had discovered that the McMichaels were no different. During a previous night surveillance, he had checked all of the obvious hiding places near the French doors, eventually finding a key hidden in a magnetic case affixed to the side of the air conditioning unit. He fished out the key now, then stepped toward the door and unlocked it.

Opening the door, Mr. Red was met with a warm waft of potpourri and the silence of an empty home. He stepped inside and closed the door behind him, turning to the alarm system. He recalled the numbers from memory and began to tap them with his gloved hand, taking his time to avoid miskeying. When the system accepted the code, Mr. Red sighed knowing that the house was his for now. Too easy. Time to go to work.

Mr. Red spent less than a minute reaching his objective, the laundry room, which he had located by looking through the room's only window during earlier recon. He scanned the room through the entryway, simple and utilitarian but refined with its mint walls, white trim, and oak flooring. The washer, dryer, and laundry sink lined the wall opposite of the entrance, while two closed doors opposed each other on the side walls. It was those doors that intrigued Mr. Red. He entered the room, walked to the door on the left, and opened it. Turning on the light switch inside revealed the home's water heater, a red stripe across the top half giving it the appearance of a robot. Close, but not quite what he was looking for, so he turned off the light, closed the door, and walked toward the other one. Opening the other door brought a smile to his face, realizing that he had found it, turning on the light to view the complexity of the furnace.

Mr. Red began the next phase of his plan. He removed his backpack and knelt in front of the furnace, opening the pack's zipper and removing a black adjustable-beam flashlight. He turned on the light and began to shine the beam along the furnace's gaps and crevices, finding satisfaction in the wide selection of hiding places.

But while Mr. Red ran through the next steps in his mind, he heard a creaking sound from behind him. He recoiled from the noise, head jerking around to look. The source of the sound was easy enough to determine—the door from the water heater had opened, the robot of an appliance staring at him as if it had been the opener of the door. This, of course, was nonsense. Mr. Red stood, walked to the open door, and closed it, tugging on the knob when shut to ensure that it was latched fully this time. Satisfied, he returned to the furnace, already deducing where among the furnace gaps he would install his little gift for the McMichaels.

Stooping to reach into his backpack, Mr. Red heard it again: the creak of the closet door opening behind him.

"Really?" he whispered to himself, turning again with equal parts annoyance and confusion. But when he saw confirmation that the water heater door was indeed open again, there was a new concern—the light inside the water heater closet was on. That was strange, since he was positive that he'd turned it off.

Mr. Red walked toward the water heater once more, pausing a few steps in front of the door to observe anything out of the ordinary, but there was nothing unusual to see. He even took the time to step inside the closet for a closer look, but nothing except empty white walls surrounded the appliance.

He turned off the light, then flicked the switch on and off, switch working perfectly. Satisfied, he left the light off and shut the door, this time yanking on the knob several times to make doubly sure it was closed. The door was secure, no doubt about it.

Returning to the furnace, Mr. Red felt himself sweating, a natural response to the stress of the mission and the warmth of his winter gear. But was there a little more perspiration than there should be? There was no way that the door should have been opening like that, much less the light turning on by itself, and the facts sat all wrong in his gut.

In any case, he had no time for this. What if Amanda had decided to cut her walk short? He needed to take care of this and fast, then make his exit as if his hair was on fire.

Fire.

The sound that now surfaced from behind Mr. Red reminded him of the crackling roar of fire. He turned toward the water heater closet. The door was still closed this time, but the strange sound was coming from inside. It was the water heater doing its work, and that was all, Mr. Red reasoned. But was it? The sputtering on the other side of that door suggested something far more sinister. He felt his legs carry him halfway across the room toward the door where he stopped and listened.

Before he could figure out what could possibly be messing with him now, the closet door hurled open as if slammed from the inside by a Sasquatch, door ricocheting off the bumper on the wall. Fight reflexes tightening his muscles, Mr. Red dropped to a crouch, drawing his pistol and aiming it decisively at the open door with both hands, index finger fighting with itself not to pull the trigger. But bewilderment at what he saw forced him to lower the weapon slowly, coming to terms with the idea that any gun was a poor defense against the oddity in front of him.

Instead of the water heater, the closet's interior was a wall of flames, like the insides of an enormous potbellied stove. The fire lurched and weaved in hues of orange, white, and blue, hissing and popping, threatening to spill out and consume the rest of the home at any moment.

"What?" Mr. Red said to himself, this lunacy really beginning to piss him off. The house randomly burning down had never entered his mind as a risk to this mission, thoughts now only of aborting and reevaluating this mess in safety.

But before he could consider that further, Mr. Red saw something else inside the fire, and it wasn't the water heater. It pushed through the inferno, a subtle mass that appeared to have a life of its own. This induced a confused grunt from Mr. Red, by now quite frazzled by his world gone weird. Then the mass spilled out, the offspring of flame extracting itself from the closet as if being hatched, sputtering in front of him in humanoid form.

Mr. Red took a few *holy God Almighty* steps back.

It began to walk toward him.

Mr. Red had no more time to check his sanity, and no logic remaining to explain this away. As the flaming body stepped closer, he could make out a face, faintly feminine, eyes squinting in anger. Her mouth opened, and a gravely screech spilled out a confusing ultimatum: "No!"

The only sensible thing left was to kill it.

Mr. Red raised his gun and popped the abomination six times, spent casings bouncing onto the floor with brassy rattles. He stopped shooting long enough to see that this defense was having no effect, but what other options were there? He emptied the rest of the clip into the mass before the pistol's slide popped open. Dropping the gun, Mr. Red reached for his Ka-Bar sheathed on his chest. He withdrew the blade and waited, the fiery blob still coming for him. Was he really going to rage-slash a walking bonfire? *Yes,* he confirmed with himself. *Yes he was.*

Mr. Red lunged at the mass with a lateral slash to what may have been the figure's neck, the smell of smoke fueled by something chemically filling his nostrils. The blade found its mark, swiping through the flames, connecting with fire-softened flesh and scattering embers. He rolled away from the strike to evade the flames, then pulled himself up to a crouch in preparation for a counterattack.

But his slash had been enough. He saw the flaming body scatter, its fiery pieces retreating into the closet of fire. The fire groaned and sputtered as if to attack again, but instead it began to shrink away with a squealing sizzle. Then it was all gone—the flames, the smell, the smoke—not a trace of it, replaced once again by the harmless water heater. Seconds into the stillness, the closet door slammed shut.

"What the unholy hell?" Mr. Red asked himself. He stood for a moment shaking, questioning just about everything he knew, thoughts of leaving right now, and when he'd be far away from there, of calling Marcela to find another sucker for this job.

But reason found a foothold in the silence of the laundry room. All he'd need was thirty seconds at the furnace to finish this. A minute beyond that and he'd be gone, exiting through the woods before Amanda returned. He could still do this, despite whatever psychotic episode he was living. He just needed to tear off the granny panties and get this done.

So Mr. Red did just that. It was simple, under the circumstances, to install his gift for the McMichaels in an ample opening next to the furnace where no one would see it. Job done, he closed the furnace door. Then he scooped up his pistol and its spent casings from his battle with a blob of fire, preoccupied with the thought that the door might still open and spill it out again. But the door remained shut.

Casings and pistol stowed, he looked around to make sure there was no other evidence of his being there. Never mind that there should have been smoke and burn marks everywhere, but there wasn't. Had it even happened? He looked at the water heater closet door again, wondering if any of his shots had penetrated through his target and landed inside the closet. But checking that would mean opening the door to look.

Mr. Red made up his mind that he was finished taking crap from a closet. He walked up to the door and yanked it open, turning on the light to show himself that there was nothing but a water heater in there. Seeing the red robotic looking tank appearing normal eased his pulse. He searched the interior for bullet holes, finding none. He didn't even want to guess where his shots had actually gone—another mystery he didn't have the will to ponder at the moment. This had all been an illusion, something conjured by his own mind, harrowing yet harmless, he surmised.

When the fire woman's gravely screech came again, ringing his ears as if she was right next to him, Mr. Red staggered back. He turned in circles to locate the source of the scream, but there was none. It was just him and the laundry room.

Mr. Red stepped forward, turned off the closet light, and slammed the door shut, then sprinted out of the laundry room. He didn't stop running until he reached the alarm control panel at the back door. The password? He struggled in a panic to remember it, glancing toward the way he had come for the flaming lady that didn't follow.

Password coming back to him, he entered it with a shaking gloved index finger, arming the system. He opened the door, closed it behind him and locked it, then returned the key to its hiding place in the magnetic air conditioner case. Then he ran away from the house, finding the trail that would lead him back to the safety of his van, hoping the logical-rational world would meet him somewhere along the way.

28

9/11

I sat at my workstation in the dead center of a cubicle world, each of us workers nestled inside boxes, nothing more than critters in square containers. Marsh and McLennan, the insurance brokerage firm where I worked, geared up around me with keyboard clacks, telephones chiming, trivial conversations. My desk clock showed 8:44, another Tuesday morning. Only I didn't believe that. Was it really a simple Tuesday?

I should have been attacking the workload stacked in front of me, my computer monitor seeming to both urge me into action and mock me for the delay. But it was beyond a simple delay, this was an inability, a barrier that kept me still while I watched the world as though I was no longer part of it. I was asleep, in a dream, but awake and present too, as if under a spell.

When I moved it surprised me, movement an ability I thought I'd lost. I turned my head and looked around. There was an urgency to my searching. I hoped to see something in common with my coworkers—some sense of abnormality, even a mild suggestion that something wasn't right here, that none of this Tuesday was normal. But there were no signs of that. If something odd was in the air, people were burying it with workloads, even some laughs among the chitchat. No, I was the only one to feel this way.

Can I put my finger on what it felt like? Ominous, sickening, tense. An uproar from within, like sirens blaring warnings deep within my soul, fear so great that it cut my breath short and flushed my face. Yet my hands were numb with cold, as if my blood refused to go there, my system too busy oxygenating my brain against whatever had a hold of me.

I stood. I had to. Was I having a heart attack? I took a breath and searched for more symptoms. There would be pain with a heart attack, yes? I would have trouble breathing too? There was neither. Gulping in air reassured me of this, my body working fine despite something tearing at my sixth senses, the unmistakable cloud that I seemed to be swimming in.

The computer judged me. Standing up was just more stalling, cursor blinking at me as if to say: Get-Back-To-Work-Pat-ty-You-Have-No-Time-For-This-Come-On-Now-Sit-Down. I ignored it, the stupid nagging machine. Work would wait, I needed a minute, just a few minutes please, to clear my head. Then I'd dive in when the dust settled, when things were right again. I'd be okay soon enough. If I could just get a handle on things first.

I left my workstation, not sure why or to where, but just away because I couldn't stay there. I let my legs do the deciding, they seemed to know where to go, as though they had something to show me. My walk took me down the aisle past coworkers who paid no attention. There was nothing unordinary about me getting up. I often strolled the floor to do my job, just one of the many busy worker bees at Marsh and McLennan.

Turning left I walked the long aisle, my path bordered by low storage cabinets and cubicle walls. Curiously, this conjured memories of the many paths my life had taken up to this point: the bike path along the ocean I used to ride when I was young so long ago, the walkway through auditorium seating and graduations, the aisle between the pews on my wedding day, the hallway of the hospital where my children were born. We're always on paths to somewhere, often forgetting what it was like to get there, more enthralled by the arriving.

"I'll have it for you tomorrow," I heard someone say over the telephone. I think it was Tom, just a kid, already overworked. "Yep, I just need to do a few more things with it. Tomorrow, I promise."

Tomorrow.

Why did that word feel like a lie? Tomorrow, the day after today, it's a certainty, isn't it? If we didn't believe it were so, it would eat at us. We guarantee tomorrow will happen. *I promise.*

The windows were calling to me, and my legs answered by leading me toward them. Tall and narrow, the windows were a hallmark of my office in the North Tower, ninety stories above the world. As I approached them, what struck me was the blue sky beyond, a fine early fall day out there, as though you'd be able to see as far as your eyes allowed. The things a person could do out there, free, wandering New York without any worries at all. Can you imagine?

I never liked looking out those windows, heights never agreeing with me, so why was I making a point of it now? Because of the spectacular view? It was breathtaking, as always, stepping to the glass to peer down on Manhattan, Hudson flowing to the left, Empire State Building in its art deco grandeur jutting up from Midtown. This was the closest thing to being a bird, up so high to see every texture and shape while soaring through the wind without effort. Looking straight down, though, I felt myself recoil from my fear, as if nothing would stop me from falling out and down. I took a step back. Better.

I don't know how long I stood there. My reflection stared back at me like a specter, faint, almost not there, like how I felt, my tired complexion in the window vague proof that I was alive.

Where had this day gone wrong? Was it the terrible nightmare the night before, the one I couldn't even recall but knew was awful? Or the pain in my lower back? Had I slept on it just the wrong way, or was it implanted from my nightmare? Rushing out to work because I had overslept a tad, skipping breakfast, scrambling to the office to begin my day, the entire commute seeming like it was fake, not there, not real.

I thought of flying in an airplane as I took my gaze from my own reflection and placed it back into the blue sky. Airplanes meant trips, exotic vacations, something I knew little about, and I found myself regretting that now. Maybe I had waited too long to indulge in such luxuries, this Tuesday unlike any other Tuesday reminding me that I needed a break, that I longed for some sort of escape, a journey maybe.

The sound of an airplane's engines penetrated through the window, and for a second I thought I had summoned it with my thoughts. But no, my mind must have heard it before I had realized it, sidetracked by delusions of travel. I searched for the aircraft out there somewhere, saw nothing, but heard it surging closer. Happy passengers aboard it, no doubt, ascending to somewhere grand or descending to see the Big Apple.

I stepped forward again, daring to be right in front of the glass. I wanted to see down there, to wonder what the masses were doing on the ground. So many places for them to be, buildings everywhere, tiny cars on the streets, endless humanity, the progress of humans without limit. Was it a normal Tuesday for them, or down there somewhere, did someone else feel it too? Was there anyone out there who knew something was immeasurably wrong?

A phone started to ring from a cubicle behind me. It sounded like any other phone at Marsh and McLennan, so why did it seem different somehow? There was urgency to it, and no one was there to pick it up. It said *look out . . . watch it . . . it's coming . . . out there . . . go now . . . run fast . . . beware.*

Why would no one answer it? Why did the caller keep trying? No one except me even noticed it. I wanted to go to it, pick it up, tell the caller to stop, but that made no sense. Why would I do that? But it **seemed** like the caller would keep at it, keep ringing, the message had to be heard.

I heard the airplane again. Closer now, low, cutting through the sky from somewhere I still couldn't see. It rattled the windows in front of me, the clatter clatter of the glass and the ring ring of the phone keeping me transfixed on the horizon.

There it was. Finally. A plane, a jet liner, a dot, enlarging fast, rushing forward as if shot from the blue sky. Where was it going? It was so low, a blot of silver flying straight, going neither up nor down, just sweeping across the city, and somehow it didn't seem to belong.

Go now . . . run away . . . leave here the phone continued to ring and warn. Why didn't I pay attention to it? Why didn't I turn and leave, right then? Because I couldn't, as if I was meant to stay. And I had to know what that plane was doing, where it was going, because it was what was wrong about that day, I knew it. It was coming right where I was standing, its destination was me.

Still I stood. The jet rushed ahead, I could see stripes of red and blue coming fast, wings leveled without hesitation. I felt my mouth fall open, air heaving in from panic that had now reached crescendo. The glass shook louder, the jet engines booming. I could see the windows of the plane's cockpit, could swear I saw men's faces in there. I couldn't read their expressions but wondered what they could possibly be thinking.

It's coming, no doubt now, it's coming here, for me. I stepped back, invisible chains that had held me there releasing at last. Too late. Far too late. The phone stopped ringing. No use now, it had tried to warn us but failed.

I retreated down the aisle, a strut at first, then the blaring sounds of the engines compelled me into a sprint. I dared not look back, knew it was coming, so there was no reason. One more path—a footrace, a sprint to cheat death, but I knew I'd lose.

"Run!" I shouted nonetheless, heads poking up from cubicles, not understanding, unable to process my madness. "Get out!"

Too late. Behind me erupted a great shattering of glass and steel, engines plunging the plane far into our cubicle world, a thunderous spewing of explosive fire. The blast lifted me, threw me forward with an anger I had never imagined possible, scorching flames carrying me off, consuming me, obliterating me. What is it like to turn to ash in a millisecond? Like nothing at all, a great shutting off.

Darkness. I died that day, a Tuesday. Nothing normal about that Tuesday in September.

29

———

FIRE

Erin jolted awake to the sound of an explosion that rocked her bedroom. She shielded her face with trembling hands against a wave of orange light, but it was a useless gesture. Fire slammed through the walls and floor, smothering the room with the reek of jet fuel and chemical smoke. The blaze scorched everything to ash from the drapes to the carpeting to the bedspread. Next it found her, the flames vaporizing her flesh before she could utter a word.

Then the fire and all of its destruction faded away, the illusion replaced by the silence of her undisturbed bedroom. Yet her body's defenses had already been triggered, gasps inducing a coughing fit as if expelling the noxious smoke. Throat cleared, she sucked in breaths of air, her pulse at full throttle but easing back with each inhale. She looked over at Conner sleeping in her bed next to her.

"Conner!" Erin shouted, nudging his shoulder. He didn't move, continued to sleep. Why wouldn't he wake? "Conner?"

Wait a minute.

Something was still wrong, fuzzy, dreamy. She felt awake and asleep at the same time, her bedroom, the bed, and

Conner just imperfect copies from her mind. But how could that be?

When she saw the woman standing in the dull light of her doorway, Erin reeled back to the headboard, her blanket an inferior defense against whatever was there.

"Conner!" she yelled again, shaking him harder this time. But there was no way he would wake, no way he could, if he was even there.

The woman stepped through the doorway. Erin saw her face in the dim bedroom light, her complexion darkened with black streaks and scars, her short hair like knotted, grungy string.

"It's coming," the woman said. "Out there."

"What do you want?" Erin tried to sound in control but it came out with a meek screech.

"To show you," the woman said.

"How did you get into my apartment?"

"Shh," the woman whispered, putting her index finger upright to her lips. She pointed to Conner, suggesting that she not wake him. That just seemed silly, Conner was comatose.

"Follow me," she said before turning toward the doorway and walking out into Erin's living room.

Diving under the covers seemed like a much better idea than following the woman. Calling the police was an even better plan. She pawed at her nightstand for her phone. She had kept the phone there every night since the day she got it, but it wasn't there. Where the hell did it go?

"Don't be afraid," the woman called from the living room. Erin could feel the woman watching her from somewhere out there, yet the voice had a soothing quality, something a mother would say to her daughter when telling her monsters don't exist. "Come on now, we have to hurry."

Erin stepped out of bed before she could dwell on the

decision. The floor chilled her bare feet, and she folded her arms in front of her against the winter draft in the room. Then she crept across the floor, dipping her head to try to peer through the darkness past the doorway. There was no sign of the woman out there.

Erin stopped at the doorway, looking back at Conner in case he had awakened, but he hadn't moved. Then she took a breath and slipped through the doorway, submerging into the blackness of her living room.

A rush of spectacular light made Erin snap her eyes shut and expel an involuntary yelp, the flash so unexpected that she wobbled and almost fell before finding her footing. Opening her eyes to the sting of the light, Erin found herself elsewhere. Not in her living room, but in a hallway that seemed familiar: polished floor, pristine artwork on the walls, a hallway of luxury she knew from somewhere. But where?

The woman stood at the other end of the hall next to two closed double-doors. Her face seemed incapable of emotion, dark eyes and lips beset with resolve. "In here, and quickly. Right now."

She turned, opened one of the double-doors, and slipped into the room without fanfare.

Erin turned around and looked behind her, for some reason still expecting to see her bedroom doorway there, but of course it wasn't. That way was more hallway, as if she had been dropped in its center like a hamster in a maze. What alternatives were there? Erin walked to the double-doors and entered.

Now she understood where she was: Larkin's library. But how? She could see its lavishness, fire blazing in the fireplace, flickers of flame reflecting off of the display cases, lingering cigar scent hinting that Larkin wasn't far away. Through the room's glow Erin saw the woman walking toward the center, circling behind a chair before stopping next to an end table. She looked down at an open laptop, its screen projecting an uneven streak of light across her maimed face. When the woman turned to face her, Erin regretted following her this far.

"Look," the woman said, pointing a shaking finger at the laptop.

Erin looked back at the double-doors behind her, hoping no one would find them there. How could that even be? She didn't even know how she got there.

"Hurry!" the woman said, stamping her foot in impatience, forcing Erin to take a step back. "Right now! Quickly!"

Erin looked down at the pentacle tattoo on her own wrist. She found herself rubbing it, something causing the skin underneath it to itch. Despite the discomfort, she took courage from the sensation, a hint that she could do this. She looked up and returned the woman's gaze.

"I don't understand," Erin said, venturing a few steps forward before stopping. "How did I get here?"

"There's no time!" the woman pleaded. "Look. Hurry now, come and see."

Erin took a breath and walked to her as fast as she dared, not quickly enough for the woman who seemed pained by each slow step that Erin took. The cold stare from the woman did nothing to quicken her pace, but Erin kept going before stopping three steps from the laptop.

"Watch very closely, I can only show you once," the woman said, reaching for the keyboard. Erin saw the screen-saver image, a cryptic looking metal sign brandishing foreign words that she didn't understand. But when the woman clicked the keyboard, the image disappeared in place of a login screen. Erin watched her type in six letters: A-M-A-N-D-A

Password entered, the login screen disappeared to reveal the desktop with a smattering of icons over a simple gray background.

"There," the woman pointed again. "Do you see it?"

Erin found herself staring at the woman rather than the screen, up close the woman's eyes unlike anything she had seen before, dark and dull, like two blank sockets. Erin tried to speak, wanting to know who the woman was and why she looked this way, but how to ask such a thing?

"Hurry!" the woman pleaded again. "Do you see it?"

Erin shifted her view from the woman's face back to the computer screen. On closer inspection, she noticed an open window with more files within. At the top of the window was a name, the name of the folder opened as a window.

"Project Amanda?" Erin said.

"Yes," the woman nodded. Something resembling a smile came to her blurred mouth. Then her expression went blank again.

Outside the door from down the hall came the echo of footfalls. Someone was coming. The woman stiffened at the sound and stared at the doorway. "He's returning," she said.

"Who?" Erin asked.

"Him."

Erin turned to look at the double-doors and listen for whoever was coming. "Him who?" She turned back to look at the woman, but no one was there. The woman had left her, vanished into the floor or the walls, somewhere Erin couldn't fathom.

"Hey, wait, you have to get me out of here!" Erin called. No one was there to hear her. The footsteps continued, shuffling and slow, the sickly walk of Reid Larkin.

Erin turned back to look at the door, feeling her heart working up in a panic. She wanted to be done with all of this, to go back to her bedroom and normalcy, but how? She was trapped, and he was coming. Five steps, four steps, three, two, one.

Erin huddled on the floor and blocked her eyes with both forearms, not wanting to see who was coming, not believing any of this.

He was upon her much faster than she thought he would be, pawing at her, grabbing her arms, speaking to her in words she didn't understand. She slapped away at him, kept her eyes closed tightly, not wanting to see whoever was there.

"Get away!" she shouted, swiping into the air blindly to protect herself. "Don't touch me!"

"Erin!" he called to her.

He knows my name!

"Don't you dare touch me!" she shouted, rolling away from him, squirming to avoid his grasp. But he was too fast, too strong, and he held her tightly, strong arms subduing her.

"Erin, open your eyes!" he shouted. "It's okay." It was a familiar voice, intimately personal.

"Conner?" she found herself saying. She opened her eyes.

The first thing she saw was Conner's face looking at her as if she were insane. The second thing she saw was her kitchen table above her, meaning she was on the kitchen floor. Conner held her, but he was trying to help, not attack. There were fresh scratches on his face and arms, blood welling from one on his cheek.

"It's just me," Conner said. "Jesus, what's wrong with you? Now you're sleepwalking too?"

Erin pulled away and studied her surroundings. This was absolutely her kitchen, her apartment, her home and not Larkin's mansion. It should have been a comfort, but all she felt were anguish and dread, something unbearable pressing down on her soul. She studied the scratches on Conner's skin, giving him the appearance of being whipped.

"You're hurt," she said, reaching out to touch his wounds.

"You were having a nightmare, and my face sorta got in the way."

Unable to hold it together any longer, she slumped to the floor in tears.

The woman watched from the darkness of the living room. Satisfied that her task was done, she turned and disappeared through the wall.

30

DELIRIUM

Conner found himself kneeling in an embrace with Erin. She was reduced to sobbing into his chest, his t-shirt becoming soaked with her tears, anguish he had never seen from her before.

"What did you see?" he asked. She responded with whimpering while clutching his shirt, so he just held her, noticing the simple red clock on the wall showing 1:19.

Then Conner felt Erin's body flinch, some realization cutting off her tears. She pulled away from him as if her surroundings were suddenly threatening. Her eyes found his, but they were distant, her senses preoccupied by mystery.

"Do you smell that?" she asked.

"Smell what?"

"Smoke!" she screamed, pulling herself to unstable feet. Conner stood with her, Erin swaying like a skyscraper threatening to collapse, so he grabbed her shoulders to help maintain her balance.

"Smoke?" He sniffed the air to humor her, but there was nothing smoky about the kitchen. "I don't smell anything."

"It's all over the place, how can you not smell it!" she

shouted. She wrenched away from him and sniffed the air with a deeper inhale, so repulsed by whatever she smelled that she began coughing and squinting. She turned to look down the hallway toward the living room, teetering before catching hold of the table. "It's coming from down there!" she shouted, making a clumsy sprint into the hallway.

"Wait!" Conner called, chasing after her. Delirious or not, the girl was fast, careening off the left hallway wall before spilling into the living room. She stopped and fought to see through the darkness of the room. Conner caught up with her there, turned on the living room light, and watched her sniff the air again. He stepped to her and held her there before she could hurt herself.

"Smoke," she said again, coughing more. "Don't you smell it?"

"There's no smoke," he said. "I think you're sleepwalking."

She shook her head in irritation as she scanned the living room for any source of the smoke. He also looked around, her certainty causing him to second-guess himself, but nothing was out of the ordinary. Her incense was unlit and nothing else was smoking that he could see. Conner stopped searching when he came to the painting of Erin that appeared to stare at him. The artist had captured her confident and cunning side, her expression suggesting that she was ready for anything that the metaphysical realm could hand her. The portrait couldn't have been farther from how she looked now—lost and terrified.

"Come on," he said, easing her toward the futon. Too dazed and overwhelmed to offer resistance, she sat with him, body going limp to the comfort of the cushion and his hold. She nestled her head into his shoulder and closed her eyes, lids fluttering as a last struggle against sleep. Then she sighed as her breathing calmed and she returned to a peaceful slumber, leaving Conner to wince from the scratches on his face that began to burn. Yet something took hold of him, a hypnotic calm swaddling his body, sleep returning nearly before he could close his eyes.

~

ERIN JERKED awake to the morning light hitting the living room.

"Why are we out here?" she said. Conner opened his eyes. She stood and looked down at him as though this was somehow his fault.

"You don't remember?" he asked, sniffling and rubbing his eyes.

"Remember what?"

"Apparently not then. Last night you had one heck of a sleepwalk. I made the mistake of getting in the way." Conner pointed to the scratches on his face.

"What? I didn't do that!"

"Um, yes you did."

Erin looked down at her hands and saw traces of blood in her fingernails. "Oh my God!" she said, holding her hands out as though they weren't hers. "I did! I'm sorry, are you okay?" She came to him to study the scratches.

"Those nails are lethal, but I'll survive," Conner said. "Are you really awake now?"

Erin put her palm on her forehead. "Of course I'm awake," she said. "With a mother of a migraine. I need some coffee. What happened to me?"

"You tell me," he said.

Erin became very still. She was concentrating on something.

"What?" he asked.

"Ssh," she said. "What's that?"

"What's what?" Conner asked. He began to wonder if she was hallucinating again until he started to hear it too: a rhythmic chiming and buzzing coming from the kitchen.

Erin walked to the hallway toward the kitchen, Conner following. When they reached the kitchen they listened.

"It's my phone," she said, stepping toward the counter where the sound was slightly louder. She reached for the oven and opened the door. On the top rack was her phone, morning alarm ringing and vibrating louder with the oven door open.

"What in the world?" She pulled out the phone and turned off the alarm. "Why is my phone in the oven?"

"Don't ask me," Conner said. "You were sleepwalking, maybe you put it there? Not the best place to keep a phone."

"Why would I do that?"

Conner shrugged.

Erin looked down at her phone and saw the time was 9:11 a.m.

"My class!" she shouted. "Oh shit, I slept through my class! The alarm was ringing in here for over an hour."

"It's just a class, it's not the end of the world," Conner said.

Erin gasped and cupped her hand to her mouth while she looked at her phone: 9:11

"She was there!" Erin said.

"What are you talking about now?"

Erin went to the table and sat down. She continued to look at her phone, deep in thought over something. Conner opened Erin's cupboard and took out the bag of coffee beans, hoping a cup would jolt her back to reality.

"A woman was here last night," she said as Conner poured the beans into the grinder.

"I didn't see anyone," he said, grinding the coffee, the noise interfering with Erin's ability to think. Finished, he dumped the grounds into a coffee filter, silence allowing Erin to explain.

"I don't know how she got in, but she was here. You were asleep. There was fire and smoke. I saw how she died."

Conner poured water into the coffee maker and started brewing. He checked the kitchen door to make sure it was locked, then he joined her at the table.

"Everything was locked, no one could have gotten in," he said. "And you saw some lady die?"

"You don't understand," she said. "It was a ghost."

"Maybe a nightmare? You were completely out of it, you didn't know where you were."

"It was too real to be a dream."

"Well what did she want?"

Erin looked at the phone again. "When I pulled the phone out of the oven, the time was 9:11. The woman who visited me died in the Trade Centers attack, September 11th. I could see it."

"You had 9/11 on your mind yesterday," he offered. "We both did."

She shook her head. "I know, but it wasn't just that. She made me see how she died, there was smoke and fire, I could feel it like she felt it. Pain and horror that you can't imagine. And then she showed me something else, something she wanted me to see so I could help her."

Conner got up and walked to the cupboard and retrieved two coffee cups. "I'll bite, what did she show you?"

"Larkin's library."

"What?" Conner turned and stared at her. "Why would she show you that?"

"She was next to a laptop. There was a photo on the screen. A gate with words in another language. German maybe."

"Wait a minute," Conner said. "What did it say?"

"I don't remember exactly. Abbott fried, something like that."

"Arbeit Macht Frei?" Conner asked.

Erin stared at him. "I think so. How did you know that?"

"It's Larkin's laptop screensaver. It's the sign outside of Auschwitz. It means 'work will set you free,' something like that. Cheery, isn't it? You must have seen his laptop before and it showed up in your dream."

"No," she shook her head. "I swear, I've never seen it before. Then she showed me things, his login password and some files."

"What files?"

"A project of some sort. Something Larkin's working on."

Conner turned back to the coffee maker and poured a cup for each of them. He brought them to the table and handed her one, but she ignored it, so he put it on the table.

"I think we're supposed to look on Larkin's laptop," Erin said.

"And risk getting caught?" Conner said, sipping his coffee.

"We don't have a choice, we have to," she said.

Erin's phone dinged with an incoming text. She held up her phone and read the message without reacting.

"I know all of this confuses and alarms you," Erin said. "But lives are at stake. We need to look on that laptop. Tonight."

Erin held out the phone so Conner could see the text from Karl Pike:

"Hey baby doll. Can you work tonight? Larkin has another gathering. I'll text your boyfriend the professor too. Let me know."

31

LAPTOP

Conner balanced an enormous silver platter loaded with holiday truffles, tarts, and cookies that looked too precious to eat. He navigated the hallway toward Larkin's library, tray wobbling from the weight, his fragile nerves complicating the task. Erin followed behind him carrying two matching silver coffee carafes, one regular, one decaf.

Reaching the closed library doors, Conner stumbled over himself, some of the pecan pie tarts and peppermint truffles launching from the tray into a broken mess on the tiled floor. Conner steadied himself and kept the tray from spilling more, then looked down at the damage.

"Pike'll murder me if he sees that," he said, looking back at Erin.

"Never mind," Erin said. "In a few minutes he'll have a much bigger problem to worry about."

"Are we really gonna do this? I mean, damn."

"Yes we are," she said. "Now calm down before you give us away. And trust me, this will work. You just be ready to do your part."

"Right," he said. "But I'm going on record to say that this idea is completely nuts. What if there are cameras in there?"

"So what if there are? We'll act before anyone is the wiser. There's no other way."

The night had already been tense in anticipation of making a move toward the laptop. The only question had been how. A few trips scouting the library to serve guests had allowed Erin to figure out a way. She had whispered her plan to him over dishes, his stomach knotting as he had heard what she had in mind. He had wanted to tell her that they should forget all about trying to get to Larkin's laptop, but he also knew that she was determined to do this, if not obsessed.

Now, waiting to enter the library, she continued to rally him. "Get a grip" she said, drawing closer to him for a kiss. Her lips meeting his reminded him of Bonnie kissing Clyde before a heist, her kiss soothing and reassuring. How could she be so calm about this? Feeling his torment, she pulled away. "Breathe, you'll hyperventilate. What's the worst that could happen?"

"Jail. Our cemented feet plunging us to the bottom of the Mississippi River. Pike peeling us slowly with a kitchen knife to make a suit out of our skin," he said.

"Dark and imaginative, but none of those will happen."

"Oh yeah? I get the feeling that Pike has the skills for that, and Larkin would be happy to let him."

"If this works, and it will, they won't know what we did until it's too late."

"Let's just get this over with," Conner said.

He took a breath, balanced the tray on his arm, and evened out the gap in desserts with his free hand. Then he reached for the door handle and opened the door to the sound of laughter from within the library. They both stepped inside as the laughter settled into more business talk among Larkin and his employees.

"Seriously, I think we have to move on this one Reid, and right now," a portly male executive said. He took a swig from his wine, creating the unintended illusion that the drink was filling his triple chins. "It's a winner, we just need the right price."

"Fine, fine," Larkin said, eyeing Conner and Erin, who stopped and waited to be called upon. In addition to the man who spoke, two other aging cronies sat in chairs around Larkin studying numbers on laptops, empty drink glasses littering end tables. Marcela sat next to Larkin as always, typing something frantically on her own laptop.

A female executive leaned forward to catch the chubby man's attention. "This better not be another one of your hunches gone wild, Robert." Her face looked like a bleached animal skin had been stretched over a fencepost, shrewd eyes penetrating Robert's with considerable doubt. "This is a huge investment, not some poker hand."

"Oh screw you Cassandra," Robert said, wiping wine from his full lips. "Reid, I've run the numbers, don't listen to her. She always gets scared before we pull the trigger."

"With good reason, Reid," Cassandra said.

The third executive broke in, thick-rimmed glasses, disheveled hair, and wrinkled shirt suggesting that he'd rather be making calculations than associating with people: "We all have reason to question Robert's judgment of late, but I've checked his numbers in my report, and it's all good. We should make the move."

"Save it, I've read your report Marcus," Larkin snapped, Marcus recoiling from Larkin's tone. "Once you suffer through the typos, it's a good read."

Cassandra and Robert chuckled at this insult, Marcus frowning.

"The deal seems sound," Larkin continued. "I already gave my approval, so go ahead Robert. But just in case you were wondering, this one is all on you. If you louse it up, you won't get another chance. Second chances are rare in this business, especially in my company."

"Reid, I won't," Robert said, voice nearly pleading.

"All right, I've noted in the minutes that we'll move on the Hawkins deal, Robert to initiate that as soon as possible," Marcela said, eying her notes. "Robert adds that he promises not to louse it up."

"Fine," Larkin said. Then he gestured for Conner to come over: "For God's sake bring the dessert, these people are intolerable when they're hungry."

Conner walked up to the group, beginning with Robert, who looked at the tray longingly, then suddenly seemed self-conscious and shooed Conner away in annoyance. Erin took the carafes to a serving table draped with a white tablecloth along the library wall, two mood candles burning on top. She set the carafes next to the bottles of fine wine and liquor that had fueled the evening's business dealings.

Conner tried not to dwell on what Erin was about to do. Candles, liquor, and the tablecloth would make for a doozy of a fire, a fitting distraction for the 9/11 ghost who had forced this act of desperation. Erin would only need a few seconds when no one was watching.

Cassandra reached over to pull a blueberry tart from Conner's tray. She took a bite and raised her eyebrows at the taste, very nearly a flirt with him that made him nauseous, and he continued his way around the group.

"How is everyone doing tonight?" Conner said. As part of the plan, Erin had told him to engage in a discussion to attract their attention, and that's what he was trying to do. Unfortunately, no one seemed in the mood to answer. Conner looked at Erin, who seemed perturbed that he would say such a dumb thing as a distraction. He began to search his mind for something else when Larkin started to cough. Marcela sat up and watched him fight through it, the executives staring with uncertainty. When finished, they all watched in silence.

"Damn cold season," Larkin said, glancing at Marcela and then at Conner as if to indicate *don't you dare give away my secret.*

But the cough had served as a much better distraction than Conner could have orchestrated, as Erin hunched at the table with her back turned to hide her work. He could feel the silver tray begin to shake in his arms as his agitation ratcheted higher.

"Have Karl make up a toddy with honey and brandy before bed Reid, it'll do wonders," Cassandra offered.

"The cure I need is for you people out of my home so I can rest," Larkin said. "We've been going in circles all night. What's next on the agenda?"

"We still have to discuss updates to the five-year plan," Marcela said as she took a truffle from Conner's tray.

Then Erin screamed. Everyone looked to her direction to see the tablecloth ignite, flames leaping three feet above the table. Conner hadn't expected her to scream, and a very convincing one at that, and his frayed nerves caused him to drop the tray into Marcela's lap.

"Fire!" Marcela shouted, standing up as the spilled desserts fell from her dress.

"What in the world?" Larkin said, pulling himself from his chair with great strain.

The others stood and watched helplessly as the flames grew higher, black smoke beginning to fill the room. Erin continued her theatrics by trying to beat the flames with a towel, only succeeding in knocking over a liquor bottle to feed the fire higher. Cassandra began to cough and howl in fear, pulling her blouse over her mouth against the smoke. Soon all of them were coughing, Larkin worst of all given his condition.

"Everyone out!" Marcela said, heading for the door with Larkin in tow before succumbing to coughing herself.

Everyone filed out of the room, Erin holding the door open for them to pass, Conner remaining in the room without anyone noticing from the commotion. Before exiting, she smiled at Conner and gave him a thumbs-up, then closed the door to leave him there.

"Holy shit, it actually worked!" he said to himself, fire growing higher still.

But how long did he have before Pike would arrive from the kitchen with a fire extinguisher? A minute? It would never be enough time, and the smoke was getting thick. This pushed him to work fast, stepping through the fallen desserts to Larkin's chair, grabbing the laptop on the end table beside it, Auschwitz screensaver confirming it was Larkin's. Conner coughed from the wretched smoke, black and chemically, and he began to breathe through his sleeve as he tapped the keyboard with his free hand to open the password dialogue box. Then he typed the password: A-M-A-N-DA. He hit Enter and the computer processed the action, forcing Conner to wonder for a millisecond whether the password had been changed, or whether Erin's experience really had only been a dream.

Then the box on the screen disappeared, revealing a slew of open spreadsheets, company portfolios, and business correspondence. He didn't take the time to be amazed or to celebrate that the password had worked. Instead he minimized all of the documents so he could see the desktop, fire crackling higher and beginning to scorch the library wall. He stole a quick look at the library doors, which remained shut, for now.

Where was the file? The desktop was a nightmare, files everywhere, Larkin clearly not a big fan of folders. Conner skimmed through them quickly but saw nothing like what he was looking for.

"Where is it?" he shouted, smoke burning his eyes and forcing him to cough again. Then he saw it: the folder named *Project Amanda*.

"My God," he whispered, almost not believing that the folder was actually there. He clicked it open, revealing dozens of files inside. Which one to open? He saw a Word doc named *Planning*, and he clicked it open, file taking valuable time to open, Conner watching the doors again as he prayed they wouldn't open yet.

When the file opened at last, Conner began reading through his coughs, wiping his irritated eyes to see the words more clearly. Jackpot. He skimmed it enough to realize that this was a detailed plan for something horrifying, and that realization coupled with fear of being caught overwhelmed him with nausea.

Then he heard Pike yelling from somewhere in the mansion. Conner pulled his phone from his pocket and began to take photos of the document. He had taken three pictures when the library doors burst open. Shielded by the smoke, Conner closed the file and folder, then returned the laptop to the end table and dove behind the chair before Pike could see him.

"What the flying fuck?" Pike yelled at the sight of the fire. From behind the chair, Conner heard the swoosh of a fire extinguisher and Pike screaming more obscenities, battling the blaze like it was hand-to-hand combat with the enemy. The extinguisher did the job well, snuffing the flames but filling the room with even more smoke. Conner couldn't help himself, he began to cough again.

"College boy, what are you doing in here?" Pike yelled, coming over to Conner.

"Trying to put out the fire!" Conner stammered through more coughs.

"Well you suck at it, stick to goddamned dishwashing!" Pike screamed, helping Conner up, Pike himself now coughing. The two exited the library, gasping the comparatively fresh air in the hallway, emergency vehicle sirens audible from outside of the mansion in the distance.

Pike looked back at the smoke billowing out of the library. "Oh good Christ, Larkin's gonna shit kittens! His library is totally screwed! What happened?"

"I don't know," Conner said, feeling the penetration of Pike's angry stare. "I was serving dessert when the tablecloth started on fire."

"Tablecloths don't just go up in flames, Mr. Professor, was someone by the table?"

"Erin was."

"And the table goes up in flames, just like my career!" Pike shouted. "Baby Doll must've done something stupid. Sorry dude, but that shitgibbon girlfriend of yours is *SO* fired!"

Four firefighters entered the house and ran down the hallway toward Conner and Pike.

"Relax boys, fire's all out, no thanks to this guy," Pike said to them, poking Conner's shoulder hard enough to leave a mark.

FOOTAGE

"Here comes Smokey the Bear now," Pike said to Conner in the foyer as Erin approached. The police and fire department had just finished questioning her. "What happened girl?" Pike asked.

Erin shrugged. "Just like I told them, I screwed up. I knocked over a liquor bottle onto a candle, and it just went up."

"Well that's a magnificent piece of work," Pike said. "You're both done here, I never wanna see either of you again, ever. And you're lucky I don't make you scrub the soot from the library walls with a toothbrush before you go."

"I said it was an accident!" Erin said.

"Then I hope the door doesn't accidentally smack your asses on the way out!" Pike shouted.

"Fine then," Erin said. "You and this place disgust me anyway." She turned and walked toward the front door. Conner looked at Pike and saw something beneath the anger. Suspicion? Conner tried to remain emotionless to avoid looking like he was concealing something, but Pike seemed to be assessing him with his squinting stare.

"I love it when she's all nasty," Pike said to Conner. "Smell you later junior. Boss might miss you, but I sure as hell won't. Keep her away from candles."

Pike watched Conner follow Erin out the front door to the pickup in the driveway. As he heard them drive away, Pike scratched his head, second-guessing himself for letting them leave. "Accident, huh?" he whispered. "Let's see about that."

A minute later, Pike found himself sitting at the workstation in the security room. Right hand on the mouse, he massaged his mouth with his left hand in anticipation of what he might see on the video surveillance monitor.

Like all of the cameras throughout the mansion, the four library cameras were expertly disguised. Visible cameras were an eyesore. Furthermore, Pike wanted them hidden for the treasure trove of secrets that they had uncovered. Larkin had hired some very questionable people over the years, and the cameras had helped flush out more than a few underhanded deeds. Pike wondered if the cameras were about to work their magic again.

Pike located the window for the feed of the camera just inside the library door and enlarged it. Then he dragged back the progress bar to see past footage. He stopped the bar and rolled the footage when he saw Erin step up to the library serving table at roughly the time of the fire. The recording showed her setting the two silver carafes of coffee onto the table and moving liquor bottles around to make room. Then she arranged the coffee cups and saucers next to the carafes. She turned around, presumably to wait until someone asked for coffee, and stood there without moving.

"You're boring me girlfriend, show me your accident," Pike said, drumming his fingers on the workstation table in impatience. He waded through another minute of inactivity before he got something completely different. The footage showed

Erin turning back to the table. Stealing a secretive glance over her shoulder to ensure that she wasn't being watched, she opened a bottle of whisky and poured it evenly over the table cloth as if watering a garden.

"Damn it, don't you do it Baby Doll!" Pike said, standing up and slamming both fists on the desk. "Oh, and that was the Macallan too, son of a bitch!"

The footage then showed Erin picking up a napkin and dipping it into the flame of the candle, napkin catching fire. Then she touched the flaming napkin to the table cloth. The screen flashed as the table cloth ignited.

"I'm gonna *KILL* that little pyro Pinocchio!" Pike shouted at the screen. "Why is this sick bitch burning up the library? And she says *I* disgust *her*? What a psycho!"

Pike paused the video and pulled at his hair with both hands before a new irritating thought occurred to him like an insect bite.

"And what was college boy doing?" Pike said, searching for a different camera that showed Conner. "You covering for her little prank you gutless jackal?" He enlarged the window for the camera that showed the center of the library and moved its progress bar to match the time from the library door camera. The recording showed Conner looking innocent enough holding a tray of desserts for the guests. Then the flash of fire caused Conner to drop the tray on Marcela's lap, guests standing and looking toward the bright shimmering light. As the footage advanced, smoke began to obscure the picture, but Pike could make out everyone leaving the room except Conner.

"Here comes our boy the fire brigade," Pike said as he watched to see if Conner would try to put out the fire. Instead, Conner reached for Larkin's laptop and began to type.

"What are you doing junior?" Pike yelled. "That's not

putting out the fire! Accident my ass! Both of these clowns are *SO* dead!"

He continued to watch until he saw Conner taking the photographs.

"Pictures!" Pike screamed. "He's taking pictures. I knew I hated him! For the love of God!"

Pike had seen enough. He pounded the desk again with his fists, mouse and monitor jolting from the impact. He kicked over a file cabinet in rage, then rushed from the security room and sprinted away to find Larkin and Marcela.

PIKE BURST into Larkin's bedroom to find Marcela sitting at Larkin's bedside. Larkin, who had refused to go to the hospital for examination despite the urging of paramedics, was stretched on his bed looking meek, Marcela affixing his oxygen tubes to his nose through his lingering coughs. Marcela and Larkin watched Pike stumble into the room panting.

"We got a big problem!" Pike gasped.

Marcela stood. "What now?" she asked.

"The girl set that fire on purpose!" Pike said. "I just watched the library video footage."

"Why would she do that?" Larkin asked.

"Boss, they're both in on it. The kid peeked at your laptop," Pike answered.

"My laptop?"

"And he took pictures of something," Pike added.

Marcela walked around to the other side of the bed to the nightstand where she had placed Larkin's open laptop after bringing it upstairs. She grabbed it, sat in Larkin's wingback, and typed in the password. Pike came over to watch, both of them seeing nothing but financial documents still open from the meeting.

"Did the video show what he was looking at?" Marcela asked Pike.

"No, it was too far off, and there was smoke," Pike said.

Marcela went into Excel and looked at the most recent files that were opened, all of which were documents from the meeting. Then she checked Word.

"Reid," she said to Larkin. "Did you open this document today?" She stood to show him the laptop screen displaying the document that Conner had seen and photographed.

"No, I haven't opened that in days," Reid said.

"Someone opened it today," she said. "That was probably what he photographed."

Marcela and Pike looked at each other. "They know?" Pike said. "How do they know? I swear, I didn't say anything to them."

"Karl," Larkin said through a heavy sigh. "They know. Lord only knows how. Where are they now?"

Pike swallowed. "I fired them and kicked them out. They're gone."

"You what?" Larkin said.

"Boss, the girl almost burned down your house," Pike said. "I was mad. I know you liked the history boy."

Larkin took an inhale of his oxygen before he spoke. "Not so much anymore, it would seem. Karl, I suggest you earn your salary for a change and find them before they go to the police. Or will that be too difficult for you?"

"No," Pike said. "I'll take care of it. Easy peasy. Don't worry."

Minutes later Pike roared down the driveway in his black Suburban and raced away from the mansion.

~

ERIN COULDN'T READ ANYMORE. She had spent the last five minutes reading aloud from the document Conner had photographed, but she was sickened by what it said. There were few other cars on the road in downtown White Bear Lake at that hour.

"Where are you going?" Erin asked.

"I need to fill up, we're on fumes," Conner said, veering the pickup toward a gas station. He pulled into the station and parked by a pump, station desolate.

"We have to call the police right away," Erin said.

Conner nodded, weary from the bizarre night that now seemed as if it would never end. "Do you think they'll believe us?"

"With this evidence?" she said, holding out his phone. "He's plotting to blow up hundreds of people. The police don't take kindly to that."

"Let's hope so, considering the legality of what we just did," he said.

"Will you stop worrying? This is going to work."

"I'm clearly not spy material," Conner said. He got out of the pickup and fed his credit card into the pump control panel. Erin stepped out and closed the passenger door.

"We may not get much sleep tonight," Erin said. "Coffee?" He nodded, and Erin walked toward the gas station minimart while he began pumping gas.

Conner looked down the road from where they had come, an uneasy feeling creeping in that they would get caught for what they had done. But the road was free of cars at the moment, so no one was following them. He further calmed himself with the realization that they had pulled off the scheme perfectly, just as Erin had planned it, so why would they be in danger? Still, the pump seemed freakishly slow, and he kept his eyes fixed on the road that led toward Larkin's mansion.

Gas pumped, Conner got back into the pickup. He started the engine and pulled up to the side of the minimart to wait for Erin, rolling down the windows to get some air. Minutes later, Erin came out. She got into the pickup and sat, taking a sip of coffee and handing him his cup.

"I think you need chocolate," she added, opening a Hershey bar. She broke off half and handed it to him. He took a bite, appetite not really there. Neither of them noticed a car pulling into the station, headlights off.

"You actually like this cloak-and-dagger stuff?" he asked through his chewing.

She took a bite of her half. "It beats washing dishes," she smiled. They finished their chocolate in silence.

"Okay, I'm calling the police, I don't think we should wait any longer," she said, pulling out her phone.

"Fine, but I'm getting us far away from here," Conner said. "It's creeping me out to be so close to that mansion." He put his hand on the stick shift as Erin dialed 9-1-1. Before she could tap the green icon to put the call through, a man stepped up to the open passenger window, snatching the phone and putting a pistol to Erin's head.

"Baby Doll, I'd love to put a ginormous hole in your dumbass noodle right now," Pike said calmly, Glock ready to fire. "College boy, cut the engine or you'll get her brain pie all over your funny face."

Pike canceled the unplaced call and stuffed Erin's phone in his pocket. Conner turned off the pickup in a daze from fear, shocked at how adeptly Pike had located and surprised them.

"Now your phone, Professor," Pike said. "Hand it over."

Conner grabbed his phone from the dash and handed it to Erin, who held it for a moment.

"Gimme, girl," Pike said, holding out his free hand. "You losers are so stupid. You think a mansion like that wouldn't have video cameras? Baby Doll using Macallan like it's lighter fluid. History Boy snapping photos like he's KGB. I can't wait for the sequel."

Erin still hesitated, so Pike shoved the gun harder into her face. "Did you already forget how much I wanna put a hole in your pretty noggin sweetie?"

Erin gave him the phone.

"Thank the Lord for guns!" Pike said smiling, putting Conner's phone in his other pocket. "Very good, Beavis and Butthead. I should take you to a pasture and beat you both to soup with a rusty fencepost. Instead you might live if you keep following my instructions. So here's what happens next."

33

INFILTRATE

Just shy of midnight inside a white cargo van parked in a vacant parking lot, Mr. Red sat back and studied the video monitor at his compact workstation, his bulldog napping on the floor beside him. The monitor displayed five video screens, four of which came from night vision cameras mounted conspicuously on the van's exterior. The aft camera showed a desolate office building behind the van, while the side cameras surveyed both directions of the street running perpendicular to the van's front. Mr. Red focused on the front camera displaying the Center for Immigration Assistance building across the street, the Arden Hills nonprofit organization founded and managed by John McMichael. The fifth camera, hidden on a tree outside of McMichael's office, showed only dark shadows inside his corner office.

Previous recon had told Mr. Red that McMichael split his working hours evenly between this office and his law firm in St. Paul. Mr. Red also knew that McMichael's personal office occupied the side corner of the building that the van now faced, intel obtained easily by spotting him there through the office's ample windows. The night before, Mr. Red had sneaked toward that window to hang the camera on the tree for a better look, that bit of spying showing everything in McMichael's office once daylight had returned. Of particular note was a large ficus on the floor in the corner of the room. An unremarkable object to anyone else, it had generated a satisfied grin from Mr. Red.

There was a final piece of intelligence that was especially critical: a three-man cleaning crew occupied the building beginning at midnight. Now, like clockwork, the workers drove up a few minutes apart and entered the building for work.

"Game time," Mr. Red said.

He stood, stepped over his dog, and made his way to the back of the van. Next to a narrow impeccably made cot was a double-door footlocker. Mr. Red opened the doors to reveal an impressive assortment of clothing and weaponry. He began changing into the gear, in minutes his body clad in black tactical clothing, his face and head covered with a lightweight black balaclava. He retrieved his sheathed Ka-Bar from the locker and clipped it to his chest, then attached his holstered pistol to his waist. Finally, he reached for a black backpack hanging from a hook, hefted all eighty pounds of it to his shoulder, and slung it around to his back, the weight teetering him at first. Then he stepped back to the front of the van.

"How do I look Mike?" he asked his dog, who lifted his head with what looked akin to annoyance. "You know what? I don't care what you think, I know I look good. Go back to sleep, you look exhausted."

Mr. Red opened the side door of the van, leaped out, and closed the door behind him before scampering into the shadows.

∾

THE REAR ENTRANCE to the Center for Immigration Assistance was a solitary glass door. Above the door was a light in desperate need of a new bulb, casting erratic flashes across the concrete walkway leading up to the door. Next to the door was a steel bench permanently mounted into the concrete.

Mr. Red knelt behind an elm tree just outside of the light strobes. Body perfectly still, he peered around the tree trunk and waited, drawing initial patience in the knowledge that one of the night crew was a smoker, and the call for nicotine was never far away. But Mr. Red's heavy pack turned the task of waiting into a minor workout, his back and shoulders feeling the strain from its weight. Sweat began to fall into his eyes from the balaclava, despite the winter chill, yet he remained perfectly still.

Twenty minutes in, body quivering from the strain, Mr. Red wondered if the worker had given up smoking. That possibility, however remote, teased at Mr. Red's patience. He shifted his weight in search of comfort that wasn't there, and from deep inside him came a plea to the tobacco gods to unleash their brutal cravings. As if his call was heeded, the door opened with a clang. Out stepped the smoker, burly and bald with a long beard, who repositioned a cigarette from behind his ear to his mouth as the door shut behind him. The man produced a lighter, flicked it to life on the third try, lit his cigarette, and sat on the bench. He took a drag and exhaled a voluminous cloud that gained life in the winter air. Then he pulled his phone from his shirt pocket and killed time between puffs browsing social media.

Smelling the smoke that drifted his way, Mr. Red issued a silent thank you to the tobacco gods, feeling foolish for doubting addiction. Never a smoker, he had gotten used to the smell of cigarette smoke from fellow soldiers during his long military career, so much that it was almost calming, the prelude to another mission. He inhaled the second-hand smoke with memories of Baghdad and Kandahar, the good old days. Now freelance, the money was there, but the challenges were not, mercenary jobs never quite the same as serving with his unit in lands that the world had chosen to neglect. But the freelance money was miles better, and that made all the difference.

The smoking worker laughed at meme after meme, snorting like a horse, nursing every second of his cigarette and the freedom from cleaning toilets. Ten minutes in, cigarette burned down, the man stood to vacuum out a final pull before snuffing the butt on the ground. He looked up at the sky to remember that there was a world still waiting for him while he worked, then he opened the door with his pass card and reentered the building.

Mr. Red rushed forward, cramping legs and weighted pack causing him to stumble through his initial steps before he regained his balance. Door shutting quickly, he sprinted the final steps before catching it inches from closing. He held it and listened, hearing the worker's steps trailing away inside. Mr. Red peered in to see the worker turn a corner and disappear back to his work.

Hallway clear, Mr. Red opened the door enough to slip through. As the door closed behind him, he scurried to the left hallway wall, hugging it close and listening. A vacuum cleaner hummed from somewhere, followed by one of the workers in the far distance uttering something in Spanish, another worker laughing in response. Mr. Red knew the hallway wasn't the place to dawdle. He saw the surveillance camera monitoring the hallway from above him, an unfortunate but benign realization. Likely by the time there would be a need to review the footage, he'd be far away from there. And he knew for certain that there were no security guards around at night, only the cleaning crew. He crouched and advanced in silence to avoid being seen by them, taking the first left down a hallway of offices.

He followed the dim hallway, multicultural artwork in dark walnut frames lining both walls. Reading the office nameplates as he walked, Mr. Red made his way past four darkened offices and a conference room before finding the corner office he was looking for, the nameplate *John McMichael* on the closed door. He reached for the doorknob but found it was locked. No matter. He pulled a lock-picking kit from his pants pocket and began to work on the lock as he kept an ear out for anyone approaching. After a minute of skilled manipulation, he turned the knob and opened the door. Then he slipped inside, closing and locking the door behind him. He listened at the door for movement in the hallway, but hearing none, he pulled his adjustable-beam flashlight from his shirt pocket, turned it on, and went to work.

The light illuminated McMichael's office that featured a sleek executive desk and bookshelf to the left, the spotless workspace reeking of a neatnik. A couch, meeting chairs, and a coffee table dominated the room's center. The large ficus claimed the right corner of the room, and Mr. Red moved up to the plant with a purpose. Securing the flashlight in his teeth, he removed his backpack with a grunt and gently rested it on the floor. He knelt next to it, opened the zipper, and took out an oblong satchel responsible for much of the pack's weight. He grimaced as he placed the heavy bundle onto the carpeting.

The ficus, tall and sturdy, lived on the floor in a wide plastic pot that was about two feet tall. Mr. Red stood up next to the pot, bent his knees, and pushed on the rim to tilt it, being careful not to spill any soil. The pot tilted until the ficus propped against the wall, pot tipped at an angle wide enough to give Mr. Red access to the bottom. The ficus held steady against the wall, but Mr. Red released his grip slowly until he saw that the pot would stay propped for as long as he needed it to.

Next he removed a towel from the pack and laid it on the floor beneath the bottom of the pot. He unsheathed his Ka-Bar and went to work on the bottom of the pot, sharp blade cutting into the plastic until he had opened a decent hole. He removed the flap of plastic and pulled heaps of soil from the pot, placing it all on the towel.

Cavern created, he reached for the satchel. Inside was an explosive device, armed and ready to be ignited with a simple cell phone call. It was capable of wiping out much of the vicinity, he was certain of that, all made by his own hands using the best demolition training the military could provide. He pushed the satchel into the hole, wiggling it, pulling out more soil until it fit. Satchel installed, he reached for duct tape in his pack and the plastic piece that he had cut out from the bottom of the pot. He reattached the plastic piece to the bottom of the pot and taped it on, sealing the hole. Satisfied, he folded up the towel of soil and placed it into his backpack, careful not to spill one grain. Then he pulled the pot back down so it was flat on the carpeting again. He returned his knife to its sheath, stood, and removed the flashlight from his mouth to shine around and inspect his work. The plant looked as if it hadn't been touched.

"Apologies mister ficus, but thank you for your sacrifice," he whispered to himself.

This confidence came too soon, as Mr. Red heard an improbable shuffling of footsteps from across the room. Had someone entered without him hearing?

He turned to look for a logical explanation in the semi-darkness. He shined his light toward the sound, seeing nothing, which made no sense. What had he heard then? He continued to shine the light around the room, but it was as empty as when he had entered.

The next sound that Mr. Red heard was far more chilling. If the walls had the ability to whisper, that's how it might sound—hundreds of whispers coming from every direction, like the room itself was scrutinizing his actions, words indiscernible.

Mr. Red flashed his light at the walls, but as his light shined around the room, he found that the room was still empty. Then the whispers hushed, room returning to silence.

A familiar feeling haunted him, one that Mr. Red thought he had left behind at the McMichael home. It was a panicky agitation that something was supremely wrong, like the opening of the closet door in the McMichaels's laundry room and the madness that followed. Was it happening again here?

"Bullshit," he said to himself, keeping his voice low.

A flash of light next to the desk caught Mr. Red's attention. It wasn't a desk light turning on or headlights shining through the window from outside. It was a faint flicker, like a hazy green camera flash.

Out from the light stepped a man.

Mr. Red jerked his flashlight toward the form, the light revealing the intruder's baggy blue coat and blue pants, the man's face so pale it almost glowed. He began to walk toward Mr. Red.

There was no time to figure this out. As far as Mr. Red was concerned, the man in blue was an enemy. Mr. Red unsheathed his Ka-Bar again, cocked it back over his shoulder, and heaved it toward the target. The knife flew end over end on course to find the man's forehead. But when it reached him, instead of a fleshy smack on impact, the knife flew right through him before plunging into a cork board behind McMichael's desk.

Then the man disappeared.

Mr. Red gasped, shining his light all over the room. No one was there.

"No no no *no!*" he whispered, refusing to believe any of it. He walked across the room, continuing to flash his light in attempt to look for a person, but it was no use, he was alone. He pulled the Ka-Bar from the cork board and returned it to his sheath, repositioning a photo on the board slightly to cover the knife hole.

Mr. Red was unprepared to hear keys jingling outside of McMichael's office door, followed by the door opening up. He dropped to the floor in time to remain unseen. The fluorescent ceiling lights turned on as a worker lumbered in with a vacuum cleaner, turning it on to begin vacuuming the office. Mr. Red slid farther behind the desk for cover, forcing himself to remain calm and wait for an opportunity. He watched the worker from underneath the desk. When the worker was farther into the office and had turned his back to the door, Mr. Red fled out and down the hallway undetected. Main hallway empty, he crept toward the exit. Before he opened the door to retreat outside, he took a final look behind him. Seeing no one, he shook his head and left.

Back at the van, Mr. Red panted, adrenaline alive in his veins. Usually he enjoyed the sensation, but not tonight.

"That didn't just happen," he mumbled.

He opened the van door, his dog lifting his head to greet him. Hopping in and closing the door behind him, Mr. Red took a deep breath.

"I may need to start thinking about retirement, Mike," he said. "Let's get out of here."

34

DEATH'S DOORSTEP

Karl Pike gripped the wheel of the Suburban as he guided the vehicle through the darkness of the Wisconsin country road. Radio blaring classic rock, Pike reached into a brown paper bag on the console and pulled out a 50 milliliter nip bottle of whiskey and a Slim Jim. Steering with his left knee, he opened the bottle and drained the nip with a sigh, then he opened the window to a rush of crisp Midwestern air and pitched out the bottle. Closing the window, he opened the Slim Jim and bit off a hunk to chase away the whiskey's sting with salty grease.

Better. The alcohol put a dent in his overanxious nerves. This level of jitters was rare for him, but it wasn't every day that he drove with two abducted college kids bound and gagged in the back of his Suburban. Nerves were good—they heightened the senses on a night when he needed to be on extra alert for cops—but too much could make a person jumpy. Any erratic driving might call attention to police, and he watched intently for speed traps, keeping the Suburban under the speed limit for once.

Pike reconciled the details of the night that had snow-balled too quickly. Those two college kids clearly had no idea who they were dealing with, so he had shown them. So quick were his actions that no one at the gas station had been the wiser of their abduction. All that had remained was to get the kid's pickup out of there, which he had accomplished with Marcela once he had secured the kids in Larkin's mansion. Pickup safely hidden in Larkin's garage, Pike's incriminating tracks had been covered long enough to accomplish what was needed next.

And what was that? The main event, of course. Larkin had decided to raise the pressure several notches by requesting to go to his cabin in the middle of the night. Still rattled by the fire, Larkin's health had plummeted, and the realization that the man had quickly reached death's doorstep had taken hold. Marcela had left with Larkin in another car a half hour before Pike had followed, Pike needing the time to gather his prisoners, load them onto the Suburban's flat rear bed, and cover them with a blanket.

In a way it was exhilarating to think that the issue had been forced tonight, Pike realized. Larkin would get his dying wish soon enough. When the old man passed, it would mean that Pike and Marcela would be without jobs, but it would also mean that they would be obscenely rich for their trouble, a thought that brought a greedy smile to Pike's face.

He reached for another nip in the bag, cracked the bottle open, and swigged it down, again tossing the bottle out the window. He gobbled the rest of his Slim Jim as he thought more about Larkin. Pike envisioned that he'd miss the guy much like someone might miss a crabby uncle who had the knack of making life interesting. Larkin's level of hate was a thing of legend, and Pike had chosen to embrace it over anything remotely similar to resistance, living out a lifetime of venting at the world through Larkin's forked tongue. So the old man deserved to go out in his own demented way, and Pike intended to make very sure it would happen. Let no one say Karl Pike wasn't good at his job.

But enough about that. Pike calmed himself by going over plans for what to do with his riches. He'd flee to somewhere remote and warm, far from the hellish Minnesota winters and the cops who'd eventually be onto him. He'd stay hidden until things cleared up, but live like a rock star while doing it, learning the marvels that stacks of cash could buy. Beaches, women, cars, boats, clothes—everything. Maybe he'd even buy a bottle of Macallan and swig it down while playing pool in Larkin's honor. That would be a nice touch, a simple show of thanks and a classy way to begin his new life. A year or two of that and he'd reenter the world a new man, rich and powerful, ready for the next challenge.

But first there was finishing this job. It was late in the fourth quarter, and all he needed to do was ram the ball into the end zone.

Pike spotted a glint on the left side of the road up ahead. There were many things that could be: a sign reflector, the glowing eyes of a buck ready to charge across the road in front of him, a cop in a speed trap. He slowed the cruise control of the Suburban, feeling certain that the reflection was nothing to worry about, but precaution was the rule of the hour. There was definitely something there; it continued to reflect from the Suburban's headlights. Pike kept studying it, every inch closer building his stress.

By the time Pike realized that the light was a reflection from a car nestled into an intersecting service road, it was too late to do much. Plus, a car parked on a service road was still likely benign—engine trouble, teenagers drinking, someone parked to look at a map. But as Pike searched for more details through the darkness, the unease surged as he began to make out the unmistakable clues of a state trooper's vehicle: a reinforced front grill and a thin rack of lights on the roof. He even thought he saw the dashboard glow of a trooper's face scrutinizing Pike as he passed. Hissing out a cautionary exhale, Pike snapped off the cruise control to lower his speed even more, knowing that applying the brake would make him look guilty. He was well below the speed limit, but still he stared at the review mirror for movement behind him.

"You stay right there, buddy," he spoke, willing the trooper to stay put. But an ominous hunch took over his rational thoughts, one that told him that the cop was somehow suspicious.

The trooper's headlights popped to life, and the car sped out of its hiding place in pursuit.

"No, you stupid ass!" Pike shouted, slapping the steering wheel. "I wasn't speeding!"

Pike wondered if there was another reason, a bum tail light maybe, and he regretted not checking that before heading out. His breath increased as he opened the glove compartment and removed his Glock. There was a familiarity to all of this, the awful yet wonderful feeling that he'd need to kill again. Kill or be killed in the name of duty.

"You could have just stayed there eating your doughnuts, but no! Now I gotta smoke your Barney Fife ass!"

The trooper gained ground quickly, Pike's distress eliciting a groan from his gaping mouth as he watched through the rearview. As if Pike knew it would happen, the trooper's roof lights ignited, strobing red and blue followed by the chirp of a siren signaling Pike to pull over.

"Son of a . . .!" Pike growled. He contemplated making a run for it, but quickly dismissed that, it would only mean more cops called onto the chase. Instead he would need to end this here, and quickly. Pike pulled over, stuffing the Glock into his coat pocket.

But to Pike's amazement, the trooper didn't follow him to the shoulder, and instead roared past, lights flashing into the roadside trees to chase another call. Whether the cop had never intended to pull Pike over, or he had gotten another call at the last second, Pike would never know, and he didn't care.

"Oh sweet Jesus!" Pike hollered, shaking his head, exhaling relief at his fortune. "Thanks for the heart attack, you sick bastard!"

He opened his last nip and drained it with a shaking hand before moving on.

PIKE PULLED into the gravel driveway of Larkin's northwestern Wisconsin cabin. He clicked the garage door opener button, and the two-car garage door opened to reveal Marcela's car occupying the left side. Pike pulled in next to the car and closed the garage door behind him.

"All in a day's work," he said, putting the Suburban into park and killing the engine. He removed the key and got out, rounding the vehicle to get to the rear hatch. He opened it to reveal the forms of his prisoners underneath a plaid blanket. He pulled off the blanket and enjoyed the moment of seeing them blindfolded and gagged with their hands bound behind their backs.

"There's my cute couple," he said. He reached for Erin and dragged her out like a bag of soil, standing her on the garage cement on uncertain legs. He did the same for Conner, setting them beside one another like downcast mannequins. Then he guided them toward the door leading inside the cabin. He opened the door and turned on the light, which illuminated a staircase landing, stairs going up to the right and down to the left.

"Okay ladies and gentlemen, we're gonna go down some stairs," Pike said. "Take it slowly, it'd break my heart if either of you were to fall."

Erin mumbled something indecipherable through her gag.

"I know, I love you too Baby Doll," Pike laughed. "Let's go."

Pike led them down the stairs, Erin and Conner taking the wooden steps gingerly in their temporary blindness. The stairs ended a dozen steps down in front of a closed door. Pike pulled his keys from his pocket, unlocked the door, stepped inside, and flicked on a light to reveal a sizable wine cellar. He guided his prisoners inside and removed their gags and blindfolds. Relieved from their sensory deprivation, Erin and Conner inhaled the cellar air freely as they squinted at their surroundings. Wine bottles glinted in the dull light, hundreds of different brands crowded into wooden racks lining stone walls. Three lights in iron fixtures hung from the low wooden ceiling, giving the place the appearance of a medieval dungeon.

"It's no bed and breakfast, but this is your home for now," Pike said. "Anyone have to pee? I don't change diapers." Pike pointed to a bathroom at the other end of the cellar.

"Does your mom know how disgusting you are?" Erin asked.

"She has no idea," Pike said. "Now do you have to pee or not?"

"I do," Conner said. Erin brooded silently while Pike undid Conner's wrist bindings and escorted him at gunpoint into the bathroom. When Conner was finished, Pike untied Erin, and she walked reluctantly into the bathroom for her turn.

Bathroom breaks finished, Pike led them back to the

center of the cellar. There he grabbed chains and locks stored neatly on a shelf where he'd left them—human restraining devices that he'd used well over the years.

"Okay, on your butts, each of you in front of a beam," Pike said, pointing to two vertical wooden support beams across from each other.

"Seriously?" Erin said.

"Yeah, *seriously*," Pike said, pointing the Glock at her nose.

With both of them seated, Pike bound them around their waists and chests to the support beams and locked each chain in place with a simple combination lock. Fully secured, he looked down at his captives with sadistic satisfaction.

"If you promise not to raise a fuss down here, I'll spare you the gags," he said.

"We promise," Conner said before Erin could get in another insult.

"Fine, that's how it's done bro," Pike said. "Be good for me and I won't make this any more miserable than it has to be."

"You're going to jail," Erin said. Conner rolled his eyes at her defiance.

"Jesus, how do you put up with her, dude?" Pike said to Conner, who didn't know how to answer. Pike held up the gag for Erin to see. "What's that I hear? You want this back on because it's so comfy?" he said.

Erin shook her head and looked away from him.

"All right then, I'll try to forget you just said that. And for the record, my mother is a fabulous lady, so leave her out of this."

Pike turned and walked toward the closed door. He unlocked and opened it. "Nighty night," he said, closing the door and locking it behind him. They heard his footsteps going up the stairs.

"Your mom is a total whore," Erin muttered toward the door.

Conner smiled and looked at her seething but beaten expression.

"And she wears combat boots," he added.

She smiled back, then sobered. "We're so screwed."

35

COMMENCE

"Reid?" Marcela called, voice gentle, as though she was addressing a sleeping child on a school morning.

Larkin was stretched out on a hospital bed that had been moved into the cabin's living room months ago in preparation for his final days. A fire burned in the far corner fireplace while snowflakes fluttered down outside, subduing the emerging daylight. Oxygen tubes continued to deliver precious air to Larkin's diseased lungs, while a monitor that Marcela had strapped to his wrist tracked his vital signs.

Larkin didn't stir from Marcela's voice, sleep aided by a heavy dose of liquid morphine from a few hours before. If Marcela allowed her imagination to mask reality, she could see through the aging and impending death on his face and envision the child that he may have been, innocent and hopeful, long before disagreeable bitterness had taken hold for the rest of his days.

Marcela turned to watch the snow falling outside. If only the situation were different, the view would be enjoyable, even beautiful. She had seen on the television news that the

Wisconsin storm would bring several inches. No matter, soon all of this would be over, and all that would be necessary would be for Marcela and Karl to get to the airport, and she knew that Pike and his Suburban were up to the task.

Being a home-care nurse was the last thing that Marcela had ever dreamed of adding to her résumé. But it had indeed come to that. After some hands-on training by a home-care nurse weeks ago, she had learned to perform the basics during Larkin's final days. But in addition to giving him medication from his hospice comfort kit that the hospital had prepared, feeding him oxygen, watching his vitals, and making him as comfortable as possible, now her main task appeared to be waiting for him to die, a prospect that she didn't enjoy dwelling upon. But there was another task, one that would quickly be front and center.

"Reid?" she called again, nudging his withered hand that rested across his abdomen. She could see on his wrist monitor that his vitals looked stable, the state-of-the-art device delivering his blood pressure, heart rate, body temperature, electrocardiograph, and other information on a tiny screen. The monitor was intended only for hospital use by trained personnel, but Marcela had gotten around that obstacle with relative ease. Money always talks. If she was supposed to witness his death, she had wanted to be good and certain that he was gone. The device would show her that in no uncertain terms.

Larkin's eyes peeled open. There was anger there, and something else: fear, surprise.

"It would appear I've lived to see another day," he said. His voice was hoarse, as though his throat was overwhelmed with decay.

"Of course," she said, not in a confident tone, but one that expressed the relief she felt. She had been up all night at his bedside, the gamble that he would live until morning taking a toll on her nerves.

"But I won't make it through the day," he said. "I can feel it."

Marcela's silence indicated her agreement.

"What time is it?" he asked.

She looked at her watch. "Just after eight a.m. Eight fifteen."

Larkin stirred in his bed as if to rise, but the movement was enough to dislodge a pathetic cough, shallow but long lasting, his face turning red from the strain. Marcela stood and reached toward him to grip his shoulders, as if her touch could somehow help him through it, until the cough at last subsided, leaving him to inhale the oxygen with wheezing breaths.

"You should really stay still Reid," she said as he recovered. She realized that it was an unnecessary suggestion, because Larkin had no intention of moving like that again. She sat again. "Do you need anything? You can have more morphine."

He winced away his suffering for the moment, swallowing hard. "Water," he said. "I'm thirsty enough to drink a gallon of camel piss."

"All right," she said.

Marcela reached for a white pitcher of ice water on the end table next to the bed and topped off the cup next to it, straw in the cup wiggling as she poured. Filled, she brought the cup to Larkin's face and guided the straw into his mouth. He sucked a few sips before pulling away, licking his dry lips, skin so tight on his face that it looked like his jaw bones would puncture through. His appetite had waned enough in recent weeks that he had lost significant weight. It occurred to her that she had never been this near to someone so close to death, and it made her uneasy, as if she could somehow catch his cancer.

Larkin turned his head to peer out of the enormous front window. "Snow," he said. "Lovely. My last day on Earth will be a Godforsaken blizzard."

"It's pretty," Marcela said. "Peaceful."

"If you say so," he muttered.

Larkin inhaled his oxygen, closed his eyes to collect his thoughts and energy, then opened his eyes to look at Marcela.

"I had such a dream," he said. "Must've been the morphine."

"You slept so soundly, I thought . . ."

"You can say it Marcela," Larkin finished her thought. "You thought I slept like the dead. Maybe I actually did. I dreamed that I was dead, or close to it."

"I see," she said.

"We have no idea what awaits us when we die," he continued. "I suspect for me it won't be pleasant, unless of course there's nothing at all, we just turn the lights out and disappear forever. But in my dream, there were people there, upon this deathbed. They were dead, too, begging me to do something against my wishes. I wouldn't do it though, whatever it was. Stick to your guns, I say, no matter what a few damn fools who I don't even know want of me. Stick to your guns."

"You always have," she agreed.

Larkin's eyes widened, as though he was seeing the dream again, almost reliving it as reality. There was fear there, regret and shame intermingled.

"Marcela," Larkin gasped. "Do you think . . ."

Larkin seemed unwilling or unable to finish his question.

"Do I think what, Reid?"

Larkin was silent in his thoughts for a moment, some sort of duel taking place inside his mind. But whatever he was fighting, he came out the victor, his wide eyes closing off the fear, restoring the angry confidence that she had come to know from Reid Larkin.

"Never mind," he said.

"Certainly."

"Marcela," he said.

"Yes?"

"Thank you. I'm grateful for all you've done for me. You've always come through for me, and you will do it this one final time."

"Indeed," she said. "And that's no trouble at all Reid. More water?"

Larkin shook his head. "I think you'd better call our man. It's time."

"Of course," she said, reaching for the phone in her pocket. It was a simple smartphone, but not her usual one—a burner phone, intended for minimal use before she would discard it for good to cover her trail. She dialed Mr. Red's number and held up the phone on speaker, volume turned up to max so Larkin could hear.

Mr. Red picked up the call after four rings. "What?" he said, voice modulator disguising his voice.

"You may proceed, Mr. Red, as soon as you're ready," Marcela said. There was a pause on the line as Mr. Red digested this.

"Ah. The final heartbeats are upon us then, are they?" Mr. Red said.

"Yours will be too one day, Mr. Red. Remember that," Larkin snapped.

"Oh it's a macabre milestone for all of us, Mr. Larkin, that's true enough," Mr. Red responded. "For some of us, it's even a happy release."

"Anyway," Marcela interrupted, "we're eager to conclude this project. Are you ready?"

"Ready and eager as a beaver," Mr. Red said. "Let me just check something. Hold on."

Marcela looked at Larkin, who had closed his eyes as he listened for Mr. Red to return.

A moment later, Mr. Red's voice returned. "The first Little Piggy is right where we want him, I have a visual on that," he said, referring to McMichael. "But the second Little Piggy is ah . . . out at the moment. I've replayed the surveillance. She left to walk the pooches—beautiful pair of Huskies, you should see those two frolicking in the snow. She'll be back in a half hour once the mutts have watered the back forty."

Marcela wondered if Larkin was imagining what Amanda might look like walking her dogs on a snowy winter morning, completely unaware of the terror that waited for her in her own home.

"The Third Piggy," Mr. Red continued, referring to McMichael's law firm office "well that one can be blown down whenever you please. So how would you like the Big Bad Wolf to proceed? It's your call, dearest Granny."

Larkin opened his eyes to look at Marcela, who was waiting for him to respond. Larkin only nodded, then closed his eyes again.

"Right, please proceed in a half hour then," she said. "When she returns, that is, but make sure he's available too. As for the third one, it goes whenever the other two go."

"Understood," Mr. Red said. "Nine o'clock, give or take, and then I'll huff and I'll puff."

"Good luck," Marcela said.

"Luck isn't a factor, Marcela," Mr. Red said. "These blemishes to Mr. Larkin's impeccable record will have to be scooped up with a dustpan when this is done, and that kind of execution is nothing but skill. That's not to say that I'm not superstitious. Take ghosts, for example. Do you believe in ghosts, Mr. Larkin?"

"I've never met one," Larkin said. "You're babbling Mr. Red, is there anything more you need from us?"

"Well I've come to believe in them, ghosts I mean," Mr. Red continued. "Very interesting job, this one. You see all kinds of strange things in my work, but this job has been different."

"Fine," Marcela said. "We thank you for your . . . unique skills and experience. Are we all set then?"

"Just one more thing, long as I have you both on the line," Mr. Red said.

"What in God's name now?" Larkin said, impatience overtaking him.

"It should be in God's name, with what you're about to inflict, or the devil's if you'd prefer. So I just want to ask, Mr. Larkin, whether you're absolutely sure that you want to do this? I mean, it doesn't matter to me, I may as well be exterminating ants in my kitchen. But I just wondered, when a man is so close to death, whether he begins to take stock of his life, and strange new insights might occur to him. Because once I lay waste to things, you can't really change your mind."

Marcela saw a millisecond of confusion take over Larkin with these words. Mr. Red had a rare skill of getting under Larkin's skin. Then she saw the same outrage she knew so well consume Larkin's expression again.

"Screw off you kooky bastard!" Larkin said. "I didn't pay for you to offer me psychiatric help. Just do the job, is that too much to ask?"

"Spoken like a man of passion," Mr. Red said. "You can consider it a free consultation from your humble hired hand. Imminent death can make people have all kinds of weird thoughts and delusions, but I'd say you're good and ready to give me the go-ahead."

"Yes, proceed, Mr. Red," Marcela chimed in. "Update us when it's done."

"My pleasure," Mr. Red said. "Yea though I walk through the valley of the shadow of death, I will fear no evil. That about sums it up, don't you think?"

Marcela and Larkin were silent.

"Have a happy, happy death," Mr. Red said, hanging up.

Larkin sighed and closed his eyes. "I'll take that morphine now," he said. "Wake me when that son of a bitch finishes the job."

"Of course," Marcela said.

From somewhere in the cellar came the sounds of Conner and Erin calling.

36

HELP

"Let us out of here!" Erin had screamed eight hours earlier.

"Are you absolutely nuts?" Conner had said. "He's probably watching us right now on one of his cameras. Do you want the gag back on?"

"Oh, I'm sorry, am I overreacting?" Erin had said. "I don't do well imprisoned in a basement by Hannibal Lecter."

"This whole thing was a really bad idea," Conner had said.

"Fine, it's all my fault. Is that satisfying to hear?" Her voice had cracked with defeat and fear.

"No," he had said, stopping short of saying more when he saw a solitary tear fall from her left eye.

"I should have called the cops first thing," she had said. "They'd all be in jail now, and we wouldn't be stuck here with all of this fancy wine mocking us."

"It's not your fault," Connor had offered.

"Let's just find a way out of here," she had said.

"How, exactly, do we do that?"

Wine cellar absent of windows or clocks, Conner had no way of knowing what time it was, but he knew that they had already been imprisoned there for a couple of hours. Conner had looked around, even though he had already done so dozens of times. The latest search had revealed nothing new. The room was spotless, with nothing readily apparent to be used for an escape. Even if there was, the chains prevented either of them from reaching anything.

"I don't know yet," she had said. "And my ass hurts, this floor is awful."

She had closed her eyes as if to find an answer tangled among her deepest thoughts. After a few deep breaths, her head had slumped forward, chest rising and falling in deep slumber.

Conner had become jealous that she was able to sleep, yet happy for her. Despite what they'd been through, she still looked beautiful, even peaceful. After a few minutes of watching her, sleep had become a slow contagion, pure exhaustion beginning to buffer his discomfort and fears. Eyes closing, his head had sunk into the cradle of his shoulder, defying his awareness, merciful sleep delivering temporary release.

"Conner!" Erin screamed. He recoiled awake, the back of his head knocking into the beam behind him.

"Ow! What?" he said, squinting in pain. She was awake but detached, as if in the same trance that she was in the night at her apartment. How long had they been asleep? He had no idea.

"Are you okay?" he asked.

Erin looked around, head bobbing as if she was intoxicated. When she focused on him after a moment, he could swear her face looked like someone else's.

"One," she said, her voice raspy and masculine. Her head snapped to the side. "Six," she continued, this time a female voice but different from her own. Her head lurched again followed by "four" in a different masculine voice.

"What are you doing?" Conner said.

Erin repeated the number sequence using the bizarre voices. "One. Six. Four."

"What's going on?" he asked. "I don't know what you're talking about."

Erin ignored him, head bobbing again until slumping forward. Conner heard her exhale back into sleep as if nothing had happened.

"Erin, wake up!" he shouted.

She raised her head and looked annoyed. "What?" she croaked, wincing once she realized her entire body was knotted from prolonged captivity.

"What did you just say?" he asked.

"I didn't say anything," she said. "And thanks for waking me to enjoy this hellhole some more."

"You said three numbers," Conner said.

"I did?"

"Yeah, you said one-six-four."

"Why would I say that?" she asked.

"You tell me. Were you dreaming again?"

Erin paused to think, then shook her head. "Out like a light. I don't remember anything."

"When you said the numbers it was like . . ." Conner trailed off to think.

"Like what?"

"It seemed like the words weren't coming from you."

Erin considered this as she glanced around the wine cellar that looked the same as before she had fallen asleep. Then she gasped when the answer occurred to her.

"It was them!" she said. "They're helping us again."

The prospect of spirits taking control of Erin and using her to speak was something he never would have considered just days before, but now it made sense, even though his logical brain still wanted to dispute it.

"That's super creepy. But if that's what happened, what do the numbers mean?" Conner asked. "A computer password again?"

"Dunno," Erin said. "The door over there has a key lock, but maybe one upstairs has a passcode?"

"Lot of good that would do us being locked down here," he answered. Then he looked down at the chain around his waist. He felt around with his hands behind his back until he grasped the cold steel of the combination lock.

"Hold on," he said. "Let me try something." He dug his heels into the floor and, an inch at a time, he began to turn himself until his back was facing Erin.

"Can you see the lock?" he asked.

"Yeah," she said. "Hey, that's it! It has three number dials!"

"Okay, still creepy," Conner said. "Do you think the combo is for yours or mine?"

"We'll try them both, yours first," she said, swagger returning to her voice. "Start spinning the first dial and I'll tell you when you get to number one."

Conner ran his thumb along the tiny number dials before settling on what he thought was the first one.

"No, that's the last one, other end," Erin said. "Go to the other end and spin it twice."

He went to the opposite dial and began to spin it.

"No, spin it the other way, but now go three times," she said. He turned the dial the other way and stopped after three turns so the dial reached number one.

"Got it!" she said.

Next he went to the second dial, and she guided him to number six. "Good, you got it," she said when he reached it. "Now the last one, you only need to turn it once."

Conner went to the last one and moved the dial to the four. "Try it," she said.

Conner pulled at the lock, but it wouldn't budge.

"Wait, it looks like the middle dial isn't quite centered on the number," Erin said. Conner brought his thumb back over the middle dial and massaged the dial until it popped more tightly into place over the six. "There," she said. Conner pulled on the lock again. With all the significance of opening an ancient Egyptian tomb for the first time, the lock opened.

"Holy shit!" he said, turning to look at Erin, whose expression was equally shocked.

A minute later, Conner had removed the chains and stood to enjoy the relief of blood beginning to return to his cramped legs. Then he thought about Pike watching his escape on a surveillance camera. If that were the case, Pike would be down there any second.

"But how do we get you free?" Conner said, kneeling next to her to examine whether there was any way he could free her.

"Would Pike be dumb enough to use the same combo?" she said. "That kind of lock can be set to whatever you want. Maybe it's his birthday or something, January 1964?"

"It's all we have," he said as he scurried around to the lock at her back. He moved the dials to one-six-four and pulled. The lock opened.

"The dumbass didn't want to have to remember two combos!" she laughed.

Conner removed the lock and her chains, then helped her to her feet where she stretched her arms and rubbed her rump.

"Oh my God, it's gonna take hours to get feeling back in my lower torso!" she said. "But now what? He locked the door."

"I've been giving that some thought," Conner said. "Grab a couple of wine bottles."

"It's hardly the time to get plastered," she said.

Conner shook his head. "That's not what I had in mind." He looked up at the ceiling lights and began to nod to himself, mentally walking through the details of his plan with a partial smile.

KARL PIKE HAD BEEN SITTING at the kitchen table, laptop open to the surveillance camera displaying the sleeping college kids, Glock on the table next to the laptop.

A knock at the kitchen window startled him. He stood and walked to it, leaning over the kitchen sink to peer outside, pistol at the ready. But nothing was out there except snow, and there were no tracks. He'd sworn that the sound he'd heard was a knuckle rapping on the window, but he deduced that it must have been a falling twig hitting the pane, maybe even a bird.

Pike stayed there for moment to make sure that no one was there. The calm simplicity outside reminded him of childhood memories playing in the snow. He stood there longer than he'd realized, bewitched by some mysterious pull to remain, not fighting it, long enough to miss the feed on his laptop showing something alarming transpiring in the cellar.

When he heard the kids begin to scream from down in the basement, Pike returned to his senses. He walked back to the kitchen table and sat, lifting his Glock from the table in one hand as he reached for the laptop mouse with the other. He clicked the mouse to bring the screen out of sleep mode, Pike only then realizing that he'd been at the window much longer than he'd thought. When the security feed returned off sleep mode, it was completely black. Some sort of malfunction?

"What's going on?" he asked himself.

"Hey, the lights went out!" he heard Conner shout, and from that Pike sneered, the benign solution now occurring to him. The basement had electric heat, and with the temperature dropping overnight, the heater must have tripped the circuit, knocking out the security camera and the lights. It was a known issue, one that he thought he had fixed last winter by reworking the electrical system. Apparently it was still malfunctioning.

"Stow it you oxygen thieves," he muttered to himself. "I'm coming."

"Problem?" Marcela called from down the hallway that led to the living room.

"It's fine, I'll handle it," Pike called back to her.

"We have a half hour, I just made the call. Be ready," she said, then returned to the living room to Larkin.

Pike left the table with his Glock in hand as he felt for the keys in his pants pocket. He'd go down there, switch on the tripped circuit in the breaker, lower the thermostat, insult the kids enough to shut them up, and be done with it well before showtime.

Pike turned on the stairway light and descended the stairs to the basement door.

"Let us out!" he heard Erin scream from inside.

"Shut it!" Pike called through the door, searching for the key to unlock the door. "It's only darkness sweetie, it can't kill you."

Nothing more came from inside, so Pike laughed to himself as he found the key and inserted it into the door lock.

He opened the door, scant light from the stairway revealing vague shadows inside the cellar. He returned the set of keys to his pocket and stepped through the doorway.

"Don't worry, Daddy's back to tuck you in," Pike said as he struggled in vain to see the kids chained to the posts. He blinked away the darkness to locate them, but his eyes weren't adjusted enough. All he could make out were the posts. "You two spazzes having a lovely morning down here?"

Instead of a response, Pike felt a blow to the side of his head, the strike clanking off his skull with a melodic clunk, the assault knocking a questioning word to the front of his consciousness: *escaped?*

Pike cowered from the blow, but his combat adrenaline forced him upright again as he raised the Glock to find a target. But before he could fire, another blow slammed into his head, this time from behind and accompanied by a feminine grunt, knocking the Glock from his hand and forcing him to his knees where he groaned.

"Oh you little shits!" Pike managed to shout through the pain.

Vision clouded from the blows and the semidarkness, Pike felt around for the fallen weapon, his hand sweeping over the Glock. He clutched the pistol's grip, mind focused on violent revenge. But before he could lift the gun, he felt someone step on his fingers. He howled as he yanked his hand free, someone kicking the pistol away.

"Fuck!" Pike roared, rising to his feet intent on breaking both of their necks one at a time. But again something crashed onto his head from behind, sending him hobbling sideways into the wall next to the doorway. As he swayed like a stubborn drunk, a final strike landed on Pike's nose, smashing him back until his head met the concrete floor.

Conner reached for the light on the ceiling and twisted the

bulb that he had unscrewed until it lit again. The light revealed Pike bleeding and out cold on the floor, Glock lying harmlessly away from the mess.

Erin stepped next to Conner as they watched Pike for movement, each of them holding a wine bottle that had inflicted the damage. Nothing, he was out cold, his nose horribly disfigured.

Erin cringed. "Now he's even uglier."

"Get the gun," Conner said. As Erin went for it, Conner knelt next to Pike and began searching the man's pockets, watching his body carefully for movement. But there was nothing to worry about. As Conner fished out Pike's keys, Pike was motionless, shallow breath coming from his battered nostrils.

Erin picked up the gun and brought it to Conner. "You ever use one of these?" she asked.

"I had a BB pistol when I was a kid," he said.

She sighed. "You're into military history and you don't know how to use a real gun?"

"I just read about the stuff, I've never owned a gun. Why would I need a gun? Anyway, all you do is pull the trigger."

"Well I hate guns, you take it," she said, handing it to him. "What's the rest of your plan?"

"We lock him down here," Conner said. "Then we get as far away from here as we can."

37

STOP IT

It's fine, I'll handle it.

From the moment Pike had spoken the words, they had stuck in Marcela's mind on repeat like grating grocery store music. As she sat with Larkin waiting for Mr. Red's call, it was all she could think about. What was going on down in the cellar?

With Larkin closing his eyes to the silent return of morphine sleep, she realized she needed to act. She left him there and walked to the kitchen, Pike nowhere to be seen, cellar now in complete silence. She stepped to the kitchen table and clicked the laptop's mouse to bring the monitor out of sleep mode. There she saw the surveillance camera feed sweeping across the cellar, revealing Larkin's wine collection before panning left toward the door.

Then her mouth fell open at what came into view. The college kids were standing by the door, free, talking about something, floor covered with blood, Karl Pike prone in the center of it all.

"Shit," she muttered to herself, glancing at the stairway down to the cellar.

Creeping carefully to avoid them hearing her from the cellar, she left the kitchen and returned to the living room where Larkin still slept. Finding her purse on the couch, she unzipped a pocket that was seldom used and removed the Ruger pistol. She pulled back the slide and switched off the safety.

"What are you doing?" Larkin said, awakened by the sound of the gun.

"They've escaped," she whispered, turning to face him. "I don't know how, but they're free in the cellar. I just saw it on the camera. They've hurt Karl, and they'll be coming up any second."

"Karl's incompetence strikes again. Well by all means clean up his mess," Larkin said. Marcela nodded and turned toward the kitchen.

"Wait," Larkin added. "Once you've recaptured them, bring them here."

"What?" she asked, turning to face him again.

"Yes, bring them here," he said. "I want them to be here when Mr. Red calls. They shouldn't miss out on the fun now, should they?"

"All right," she said. "Of course not."

As Marcela turned again, the cabin filled with a familiar but unexpected rumble. Someone had just opened the automatic garage door.

"I suggest you hurry," Larkin said.

Marcela raced toward the sound.

Conner started up the Suburban after he had clicked the garage door opener. The door opened far too slowly, the steel door creaking, heavy duty opener seeming to rattle the entire garage.

"Jesus that's loud!" Erin said from the passenger seat. She peered over her shoulder to see the garage door opening, unveiling a sliver of white snow outside.

"Come on, open up!" Conner yelled impatiently. As he reached for the gearshift, his peripheral vision caught something to his right, movement at the door leading into the cabin that he couldn't decipher. He turned his head fully, but before he could focus, he saw bright flashes followed by three resounding blasts. The side window of the Suburban blew in, glass scattering into the interior and all over Erin, Conner feeling a pathetic cry of terror coming from his lips as he cowered from the assault.

"Turn it off and get out," Marcela called. Conner saw her creep in close to the passenger door with a pistol pointed at Erin's temple. "Now!" Marcela shouted. As another show of her authority, she directed the pistol to the right and squeezed off another shot, bullet imploding the windshield, Erin plugging her ears from the blast.

"All right!" Conner said, turning the key to shut off the motor, holding up his hands. He saw Erin's entire body quake in fear.

Marcela opened Erin's door and pulled her out, holding the gun to her ear.

"Now you," Marcela said to Conner. "Get out and come around slowly."

Conner obeyed, feeling the Glock still tucked into his pocket.

"Now we go inside, both of you first, me following," Marcela said. "Mr. Larkin would like to speak to you."

~

WHEN KARL PIKE regained consciousness in the wine cellar, he felt like he had just been mauled in a mixed martial arts match. His head from front to back throbbed from the assault. His nose, which had taken the brunt of the damage, was badly broken, the center of his face bloody and swollen.

Yet Pike pulled himself up, forcing his way through the disorientation with reserve energy from boiling anger and duty. He stood as the room swayed, or maybe it was his brain seesawing as he tried to keep his balance.

Pike reached for his nose to hazard an inspection with thumb and forefinger, but when applying a feather's touch sent an unbearable twinge right to his spinal cord, he yanked his fingers away. Blood dripped from his nose over his lips, the red drops plopping to the red puddle on the floor. To remedy that, Pike lifted up his shirt and stretched the neck hole to avoid angering his nose, pulling off the shirt and wadding it up. He held it to his mouth to sop up the blood, then pushed it under his nose as far as he dared to stop the bleeding.

Pike turned around to see the wine cellar door locked behind him. Holding his shirt to his face with his left hand, he searched his pockets with his right for his keys. Of course they were gone, and so was the Glock. The kids had orchestrated a legitimate smash and grab, and by now they were probably joyriding through the Wisconsin countryside in his Suburban, ready to call the cops at the first occupied cabin they could find. Perfect.

"Marcela!" Pike called, yanking at the doorknob, his voice hardly audible through the shirt. Even talking pained his shattered nose, and he groaned from the sting that resulted, closing his eyes to try to shut it out.

He had somehow allowed himself to be bamboozled into this mess, Pike realized, so now it was up to him to get out of it, and fast. He reached for his back pocket to find that his wallet was still there. The kids hadn't had a use for it, he surmised, as he pulled it out and flipped it open. One handed, he fished out his American Express card, his mind remaining witty by replaying the slogan: *Membership has its privileges.*

This wasn't the first time he'd attempted to open a locked door with a credit card, a party trick he had perfected years ago when bored. He was glad for that now as his jimmied the card into the crack of the door above the lock, knee pushing into the door so he could view the bolt latch better in order to work his magic. A minute of fishing the card around, bending it to and fro, and the bolt slid in. He yanked the knob and opened the door.

As he stepped through the doorway, he listened for sounds from upstairs. There was only silence at first, which was not a good sign. But then he heard voices coming from the living room. First it was Marcela, then a nearly inaudible grumble that was likely Larkin. But then came voices he hadn't expected, the sounds rejuvenating him into action: the kids. They were still in the house!

Pike lunged up the stairs, stopping at the closet on the landing just a handful of steps below the kitchen. He opened the closet door to find the pistol grip riot shotgun leaning against the wall in the back, twelve shot extended clip attached and loaded. He grabbed it and the spare magazine resting beside it and ran up the rest of the stairs, trigger finger itching for sweet revenge.

∼

"Marcela dear, the time?" Larkin asked.

Marcela, who stood at his bedside, looked at her watch. "8:38."

Larkin nodded, eying Conner and Erin standing at the foot of his bed.

"The funny thing about time is not all minutes are created equally," Larkin said, appearing to find new energy with the arrival of his visitors. "Some pass too quickly, others tick away like they're pretending to be hours. Life is like that. Soon enough you, too, will wonder where all of the time went. But for the next twenty-two minutes we'll wait. At nine the fireworks, my show that you two have stumbled across, will begin."

"Mr. Larkin, I know we know too much, but there's nothing we can do to stop your plan," Conner said. "Please, just let us go, we didn't do anything to you."

Larkin squinted. "Besides very nearly burning down my house, me and my associates along with it, and mangling poor Karl you mean?"

"You're going to murder innocent people!" Erin shouted. "Isn't there anything in your sick brain that sees how demented that is?"

"It's none of your concern what goes on in my brain," Larkin said. "And anyway, soon enough you two won't have any concerns at all."

"Come on, there's no need for that," Conner said.

"Why? Because you won't say a word to the police? You'll pretend you know nothing?" Larkin scoffed. "Doubtful. No, I'm afraid you're both collateral damage now. And to think I even paid for your trip to Hawaii, all the time both of you conspiring. You had your chance."

Conner swallowed hard at the realization that Larkin had no intention of releasing them. Pike, if he was still coherent, would gladly take care of them when this was over, and Conner sensed that the man would come up with a hideous way to accomplish that.

As if Conner's thoughts had summoned the devil, they all heard heavy footfalls across the kitchen floor. Plunging out of the hallway into the living room was Karl Pike holding a bloody shirt to his nose, shotgun pointing forward in his free hand.

"Collateral damage all right!" Pike huffed. "I'm gonna bludgeon you two shits with every goddamned wine bottle in that cellar!"

"Calm down Karl," Larkin said. "So they outsmarted you, it's not all that difficult. But your time for payback will come."

Pike shambled his way to the bar just inside the living room entrance. He removed the bloody shirt from his nose and set it on the bar. Shotgun still in hand, he reached for a bottle of Bourbon behind the bar, opened it, and took a long swig right from the bottle. Then he set down the bottle and wiped the blood and booze from his mouth with the back of his hand.

A stillness captured the cabin living room, with nothing more to be said or done for the moment as the precious minutes elapsed. But eventually the quiet brought with it a transformation, subtle at first with the continued darkening of heavy snowfall outside, intensifying as winter winds surged without warning, pelting the windows and rocking the cabin's foundation.

Conner looked up at the vaulted ceiling to see the copper chandelier begin to sway ever so slightly. He looked at Erin and saw that she saw it too, eyes wide with the significance. A draft flowed throughout the cabin, and it wafted in a complicated assortment of oil, sweat, and decay.

"They're with us," Erin said.

"What's that supposed to mean?" Marcela asked, Ruger still at the ready. She looked around the room, seeing nothing but the rustic couch, chairs, and end tables in hues of green and brown. The flame in the fireplace jumped and popped, as if fanned by an unseen bellows.

"They've come for you," Erin continued. "They know what you're planning to do."

"Quiet girl!" Pike snapped. "No one knows we're here." Erin glared at him.

Even as the words of confidence left Pike's lips, he began to scan the room as if he was second guessing himself. Then he sniffed through his broken nose, brow wrinkling in disgust.

"What reeks?" he said. "You smell that? Or is my busted nose playing tricks?"

But clearly the odor had also spread to Marcela, who covered her mouth and nose with her free hand.

"Septic tank?" Marcela asked. Pike didn't look convinced.

From the lamps on the side tables to the chandelier on the ceiling, all of the lights in the living room dulled. For a moment it seemed as though they would go out entirely before regaining strength and remaining on. Everyone looked at the lights in silence.

Then Pike gasped and swiveled to his left from some threat that no one else could see. He raised the shotgun as if to fire, waving it to and fro to search for a target. At first it appeared that he was aiming at nothing at all—the wall or something outside—but then all of them saw it. Some sort of white shadow rushing toward him, a light source that floated relentlessly forward, closing quickly onto Pike.

The shotgun erupted, sending a blast into the approaching mist, but the shot passed right through it, punching a scatter of buckshot into the wall. The shadow of white still came forward, so Pike pumped another shell into the chamber and fired, but to the same effect, the wall taking a beating from the shots. Pike screamed toward the cloud in fear, then pumped and shot twice more before the attacking anomaly wilted and disappeared.

But this odd display wasn't over. As soon as the first one vanished, something else rose up from behind the bar, another shadow, like a phantom bartender come to collect Pike's expensive tab. Pike turned the shotgun on the new nemesis and shot at the shadow again and again, the blasts obliterating bottles and glasses and shattering the mirror on the wall behind the bar. Four shots later and the second shadow disappeared.

"Karl!" Marcela shouted, helpless to control him or understand what was attacking him. He ignored her as a third figure emerged from the hallway. Pike turned and met it with four more shots, a pile of expended shells now smoking at his feet. He howled with each shot, stepping slowly backwards as the figure kept advancing. But with the fourth shot, this shadow too disappeared in front of him, leaving nothing but shotgun smoke and silence.

"Jesus Karl!" Larkin cried when the shooting stopped, which sent Larkin into a dizzying barrage of coughs as everyone else watched Pike. But Pike was too rattled now, removing the spent magazine from the shotgun and replacing it with the spare before pointing the weapon every which way like a madman.

"Karl, relax!" Marcela urged. "What's wrong with you?"

"You saw them, right?" Pike growled, still training the shotgun around the room. "Tell me you didn't see them?"

"I saw . . ." Marcela began, searching for a way to explain that she saw something, but that she wasn't certain it warranted him shooting up the cabin. "Just stop shooting before you kill us all!" she urged.

As Larkin continued to cough, Marcela turned to him and

reached to adjust the oxygen tubes tighter to his nose. "Easy Reid, just breathe," she soothed.

But at that moment, nothing mortal seemed capable of helping Reid Larkin, death abruptly grabbing hold like a constrictor to a rat. The suffocating coughs reached a crescendo, Larkin having no more air to give, and his mouth went limp, eyes widening as if witnessing his own impending death. His entire body shook as he wrestled against discomfort, his gaze fixed upon the ceiling in a daze, completely overtaken by a living nightmare only he could see.

"Reid?" Marcela said, but he seemed painfully far away, his soul being pulled in three different directions. "Reid?"

Larkin gasped, not from his coughs but from what he appeared to see deep in his thoughts, something being shown to him for the first time. The unknown stench swirled about him, a renewed blast of stink that caused Marcela to take two steps back from Larkin's bed, not bothering to hide her concern for whatever brought the odor. Somehow Larkin managed to scream, and it was the cry of a helpless, pitiful man. Then he was perfectly still, something inside him building up speed, a freight train of anguish slowly surging up until words spilled from his mouth as a forewarning:

"Oh no," he whispered. "Oh no, no. I . . ."

Larkin's upper body lurched forward, breaths coming in desperate puffs, eyes bulging in horror. His body trembled again, and he shook his head, seemingly staring at something so hideous that he refused to believe it was possible.

"Reid?" Marcela called again, reaching a hand toward him but not daring to step back to his side. "What is it?"

Larkin saw her now, his most trusted employee, the woman who would do anything he asked for. Words hung up in his throat as if speaking would pain him physically and spiritually, but there was something he most desperately needed to communicate. But could he do it? Should he do it?

"Marcela . . . Marcela . . . please . . . call . . ." he said.

And then Reid Larkin collapsed back onto the hospital bed, his last breath escaping his mouth with a croupy gurgle.

38

A DYING WISH

The vital signs monitor on Reid Larkin's wrist went berserk, the leads connected to his chest communicating a dire condition. Marcela stepped closer to view the device, already knowing what it would show her. Even though she had known for some time that this moment would arrive, the flatline of the EKG signaled a cold finality that ceased all of her movements except a seep of tears from her eyes. She had never expected Larkin's passing to unfold like this, death sweeping him away in an excruciating and enigmatic instant. So much for the idea that he would die slowly on a cloud of morphine, welcoming the peace of his final breath and sweet revenge.

Marcela watched the flatline for a return to stability that wouldn't come. Soon the repellant rings from the wrist monitor broke her free of her trance, each beep reminding her of Larkin's death gape and the words he had spoken: "Please . . . call."

She reached for the device to turn it off. Hand inching closer, she looked at Larkin's face that still revealed the torment of his passing, eyes frozen open in an unseeing gaze.

It occurred to her that the odd aroma was now absent, yet the smell had brought back the memories of her swim in Larkin's pool that had taken her to a place that she still didn't understand. She pressed and held the power button until the device powered down, hushing its cries.

"What did he say?" Conner spoke.

Marcela stepped away from the bed again, wiped her eyes dry with the back of her hand, and turned to look at Conner.

"Call," she heard herself say.

"I know what he was trying to say," Erin said. "He was telling you to call it off. In his last seconds of life, he had a change of heart."

"Nice try, Baby Doll," Pike said, stepping closer with the shotgun still in hand. His tone was closer to his usual brash self. "If you knew Reid Larkin, you'd know that he'd never do that."

"Then what did he mean by call?" Conner asked. "Call who?"

"You saw what happened," Pike said. "The man was delusional, you'd be too if you died like that. Hell of a way to go. He could have been asking someone to call for a pizza for all we know."

Conner and Erin looked at Marcela. She raised her left hand to her face and brushed three fingers over the scar. Her caresses evolved into gentle itching, the scar reddening as her long nails did their curious work. She looked at Larkin's body again, maybe hoping he would awaken for a few more seconds by some miracle to tell her what to do. But the man was long gone, leaving her profoundly confused.

"There's still time to call it off," Erin said to her. "You have to understand what just happened here. He was shown something, you could tell. They showed him."

Marcela looked at Erin, words trying to form a response, but she seemed paralyzed in conflict.

"What are you even talking about?" Pike said. "Who showed what?"

"We saw what you were shooting at," Conner said. "You saw them too. Spirits were here to try to stop Larkin's plot."

"Oh BS!" Pike hissed. "I don't know what kind of trick you two are playing, but I'm not stupid."

"Then what were they Karl?" Marcela said at last. "What was here?"

"Jesus Marcela, just stop where you're going with this," Pike said.

Once again the cabin lights dimmed before regaining power, the fire surging in the fireplace by a curious draft. The wind from the snowstorm outside sounded vaguely like whispers.

"They haven't left," Erin said. "Marcela, you have a chance to make this right. Call this off, it's what Larkin was asking for, as hard as it is to believe. If you don't, innocent people will die, and for what purpose? Some twisted act of revenge by a sad excuse for a human being?"

"Shut it girl!" Pike shouted, pointing the shotgun at Erin. "It's about time I take care of you two twerps for nearly hosing up this whole thing. Any last pathetic words?"

"No," Marcela said. "We're letting them go."

Pike glared at Marcela, his mangled face looking like an angry prizefighter fighting for his life on the ropes. "What? We can't let them go, they know everything we've done!"

"I'm still in charge Karl," she said, pointing the Ruger at him.

"Goddamn it Marcela, what has gotten into you?" Pike said.

"She's come to her senses," Conner said, pulling out the

Glock and aiming it at Pike. "So should you. All of this is over."

"Oh, that right, junior? Put that down before you hurt yourself!" Pike said. "Pointing my own gun at me? You mousy little bitch!"

"Two against one Karl," Marcela said. "Put it down."

"Like hell! " Pike scoffed.

Everything in the cabin seemed to slow down as inevitable violence won over common sense. Pike raised the shotgun toward Marcela and shot. Marcela dove to the side and shot back, the intensity of the blasts causing Conner to flinch and fire the Glock. Conner's shot went wild, shattering a glass lamp while the Glock's recoil knocked the gun from his hand, the pistol falling harmlessly to the floor. But Pike's blast had found its mark, clipping Marcela's side. Yet Marcela's shot was far more devastating, finding Pike's forehead with a sickening smack. Marcela crumpled to the floor by Larkin's bed and groaned. Pike teetered from his mortal wound, nerves refusing to give in, fighting against all odds to remain upright. He dropped the shotgun and fell dead onto the hardwood floor.

Erin and Conner scrambled to Marcela's side, blood already pouring from the many holes in her abdomen. Conner ripped the blanket off of Larkin's corpse and brought it to Marcela, both Erin and Conner pressing the blanket onto the wounds.

"My phone," Marcela said, reaching toward her pocket with a hand that quivered in shock. "I need my phone."

Erin pulled the phone from Marcela's pocket, turned it on, and gave it to her. Marcela took a breath to calm herself, then found the only number in the contacts and called.

~

At 8:57, Amanda McMichael and her two huskies returned home from their walk. Mr. Red, safe inside his van in a parking lot, smiled in satisfaction when they appeared on the surveillance cameras just as he'd said they would. With the other camera revealing that John McMichael was still at his desk, it was time for all of his work to come to fruition.

Mr. Red fished out a cell phone from his shirt pocket, turned it on, and placed it on the workstation in front of him. Each of three phone calls would detonate a target, and then he would only need to destroy and discard the phone and head for the hills. He would then be on the run, but that was the easy part. In less than twenty-four hours, he'd be back in his bunker a very rich man, and no one would be the wiser. In all, it was easy money wrapped in a perfect little package with a sweet little bow on top.

But when Mr. Red's other cell phone, the one he used to communicate with Marcela and Larkin, rang from inside his pants pocket, something didn't sit right in his gut. He pulled out the phone and answered the call: "It's not nine o'clock yet," he said.

"I know," came Marcela's voice. Something was wrong with it, a subtle strain that stank. "Don't detonate, we're calling it off."

Mr. Red dissected her words mentally, each deduction he made only increasing his suspicion.

"Now, why would I go and do a silly thing like that, minutes before the big show?" he said.

He heard Marcela's labored breath: somehow she wasn't in control, either coerced or injured.

"Because I'm ordering you to stand down!" she said. "None of your damn business why! I'm the client here. You'll still get your money, but I demand you to abort. Do not detonate!"

Mr. Red rubbed his lips with thumb and forefinger as he

looked down at the detonator phone. This unexpected crisis was as unwelcome as a gator in a kiddie pool.

"I need to hear it from Larkin," Mr. Red said. "Forgive me for doubting that he'd agree to such a change in direction."

"Not possible," Marcela sighed. "He's gone, he died a little while ago."

Now Mr. Red understood. "And now that the cat's away, the mice play, is that it? No more doing someone else's dirty work now that you hold the reins?"

"No, he told me before he died that he wanted to call it off," she stammered. "Simple as that."

"You're not exactly convincing," Mr. Red said. "Where's that other fellow from your team, the ex-military stiff who washes Larkin's balls?"

"Not here," she said.

"Also dead then," Mr. Red said, and he wasn't stating it as a question.

"No," Marcela lied. "He stepped out."

As Mr. Red contemplated how to handle this coup, he saw his bulldog Mike, who had been lying on the floor, jump to his feet and begin whining toward the back of the van. Normally the dog didn't move that quickly even for his favorite thing of all time—dinner—so this gained Mr. Red's attention. Both of them looked toward the back of the van and saw nothing.

When the van's alarm system tripped, horn honking and lights flashing, Mr. Red bolted upright. He plunged his hand into his pocket to retrieve his keys, pulling them out and fumbling to turn off the van's panic button. He found it and pushed five, six, seven times, but the button was useless, the horn continued to sound the alarm cadence.

Earthquakes in Minnesota are extremely rare, but when the van began to shake inexplicably, it was the only conclusion that Mr. Red could make. The security cameras outside of the van showed without doubt that no one was around the vehicle, so an earthquake it was. But why were no other nearby cars shaking?

The angry barks that erupted from Mike were fight barks, a kind that Mr. Red had rarely heard from his subdued companion. They were directed at the back of the van, which remained empty to Mr. Red's eyes.

Muting the phone, Mr. Red shouted for Mike to stop. The dog cowered from the command, but nonetheless continued barking as if under attack. But just as abruptly, Mike stopped and sniffed the air, meeting it with a suspicious growl. Mr. Red then caught the aroma that Mike had already sensed: something rotten, oily, burned, a stench so intolerable that he covered his mouth and nose with his shirt.

"Jesus Mike, what did you eat?" Mr. Red said, realizing full well that the aroma wasn't Mike's doing.

Mike's growls simmered before giving way to an onslaught of barks again while the van continued to shake and the horn alarm beeped without sign of stopping.

Something began to appear in the back of the van like an intensifying 3D projection. There were three of them, vaguely humanoid. As they materialized more, Mr. Red saw the sailor suit, the military uniform, the tattered civilian clothing, and the faint impression of three illuminated figures.

Mr. Red drew his pistol with western outlaw speed and pointed toward the intruders. While he tightened his finger to the trigger, he stopped himself from shooting, realizing from experience that bullets were useless against whatever had just popped into his world.

"Who the flying fuck are you?" he said, waving the pistol from target to target, gaining no reassurance from the weapon.

The sailor began moving his head to and fro, to and fro, an emphatic no. The soldier followed suit, and soon all three of them were doing it, shaking their heads no, a message that Mr. Red had trouble interpreting.

"No? No what?" he said.

The sailor stepped forward, the face of a young man, eyes bulging as if in suffocation. He pointed to the detonator phone on the workstation. The other two pointed now too, Mike snarling and barking at their pointing like the cornered animal he was.

Mr. Red looked down at the phone, trying to keep his balance as the van shook more violently now, or was he shaking from his own frazzled inner core?

They screamed. Jaws dropped in unison, all three intruders howled at Mr. Red, screams of the dead, a demand, an order, a warning in the most raw of deliveries from tormented souls.

Mike had had enough. He screeched and bolted for the front of the van, finding refuge in the passenger seat footwell. Mr. Red felt himself buckling from the unbearable sound, pistol and phone falling from his grasp and dropping to the floor as he sank to his knees to plug his ears. But the shrieks persisted, easily found passage to his ears and mind through the insufficient barriers of his fingers, and the noise infested his thoughts with a hopelessness unlike anything he had known to be real.

And then everything stopped. The horn alarm, the shaking of the van, the deathly howls, the stench—everything returned to what it had been before.

"Mr. Red, are you there?" came Marcela's voice from the phone on the van floor. "Mr. Red?"

He picked up the phone, unmuted it, and put it to his ear. "Here," he said.

"Please tell me you'll abort," she said. "I'm ordering you to abort. Then go back and remove the bombs. I want no trace of them being there."

"Understood," he said, trying to compose himself. "You're the boss, sweetheart. It's been a pleasure doing business with you, sort of. My condolences on your loss."

"You promise you'll abort?"

"Cross my heart and hope to die," Mr. Red said. "It'll be as if nothing ever happened."

"Thank you," she said, ending the call.

Mr. Red pulled himself up underneath legs that still shook in terror. He turned to see Mike peering from behind the passenger seat up front, tormented whines coming from his saggy jowls.

"Oh Mike, get a hold of yourself," he said. "We have to get a grip here."

He glanced down at the detonator phone on the workstation, image still in his head of those three spooks pointing at the device as if it were evil itself. Mr. Red picked up the pistol and held it by the barrel like a makeshift hammer. Mike went back into hiding as Mr. Red pounded the detonator phone with the pistol grip until the device was a thousand shards and scraps and worthless bits of technology.

Marcela turned off the phone. Erin and Conner had heard the conversation through the speaker.

"Thank you," Erin said. "It was the right thing to do."

She took the phone from Marcela and returned it to Marcela's pocket.

"We have to get an ambulance out here," Conner said.

Marcela struggled through the pain to pull herself up to a sitting position, Conner and Erin helpless to keep her still. "If it's just the same to you, I'd rather not," Marcela said. She clenched her teeth and issued a pained hiss as a twinge seized her momentarily.

"You could die, you've lost a lot of blood," Erin said.

"Maybe you forgot that I killed Karl," Marcela offered. "And once the questioning begins, the police will find out just what we had intended to do here. That's going to get messy."

Marcela reached for the Ruger, picked it up, and turned it on Conner and Erin. "So this is the plan. I'm leaving here, right now, and you're staying. Call the police when I'm gone, I don't care. Tell them what you saw here, I don't care about that either. But I'm not going to jail for this."

"You don't need to point that at us," Conner said. "We won't stop you."

Marcela managed to stand, still holding the blanket to her wound, pointing the pistol at them with her other hand. "Yes, I do," she said. "When the police ask, now you can tell them that I left against your will. You don't need to be caught aiding and abetting a fugitive. But there will be no more bloodshed today."

Erin and Conner stood. "You saved a lot of people today," Erin said. "Thank you."

Marcela nodded as she found her balance and summoned strength for what was needed next. She glanced down at Karl's corpse to her right, then toward Larkin's body in the bed to her left. With another nod, she stumbled through the living room, drops of blood trailing behind her, disappearing down the hallway toward the kitchen. Erin and Conner heard the garage door open, followed by the engine of Marcela's car revving. Then they heard her speed away into the snowy morning.

Conner looked at Erin, her face pale and weary, but also peaceful, relief taking over. He went to her, both of them falling into a tight embrace of silence to chase away what they had been through. She pulled away enough to put a hand on his face, gently pulling his mouth to hers.

"I love you," she said between kisses.

"I love you," he said. "But the last time you said that, you were delirious."

She smiled. "I'm still delirious, but it doesn't mean I don't mean it."

"You were right about everything," Conner said.

"Of course I was," she said. "You'd be smart to stop second-guessing me."

"Working on it," he smiled, and kissed her again.

The considerable Wisconsin blizzard continued to blow and dump icy snowflakes onto the lake and woods surrounding the cabin. They held each other and watched nature carry out its onslaught until some sense of normalcy urged them to search the cabin for a phone.

39

THE GIFT

FIVE YEARS LATER

The starter home master bedroom brightened with the coming of dawn. Conner and Erin huddled together in deep sleep after staying up much of the night waiting and hoping.

When Erin sprung upright, Conner went on the defensive, wondering if the spirits had returned again for some unknown and unfinished business. It had been years since he'd experienced that fear, and he recoiled from the memories. But when she reached for her phone, he knew exactly what was going on, and it had nothing to do with ghosts, at least not directly. She was just looking to see if the election results were in.

She turned on the phone, then looked to see that Conner was awake.

"I'm terrified to even look," she said. "Do you think it's decided by now?"

Conner sat up with her and kissed her cheek, feeling the strain in her jaw. "It's just an election," he said.

He reached for her left hand and held it in his, diamond on her wedding ring glinting even in the dull light of morning.

Whenever he saw it, he still couldn't believe that they were married, newlyweds for a month now.

"It's not *just* an election, and you know it," she said.

Erin opened her *USA Today* app and stared as it loaded. Then she held the phone to Conner so he could see the headline in large text across the screen:

McMichael Wins

"Wow, he did it!" Conner said, looking at Erin, whose nervousness had turned into an intensely satisfied grin.

"I knew it all along," she said.

"Oh *sure* you did," he said. "Why were you so nervous about it then?"

"It was much closer than I thought it would be, he barely won," she said.

"A win's a win, especially these days," Conner said.

She nestled into him as they laid back down to digest the significance. Now it was official, they had helped save the lives of the President of the United States and the First Lady five years before being elected. What they had been through had been amazing enough without this new reality, but now they'd helped fulfill a prophecy of sorts that neither of them fully understood.

"I hope he does a good job," Conner said.

"He will," she said. "God knows this country can only improve from here. He has a lot of great ideas, things that people before him had never even considered."

"Hope so."

"Let's call in sick today," she said.

"Are you crazy? I can't do that, I have classes to teach," he said.

"I know," she said. "The goody-good professor never

misses a class. I have a full schedule of clients anyway." Erin had switched her academic path to psychology years before, and now she worked at a counseling center. Conner taught history at a private college in St. Paul.

"Right," he said. "You don't want to leave your wackos in the lurch just so you can play hooky."

Erin slapped his chest. "Don't call them that!" she scolded.

"Ow," he said.

"Besides, you could use some counseling yourself, you wacko."

"Well, I don't know, do you have any openings?" he asked.

"Not at the moment," she said, sliding on top of him, kissing his neck. "But I might be able to do house calls."

"Sounds expensive," he said.

"Oh I am," she said.

"Whatever it is, I'll pay it."

The wake-up alarm on Conner's phone sounded, and both of them stared at the chiming device in disgust.

"Time to get ready for school, Mr. Professor," she said.

"Let it ring," he said, kissing her.

CONNER THUMBED through the neglected pile of yesterday's mail as he waited for the coffee maker to brew enough to fill his cup. Mixed in with the junk mail was a package without a return address. He tore it open to see an envelope taped to another sealed package. He opened the envelope to see a greeting card with silhouettes of a bride and groom on the front, *Congratulations* embossed in silver above the image.

Inside was a handwritten note below the card's words of congratulations:

"Heard about your wedding. Congratulations both of you! I read your book, Conner. Reid would have hated it, a book about ending the cycle of evil throughout history. But I thought it was genius. May you both have long and happy lives together. I trust you will know what to do with the item in the package. Consider it a wedding gift. -M"

Conner had never expected to hear from Marcela again, whether she had died from her wounds or just disappeared entirely, but clearly she had survived. She was referring to his book, which was based on his master's thesis.

He opened up the package and looked at it, jaw dropping.

"Coffee ready yet?" Erin said, entering the kitchen in her bathrobe, patting her hair dry with a towel. When she noticed Conner's look of shock, she froze. "What?"

"It's from Marcela," he said, handing her the card.

"It is?" she asked, taking the card and reading it.

"She's alive, and she gave us this," he said.

"What?" Erin looked at the object in his hand: Larkin's playbill for *Our American Cousin* signed by John Wilkes Booth.

"Oh my God!" she said.

"I know!" he said. "What do we do?"

Erin shrugged. "You're the history geek, you figure it out."

"I'll have to authenticate it somehow, or disprove it," he said.

"Sounds super fun," she said sarcastically. "Maybe the subject of your next book?"

"Maybe," he said. "I'm really glad she made it."

"Me too," Erin said. "But I always figured she had, somehow."

"I wonder where she is?" he asked. "There's no return address."

"Doesn't matter really, she's away from Larkin, so anywhere would be paradise," Erin said.

Conner rubbed the frame, then tucked the playbill into a kitchen drawer for later.

~

THE VOID LACKED any sense of place and time, a simple passageway and not a space to linger. Stepping across it was like passing through nothing at all, an ethereal no-man's land separating the living and the dead.

But it was the magnificent light beyond the void that beckoned them forward. Imagine a light so inviting that nothing can prevent its draw, the desire to be deeper within its shine greater than any human need.

The sailor, the soldier, and the secretary stepped toward it as if spellbound, an invitation years in the making that promised an end to their hopeless wandering. Only the universe knew why they had never seen this light before, but there it was at last—their light.

They entered it, their bodies instantly blanketed in thick light that seemed alive. A flash melded the three forms with the light, the bodies no longer discernible, the brilliance so bright that for a second it overtook the void entirely. Then all went black, leaving the void to its usual oppressive murk, and the three were gone.

ACKNOWLEDGMENTS

Thank you to those who provided their expertise and assistance with this novel.

Charles Pederson for copy editing the manuscript. As always, his meticulous edits were critical in making the novel the best it could be.

Brandi Doane McCann for providing yet another wonderful cover design.

Susie Keithahn for reviewing the manuscript and providing countless consultations throughout the writing of this novel.

Glenn Diedrich for his information about attending graduate school and writing a thesis.

ABOUT THE AUTHOR

Patrick Keithahn lives in Massachusetts with his wife and three children. An editor for nearly 30 years, he's an editorial manager for a large educational publisher in Boston, where he develops social studies materials. Born in Minnesota, he is a graduate of Hamline University. He grew up in Huntington Beach, California. He has lived in Massachusetts since 2008. In addition to *Thesis of Evil,* his other novels include *Ring of Ages* (2016) and *Enter the After* (2018). He enjoys history, football, baseball, reading, and fishing.

Author's note: Many thanks for reading this book! Please consider leaving a review on a platform where the book is sold. Authors depend on your feedback and ratings! *-PK*

www.pkeithahn.com

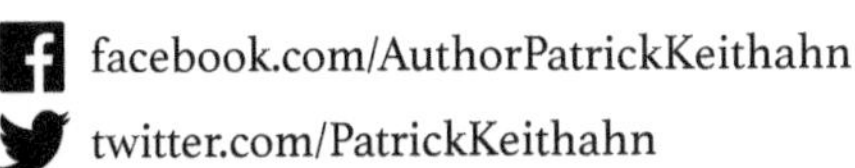

facebook.com/AuthorPatrickKeithahn

twitter.com/PatrickKeithahn